THE GAZEBO

There was a solid oak table in the middle of the room. There was a wooden bench, and some deck-chairs stacked against the wall. The floor boards were dusty and in the corners there were cobwebs. There was the body of Winifred Graham. It lay on its face, bare ankles showing beneath the black cloth coat. From the very first moment Althea had no doubt that her mother was dead, but she knelt down, found an ice-cold hand and wrist, and felt for a pulse that wasn't there.

**Also by the same author,
and available in Coronet Books:**

The Gazebo

Patricia
Wentworth

CORONET BOOKS
Hodder and Stoughton

Copyright © 1958 by Patricia
Wentworth

First published in Great Britain
in 1955 by Hodder & Stoughton
Ltd.

Coronet edition 1973
Fifth impression 1988

Printed and bound in Great Britain
for Hodder and Stoughton
Paperbacks, a division of Hodder
and Stoughton Ltd., Mill Road,
Dunton Green, Sevenoaks, Kent
TN13 2YA (Editorial Office: 47
Bedford Square, London WC1B
3DP) by Richard Clay Ltd.,
Bungay, Suffolk.

ISBN 0-340-16949-4

1

Althea Graham slipped back the catch of the front door. Her
mother had recalled her three times already. Perhaps this
time she would really get away. But before there was time for
her to think that it looked as if it was going to be fine, there
was Mrs Graham's sweet high voice with its note of urgency
– 'Thea! Thea!'

She turned back. Mrs Graham, having surmounted the
fatigue of dressing, now sat very comfortably in her own
particular armchair with her feet on a cushion and a pale
blue spread across her knees. She was a small, frail creature
with fair hair, blue eyes, and a complexion upon which she
lavished the utmost care. As a girl she had had a good many
admirers. Not, perhaps, quite as many as she liked to believe.
Their number and the extravagance of their attentions
tended to increase when viewed in retrospect, but she had
been 'pretty Winifred Owen', and when she married Robert
Graham the local paper described her as the loveliest of
brides.

It was now a good many years since Robert had died
leaving her with an income no longer so adequate as it had
been, a devoted daughter – she always told everyone how
devoted Althea was – and an abiding sense of injury. She
hardly remembered him now as a person, but she never forgot
the grievance. There was a good deal less money than she had
expected. There were death duties, and there was the rising
cost of living. These things were somehow Robert's fault.
When the lawyer tried to explain them it only made her head
go round. She gazed at him out of limpid blue eyes and said it
was all very difficult to understand. And he didn't mean, he
surely couldn't mean, that the house had been left to Althea
and not to her! She couldn't believe it – she really *couldn't*!
A mere child not ten years old – how could Robert do such

a thing! And why was it allowed! Surely something could be done about it! It had all been most dreadfully trying.

And it didn't stop there. Incomes went down and prices continued to go up. Of course there was the house. Houses were worth more than they used to be, and she had almost succeeded in forgetting that The Lodge did not really belong to her.

Althea came a little way into the room and said,

'What is it, Mother?'

'Darling, if you will just shut the door – such a draught! Now let me see, what was it? Will you be passing Burrage's? Because if you were, I thought I might just try that new Sungleam hair-rinse. I thought of it this morning, and then I wasn't sure, but after all it wouldn't do any harm just to try it, and then if it didn't suit me there wouldn't be any need to go on.'

Time was when Althea would have pointed out that going to Burrage's would take her at least another twenty minutes, and that she was already late in starting because Mrs Graham had mislaid a pattern of embroidery silk which had had to be looked for, and had then called her back to say that she thought the last apples from Parsons' were not very good and why not try Harper's, and – yes, after all, she did think her library book had better be changed.

'And, darling, why don't you try some of that Sungleam stuff yourself? They have it in all shades. And really I don't think you take enough care of your hair. It was such a disappointment to me when it didn't stay fair – there really isn't anything like fair hair to set a girl off. But it had a nice gloss, and it used to curl quite naturally. You know, it's a mistake to let those sort of things go – it really is.'

Althea did not respond. She said briefly, 'I'll go to Burrage's,' and got herself out of the room.

This time she got herself out of the house too. As she walked down Belview Road she found herself shaking. It was not very often that she had one of those blinding flashes of anger now. She had learned to endure them and not to show what she felt. She had not learned, and would never learn, not to suffer when they came. *'It's a mistake to let those sort of things go – it really is.'* When her mother said that, there had

6

been the lightning stroke of anger and the old searing pain. She had let everything go because she had to let it go. She had let it go because her mother had taken it from her. It wasn't just her youth and the gloss and curl of her hair. It was freedom, and life, and Nicholas Carey. She had had to let them go because her mother had wept and pleaded, and backed up the weeping and pleading by a series of heart attacks. 'You can't leave me, Thea – you *can't!* I'm not asking very much – only that you will stay with me for the short, short time I shall be here. You know, Sir Thomas said it might be a very short time indeed – and Dr Barrington will tell you the same. I don't ask you not to see Nicholas – I don't even ask you not to be engaged to him. I only ask you to stay with me for the little, little time I've got left.'

All that was five years ago – it was dead. The dead should stay in their graves. They have no business to rise and walk beside you in the face of the day. They are not suitable companions as you go down Belview Road and let the bus catch you up, and do your errands. You must get rid of them before you change the library book, and buy the fish, and match the embroidery silk, and ask the girl at Burrage's for a packet of Golden Sungleam.

She got on to the bus, and found herself just behind the second Miss Pimm. There were three Miss Pimms, and almost the only time that they were ever seen together was at church. Not because they were not on the most affectionate terms, but to do their shopping and change their books individually gave them more scope. Neither a friend nor a shop assistant can talk or listen to three ladies at once, and all the Miss Pimms were talkers. If there was news to be had they picked it up, if there was news to be given they were forward in imparting it. Althea was hardly in her seat, when Miss Nettie had screwed her head round over her shoulder and was telling her that Sophy Justice had had twins.

'You remember she married a connexion of ours about five years ago and went out with him to the West Indies – something to do with sugar. Such a pity you couldn't come to the wedding. Your mother was having one of her attacks, wasn't she? Sophy really did want you to be a bridesmaid, but in the circumstances of course she couldn't have counted on it, and the dress wouldn't have fitted anyone else, but I know she was very sorry. They have three children already, and now these twins – a boy and a girl. Really quite a handful, but her mother tells me they are very much pleased. Of course they never write – just a card at Christmas. And we used to see her going by every day. Such a bush of red hair, but it lighted up well under her veil at the wedding. Dear me, it doesn't seem as if it *could* be five years ago!'

For Althea the five years dragged out in retrospect to three times their actual length. The attack which had kept her at her mother's bedside during the week of Sophy's wedding had marked the end of her own struggle. However often and however bitterly she looked back, she still couldn't think what else she could have done. Dr Barrington had been perfectly frank. If Mrs Graham ceased to agitate herself there was every prospect of her recovery. She would have to lead a quiet, regular life, but there was no reason why she should not live to a good old age. If, on the other hand, she was to be subjected to any more scenes, he really could not be answerable for the consequences. There must not, for instance, be another such interview as had precipitated the present attack.

The interview had been with Nicholas Carey, and it had ended with his banging out of the house. It was almost the last time Althea had seen him. The very last time was when she had gone up through the wet garden to the summerhouse and heard the rain fall mournfully outside as they took their last farewell. She had withstood his anger and his pleading. She had withstood her own crying need of him. She had lived through the moment when he put his head down on her shoulder. His hot tears had run down and soaked the thin stuff of her dress. It was the hardest moment of all, because she could feel his need of her. It was almost a relief when his anger came on him again – a cold, proud anger that sent her away and slammed the door between them.

All this because Nettie Pimm had told her that Sophy Justice had had twins! She could feel a little bitter stab of humour over that. And then Miss Nettie was saying,

'Mrs Craddock tells me she ran into Nicholas Carey the other day – in a lift at Harrods. She said he seemed to be in a great hurry, but of course one always is in town. He had just got back from abroad – but perhaps you have heard from him?' Her little birdlike face had an effect of pecking curiosity.

Althea said, 'No.'

Miss Nettie went on in her light, bright voice.

'Oh, well, people drift away, don't they? And one hasn't really got the time. But you used to be friends – really very great friends, weren't you? Only of course you are so fully occupied with your mother. And, by the way, do you want a very good daily – because Mrs Woodley is leaving the Ashingtons. Fancy, after all these years! But, you know, we have her cousin Doris Wills, and she says . . .' Here Miss Pimm leaned right over the back of the seat and dropped her voice to a buzzing whisper. 'The old lady, you know – quite, quite off her head, and Mrs Woodley says if she doesn't get away she'll be going queer herself and that's a fact. So if you do want any-one . . .'

They couldn't afford to have Mrs Woodley every day, and Miss Pimm knew it as well as Althea did herself. She didn't mean to be unkind, but she had a darting, probing way with her. She believed in frankness. People oughtn't to mind saying if they were hard-up. Althea could say so, couldn't she? And then she could sympathize and say how dreadfully dear every-thing was, and she would go home and be able to tell Mabel and Lily that the Grahams really did seem to be hard up, and what a pity it was. The fact that everyone on the bus would be listening did not trouble her at all. Neither she nor her sister had anything to hide, and why shouldn't everyone be as open as they were? There was, of course, no answer to that. Althea at any rate did not seem to have one. She leaned back as far as she could in her seat and said in a tired voice,

'Thank you – we have Mrs Stokes.'

'But only one day a week, I think, and I have never considered her really thorough. Now Mrs Woodley *is* first-class, and you would find her such a comfort. And you really do look very tired. You can't afford to neglect yourself, or what would happen to your dear mother? Now with Mrs Woodley . . .' It went on until Althea got out at the top of the High Street.

She concentrated on doing her errands. That was something

she had learned to do in the last five years. If you made yourself think about what you were doing, not just with a surface attention but as if each thing really mattered, it did help you to get through the day. She got the embroidery silk, refusing a near match at Gorton's and finding what she wanted at the little new shop in Kent Street. She bought fish and she changed the library book, and made the long detour to the hairdresser who sold the Sungleam preparations. There was just a moment when the drilled routine of her thoughts was broken through. She inquired about the shampoo for her mother.

'It's not a dye, is it?'

'Oh, no, madam. Is it for yourself?'

'No ... no ...' She was surprised at the sound of her own voice. It was just as if she was pushing something away. She went on hurriedly. 'It's for my mother. She has fair hair with just a little grey in it – really not much at all.'

The new salesgirl was a good saleswoman. She said she knew just what madam wanted and produced it.

'It's really good,' she said in a pretty, friendly voice. 'People keep on coming back for more. Now why don't you try it for yourself? I'm sure you'd be pleased. It's wonderful how it brings up the lights in the hair. Makes it ever so soft and pretty too.'

It was the girl's 'Why?' that pushed its way in amongst Althea's ordered thoughts. It hadn't any business there. It just gate-crashed and stayed – a determined and shameless fifth-columnist. Before she knew what she was going to do she heard herself say, 'Oh, I don't know ...' in the kind of tone which is a positive invitation to the enemy to come in.

The girl smiled up at her. She was an engaging little thing with dimples.

'You'd like it really – I'm sure you would.'

Althea came out of the shop with two bottles of Sungleam, one for fair hair and the other for brown. The girl had also sold her a pot of vanishing-cream, and had tried to persuade her into lipstick and rouge, but she had come to with a jerk and made her escape. Locked away at the back of her mind there were things which must on no account be allowed to push their way out. She was aware of them there, stirring, rising, struggling. Something in the hot scented air of the shop, the whirr of driers in the background, the rows of bottles, the creams and lotions, the vivid scarlet of nail-polish, the whole array of all the frivolous things that minister to beauty, encouraged them to struggle. It was years since she had had her hair done at a shop. It was years since she had stopped using make-up. It was years since she had stopped taking any interest in how she looked.

Five years, to be exact.

She walked on a little way, and then stood still. You can't just stand still in a crowded street. There has to be a reason for it. She turned and stared into a bookshop which was displaying about twenty-five copies of a book with a jacket where a scarlet skull grinned from a bright green background. It might have been twice as bright and Althea wouldn't have noticed it. If anyone saw her, she was just looking in at the window. No one was to know that it was because she could no longer turn her face to the street. Civilization has not destroyed the primitive emotions, but it insists that they should function in private. The extremities of happiness, pain, despair, and shame must not affront the public gaze. It was shame, burning and overwhelming shame, that had come upon Althea.

As she walked away from Burrage's with her shopping-basket heavy on her arm, two things came together in her mind. She had not consciously connected them, but suddenly she saw them in their true relation. Nakedly and plainly, there they were, inextricably linked. Nettie Pimm said that Nicholas had come home – he had come home, and she might meet him at any street corner. So she had bought face-cream and a brightening wash for her hair. If she had stayed in that shop for another five minutes she would have come away with lipstick and rouge as well. She hadn't thought of it that way, but that was the way it was, and she was shamed right through to her bones. It was like one of those dreams in which you find yourself stripped and bare in the open street.

She took hold of herself with an effort. The open street was here, and she had got to face it. And catch a bus, and go back to Belview Road. She became really conscious for the first time of the twenty-five scarlet skulls glaring at her from the shop window. Once you had seen them it was quite impossible to lose them again. They insisted on being seen and disliked, they forced their way in amongst your thoughts and occasioned an extraordinary revulsion there. Here was murder and sudden death. Crude violence violently displayed. And she was letting herself be worried about a hair-lotion and a pot of vanishing-cream! All at once something in her kicked and it seemed damnably silly. To start with, she probably wouldn't see Nicholas at all. People in the suburbs go up to town, but no one comes down from town to a suburb unless there is something to bring him there. There was nothing to bring Nicholas to Grove Hill. The aunt with whom he used to come and stay had gone to join a sister in Devonshire. There was very little likelihood that Althea would meet him round any street corner. But if by any chance she did, why should he see her looking as if she had been feeding an empty heart on ashes for the five longest and loneliest years of her life? It was true, but the naked truth could be a terribly shaming thing. She would never see Nicholas again, but if she did see him she would contrive to fly a flag or two.

As she turned away from the shop window, Myra Hutchinson waved to her from across the street. She was a decorative creature, vivid as a poster in brown corduroy slacks and an orange cardigan above which her hair glowed like a newly minted penny. When they were at school together she had been a wisp of a white-faced girl with sandy eyelashes. Those days were gone. The lashes were now dark enough to set off the grey-green eyes. There was colour in the cheeks, there was a brightly painted mouth. The effect was cheerful and attractive. She had been married for five years and she had three children. She was a couple of years older than Althea, and she looked half a dozen years younger.

Althea turned round and went back to Burrage's.

2

It was when she was walking up the High Street on the way to the bus stop that she encountered Mr Martin. She was passing his office – Martin & Steadman, house-agents – and he was seeing a prosperous-looking client out. The client went off in the direction from which Althea was coming, so that Mr Martin really couldn't help seeing her.

He was a sidesman in the church which Mrs Graham attended, and they had known each other since she was a little girl. A couple of years ago he had let their house for them, and she had taken her mother down to the sea for three months. It had not been a very successful experiment, and she had no wish to repeat it. She bowed, gave him a grave smile and was about to pass on, when he said,

'Oh, Miss Graham – good morning. How very fortunate, running into you like this. Could you spare me a moment?'

She said, 'Well . . .' and found herself being ushered across the threshold, through the outer office, and along the narrow passage which led to his private room. The house was an old one. There were two meaningless and inconvenient steps down at one end of the passage and two more up at the other end, but the room itself looked pleasantly out upon a garden full of old-fashioned flowers. As she sat facing Mr Martin across his writing-table she could see a round bed full of roses set in a square of crazy paving, and beyond it two wide borders full of phlox, helenium, carnations and gladioli, with a paved path running between them. Mr Martin fancied himself as a gardener. His own garden up the hill was a show piece, and nothing pleased him better than to hear people stop and admire it as they went by. He beamed at Althea and said,

'Now I expect you are wondering why I wanted to see you.'

'Well, yes . . .'

He leaned back in his chair and put his hands together in a professional manner.

'Of course I could have rung you up, but I didn't want to make it too formal, if you know what I mean.'

Since she hadn't the least idea, she said nothing at all. After a moment he went on again.

'Well, as a matter of fact, I have had a client making inquiries about house property in this neighbourhood, and it did just cross my mind to wonder whether you would be interested.'

'I'm afraid not, Mr Martin.'

13

Well, he had put it to her, and she had come out with what looked like a flat enough 'No'. He frowned, pushed out his lips, and said in a casual tone,

'It's a Mr Blount and his wife – delicate sort of lady – Fanciful, if you know what I mean, and it seems Grove Hill has taken her fancy. Thinks it's healthy, which of course it is. Thinks it suits her. They are staying at that guest house of Miss Madison's half way up the hill, and she says she doesn't know when she's been anywhere that suited her better. She says she doen't know when she's slept better anywhere, so they are all set to buy and it just crossed my mind to wonder . . .'

'Oh, no, Mr Martin, we haven't any idea of selling.'

'No?' said Mr Martin. 'Now you know, your mother gave me quite a different idea. Just a few words I had with her over the hedge the other evening. I was passing, and I stopped to admire your begonias in the front garden – very fine indeed, if I may say so – and Mrs Graham certainly gave me to understand . . .'

'What did she say, Mr Martin?'

He searched his memory.

'Oh, nothing definite of course. Pray do not think I meant to imply that there was anything definite. It was just she gave me the impression that the house was larger than she required – in point of fact that it gave you too much to do, and that she would not be averse to a sale if the terms were sufficiently advantageous.'

A little colour had come into Althea's face. Mr Martin admired it. He had a benevolent disposition, and he had known her since she was ten years old. She had had quite a bright colour then. He liked to see a girl with a colour. He was afraid Althea Graham had a very dull time of it, shut up with an invalid mother. Very charming woman Mrs Graham, of course, but a girl needed younger friends. She was the same age as his Dulcie, and Dulcie had been twenty-seven a month ago. Married young, both of his girls, and no good saying he didn't miss them, because he did, but a young woman needed a home of her own and a husband and children. He looked at Althea who had none of these things and said,

'Mr Blount would give a very good price . . .'

Mrs Graham was pottering in the garden when Althea came

14

up the road. It was a warm sunny day, and other people be-sides Mr Martin stopped and looked over the hedge to admire the begonias. Mrs Graham had a pleasant feeling that the admiration did not stop at the flowers. A garden was the most attractive setting a woman could have. Her hair was hardly grey at all, and she had kept her complexion and her figure. She had a picture of herself, graceful and fragile amongst her flowers.

She came into the house with Althea and told her about the people who had passed and what they had said.

'And the Harrisons and Mr Snead will be coming in to bridge. Well, you must make a cake and some of those nice light scones. It really was very pleasant in the garden. Did you get that Sungleam stuff? Now I wonder would there be time to get my hair washed and set? It would have to be before lunch, because of my rest in the afternoon.'

'Mother I've got to cook the lunch. Of course if you could manage it yourself . . .'

There was a pause, after which Mrs Graham said gently,

'You are sometimes a little thoughtless, dear. Do you think it is kind to remind me that I am a burden to you?'

'No, Mother . . .'

Mrs Graham smiled bravely.

'It's all right, darling – I don't want to complain. It's just – Mrs Harrison is always so well turned out, and it would have been rather nice. I'm really longing to try the Sungleam, but of course, as you say, there's lunch.' She broke into a sudden smile. 'No, darling, I've had an idea. You've been rather a long time this morning, but we can manage if we are quick. We'll do my hair, because I do feel that is important. You know, Mrs Justice is having her cocktail party on Satur-day, and I don't like to leave trying a new thing like the Sun-gleam to the last minute in case it didn't turn out all right, so we'll get on with it now. We'll just have an omelette for lunch, and some of that last cake you made. It is a particular-ly good one, and there isn't really enough of it to come in for tea. So hurry, darling, hurry, and you'll see it will all fit in beautifully.'

The Sungleam proved very successful. It was while she was setting the abundant fair hair that Althea said,

'What did you say to Mr Martin to make him think that we should be willing to sell the house?'

Mrs Graham said in an absent-minded voice,

'Mr Martin . . . Oh, dear I don't think that curler is right. You'll have to take it out again.'

Althea undid the curler and repeated Mr Martin's name.

'He admired the begonias – over the hedge – and you seem to have given him the idea that we should be willing to sell.'

Mrs Graham picked up the hand-mirror and twisted round to see the curls at the back of her head.

'Well,' she said, 'I've sometimes thought – houses have been fetching such very good prices . . .'

'We should have to buy another, and that would fetch a good price too.'

'Oh, there wouldn't be any need to settle down again at once. I have wondered about a cruise. I believe one meets the most charming people. The Harrisons went last year, and they enjoyed it so much. They missed all the cold weather and came home again in the spring. It sounded delightful.'

'The Harrisons could afford it. I don't see how we could.'

'Oh, it would have to come out of the money we got for the house.'

'And what do we live on when we have spent our capital?'

'But, darling, what else is there to live on? It's the only possible way. The Harrisons have been doing it for years – she told me so herself. Suppose it costs us five hundred pounds. I don't know that it would, but just for the sake of argument suppose it did. I don't know how much interest we get on that for a year, but by the time the income tax has come off there is so little left that I can't see that it really matters whether we get it or not – and we should have had our cruise. You know, darling, it is all very well for you – you get out a great deal more than I do – but there are times when I feel that I might have better health if I could get away from Grove Hill. I said so to Ella Harrison, and she said of course what I really needed was to meet fresh people and to have more interests in life. As she says, I am really quite a young woman still. I was only seventeen when you were born, and even so, she wouldn't believe me when I told her you were twenty-seven.'

Althea gave a short laugh.

'Was that intended as a compliment for me?'

Mrs Graham had a small satisfied smile as she said,

'Well, darling, I am afraid *not*. She just couldn't believe I had a daughter as old as that. She said she always thought your father must have been married before, and that you were a step-child. Very ridiculous of course, but I could see she meant it.'

Standing behind her mother and looking into the mirror on the rather elaborate dressing-table, Althea could see the two faces reflected there. Even with her hair full of setting-combs and curlers Mrs Graham was a pretty woman. The legend of her marriage at sixteen was of course apocryphal. She had been twenty-one, and Althea was born the following year. Mrs Graham was therefore forty-eight, and she knew perfectly well that Althea was aware of it, but she had been moving the date of her marriage back for years. Beyond sixteen she would, unfortunately, not be able to go, and the trouble was that Althea looked her age and more. She must be induced to take more interest in herself – to encourage the wave in her hair and use a little discreet make-up. She had been an attractive girl – some people had even called her beautiful. It wasn't a style Mrs Graham admired. Men preferred blondes, and so did she. But Thea had quite good features, and if she were to give herself a little trouble she ought to be able to take five or six years off her age. Of course it wouldn't go down at Grove Hill, which was full of girls who had been at school with her, but on a cruise among quite fresh people where she could allude to her as 'my young daughter' and throw in a smiling remark about girls always being too serious when they had just left school. . . . She went on thinking along these lines, and presently came back to Mr Martin.

'I think I might really ask him to come and see me. He will know that I cannot get down into the town.'

Althea had finished with the combs and the curlers. She was now putting things away in the washstand drawer. She said over her shoulder.

'Why do you want to see him?'

'Darling, to ask him about getting a good price for the house.'

A thought knocked insistently at Althea's mind. She didn't want to let it in, but it was difficult to keep it out. She couldn't help wondering whether Mrs Harrison had told her mother that Nicholas Carey was back from wherever he had been for these five long years. It meant nothing, it couldn't mean anything, but if Mrs Graham thought that it might, it could be a reason for her interest in a cruise. She said a little more sharply than she had meant to.

'I saw him this morning, and I told him we didn't want to sell.'

Mrs Graham turned round on the dressing-stool. She was flushed and shaking.

'You never told me!'

'I didn't want to worry you.'

'You didn't want to tell me because you knew what I would say!'

'Mother . . . please . . .'

'You knew I would like to sell. You knew I wanted to get away from this place that was making me ill.'

'Mother!'

'You think of no one but yourself. Do you suppose I don't know why you don't want to go away? You'd have jumped at it any time during these five years, but now just because Nicholas Carey is home again you don't want to go!' She laughed on a high, angry note. 'Do you know so little about men as to suppose that he ever gives you a thought? Darling, it's really very stupid if you do. Five years!' She laughed again. 'There will have been dozens of girls since you. That's what men are like. Have you looked in the glass lately? When Ella Harrison told me he was back I wondered if he would even recognize you.'

'Mother, you'll make yourself ill.'

It was her only defence, her only weapon. If she answered back, if she let the sick hurt in her turn to anger, the scene would end as other scenes had done – her mother suddenly frightened at the storm she had raised herself, gasping for breath, alternately clinging to her and pushing her away. There would be the dosing, the getting her to bed, the telephoning to Dr Barrington. It had happened so many times, and she knew her part in it, a part in a play which has been played so often that her response to the cues had become automatic. She must keep her voice low, she must avoid saying or doing anything that could offend, she must produce the sal volatile and the smelling-salts at exactly the right moment, and when the time came she must allow herself to be forgiven.

She went through with it now. It wasn't, after all, to be one of the worst scenes, since Mrs Graham had fortunately remembered about Mr Snead and the Harrisons coming in to bridge. She had had her hair done on purpose, and she didn't want to waste the Sungleam, so she checked herself, pressed her hand to her heart, sighed, closed her eyes, and said faintly,

'I'm not really strong enough for this sort of thing, darling – you ought to know that. If you will just help me to the bed . . .'

There was a good deal more to it than that – the salvolatile of course, the careful arrangement of pillows, the bed-jacket – 'no darling, I think I would rather the blue one' – the fetching of a hot-water-bottle, the spreading of a coverlet, the drawing down of the blinds, the quotations from what Dr Barrington had said upon other occasions, to the final brave 'I shall be all right if I can be perfectly quiet for a little' before an erring daughter was dismissed to make the cakes for tea.

3

Mrs Graham was able to enjoy her tea-party and the bridge which followed it. The Sungleam had done all and more than she had hoped, and really she had to admit that Thea had a talent for doing hair. The soft gold waves in front and the curls at the back were quite delightful. Now if she were to take as much trouble over her own! It had been a very pretty golden brown when she first grew up, and a natural wave is such a useful thing to have. It was a pity that she had got into such a dull uninteresting way of dressing – quite ageing. She really must be roused into taking more interest. Looking as she did now, no one would take her for under thirty. Ridiculous to suppose that she could have a daughter over thirty!

Mrs Graham's bridge circle did not rule out conversation. Mr Harrison was a quietly depressed little man who was apt to revoke. Mr Snead was dry and grey. Mrs Harrison combined showy good looks with a vivacious manner. She regarded bridge as a convenient means of getting three people round a table who would be more or less obliged to listen to her. Althea wondered how any of them could bear it, but her cakes had been appreciated and they appeared to be enjoying themselves. She was on the point of taking out the tea-tray, when Mrs Harrison said,

'Nicholas Carey? Yes, I told you. Here, Thea – wasn't he a friend of yours way back in the dark ages before we came to Grove Hill? Benighted place it must have been! But I'm sure somebody told me he used to be a pal of yours. Heartless the way they go off and leave us, isn't it? However, lots of good fish in the sea is what I say. I was telling your mother she ought to take you off on a cruise.'

Althea pushed open the door and went out with her tray, but when she came back for the cake-stand they were still talking about Nicholas. She heard her mother say,

'I always thought he was wild.'

Mrs Harrison laughed.

'Most young men are. Or else just dull. Of course I only met him once, quite a long time ago, but his aunt Emmy Lester is a sort of cousin of Jack's. I used to say he ought to have married her – didn't I, Jack?'

Mr Harrison said, 'Yes.' No one could have told that he was filled with a burning resentment.

'They'd have suited each other to a T,' said Mrs Harrison brightly. 'A pity about me, but I couldn't very well die to oblige them – now could I? And after all, Jack and I are very well as we are. We took the house over from Emmy, you know. She had a lot of Nicholas's things there up in the attic, and she asked if she could leave them, so I expect he will be coming down to sort them out. You'll have to come up and meet him, Thea.'

Every time Mrs Harrison came to the house Althea was convinced all over again that she was the most blatant woman she had ever met. She removed the cakestand and took as long as she could over washing-up.

In the drawing-room Mr Harrison had misdealt and the cards had to be shuffled again. Mrs Graham dropped her voice and said in a sweetly confidential tone that Nicholas had behaved very badly and she didn't think Thea would care to meet him again.

'Just a boy and girl affair, you know – nothing in it all. But I don't think she would care to be reminded of it, Ella. She was quite ridiculously young.'

Mrs Harrison said tolerantly that she had broken her heart at least six times before she was fifteen, and they picked up their cards and began to play.

It was the following morning that Mr Martin had a telephone call from Mrs Graham. He recognized her high fluting voice as soon as he picked up the receiver.

'Oh, Mr Martin, is that you? I am so glad, because I really did want to speak to you ... Yes, about the house. I believe you spoke to my daughter about it yesterday, and I am afraid she may have misled you. Not intentionally of course, but it is really so easy to give a false impression without meaning to. And when she told me about her conversation with you I was afraid that was just what she had done. Of course the house is a very nice one and we should want a very good price for it.'

Mr Martin diagnosed a difference of opinion in the family circle. He said in a soothing voice,

'Oh, yes, Mrs Graham, I quite understand. I believe Mr Blount would be prepared to make a very reasonable offer. He seems to have taken a fancy to the house, and so has his wife.'

Her voice sharpened a little.

'I didn't understand that anyone had actually made a proposal.'

Mr Martin continued to soothe.

'Well, it hardly amounted to that. Mr Blount said they had walked down Belview Road, and that he and his wife were particularly taken with The Lodge. They liked its being a corner house and they were greatly taken with what they could see of the garden. There was no actual offer made, but

21

I formed the impression that they would be willing to pay a good price.'

'And what would you call a good price, Mr Martin?'

'Well, No. 12 fetched five thousand and five hundred, but that was some years ago, and there has been a considerable drop in prices since then.'

Mrs Graham gave a high, sweet laugh.

'Oh, but, Mr Martin No. 12! It doesn't compare in any *way*!'

'Ah, yes, but the Forster estate hadn't been opened up then. Those modern labour-saving houses have made a lot of difference to what the older ones will fetch.'

'Everyone says they are jerry-built.'

'Now, now, Mrs Graham, that is really quite a mistake, if you will allow me to say so. There has been very good work put into them, I can assure you.'

Mrs Graham was not in the least interested in the Forster estate, which had been thrown on the market by an impoverished peer. She said quite tartly,

'How much would Mr Blount pay? If he doesn't make an offer, how am I to know whether it would pay us to accept it or not? We might go away on a cruise, but we should have to get something to live in when we came back. My daughter doesn't think I am businesslike, but I have thought about that! And I think that a cruise would be very good for us both. A little change, you know – fresh people – not just seeing the same dull faces every day. I'm sure I get quite tired of seeing them go by!'

Mr Martin being one of the people who passed by her windows every day, he could hardly escape the implication. It occurred to him, and not for the first time, that Althea Graham must have a trying time of it, and that it would be good for her to get away for a change, though what she really needed was to get away from her mother.

Mrs Graham's voice was fluting again.

'So perhaps you will just find out what he is prepared to offer.' A click at her end of the line informed him that she had rung off.

Althea was out when this conversation took place, but she was at home at two o'clock when Mr and Mrs Blount arrived with an order to view the house. She was not pleased, and perhaps her manner showed it.

'I am sorry,' she said, 'but I told Mr Martin yesterday that we are not thinking of selling.'

Mr Blount was a heavily built, ruddy man with a well-to-do kind of air about him. He put a hand under the elbow of his flabby, drooping wife and guided her past Althea into the hall. Without absolute rudeness it would not have been possible to keep them out. Mr Blount's voice was resonant and good-humoured. He said,

'Well, well – what a pity. I certainly understood from the house-agent . . . You are Mrs Graham?'

'I am Miss Graham.'

He beamed.

'Ah, then there is some little misunderstanding. Mr Martin said it was Mrs Graham he had been talking to. Perhaps we might see her . . .'

'My mother is resting.'

'Now isn't that a pity! We certainly understood that she might be disposed to consider a favourable offer. Perhaps as we are here we might just have a look round. The fact is my wife has taken a wonderful fancy to the neighbourhood. Up and down and all over the place we've been, looking for somewhere to settle down now I'm retiring, and there's been something wrong with all of them. Either the water or the soil, or too high or too low down – there's always been something that didn't suit. And what all the doctors say is, "Let her do as she wants, Mr Blount. Don't push her, or you'll be sorry for it." Very interested in her case the doctors are. And what they say wrapped up in the doctor's language, which I'm no good at and I don't suppose you are either – well, it amounts to this, if there's anything she wants, get it for her, and if she wants it badly get it for her quick. Now this house, we've been walking past and looking at it and she's taken the biggest kind of fancy for it – haven't you, Milly?'

Mrs Blount had sunk down upon one of the hall chairs. She had a limp discouraged look, from her stringy sandy hair to her toed-in feet. She drooped on the upright chair and looked past Althea with pale watery eyes. She didn't seem capable of having a violent enthusiasm about anything. She opened the

23

lips which hardly showed in the general pallor of her face and said,

'Oh, yes.'

Althea found herself saying in the voice she would have used to a child, 'I'm sorry, but we really don't intend to sell,' and with that the drawing-room door opened and Mrs Graham stood there. There could have been no greater contrast to the sagging Mrs Blount. Mrs Graham wore her invalidism in a very finished and elegant manner, from her beautifully arranged hair to the grey suède shoes which matched her dress. It is true that she wore a shawl, but it was a cloudy affair of pink and blue and lavender which threw up the delicate tints of her face and complimented the blue of her eyes.

'Darling, I heard voices. Oh . . .' she broke off.

Mr Blount advanced with his hand out.

'Mrs Graham, permit me – I am Mr Blount, and this is Mrs Blount. We have an order to view, but there seems to be a misunderstanding. Miss Graham . . .'

Mrs Graham smiled graciously.

'Oh, yes. I had a little chat with Mr Martin this morning, Thea darling. I ought to have told you, but it slipped my memory. I didn't think he would be able to arrange anything so soon. Perhaps you will take them over the house.' She turned a deprecating look upon Mr Blount. 'I am not allowed to do the stairs more than once a day.'

Impossible to have a scene in front of two strangers. Althea took them over the house, Mr Blount talking all the time and Mrs Blount repeating in every room the same two words – 'Very nice.' When she had said it in four bedrooms, a bathroom, the dining-room, the drawing-room, and the kitchen, they went into the garden, where two bright borders and a strip of grass led up to a shrubbery and a summerhouse. The slope was really quite a steep one, so much so that Mrs Graham considered it beyond her. Althea's conscience took her to task for the feeling of gratitude which this induced and she had no defence against it. The place was a refuge, and the house afforded her none. There was no room in it where she could turn a deaf ear to the sound of her mother's high, sweet voice calling her, or to the tinkle of her summoning bell.

Mr Blount looked at everything. He obviously didn't know

a delphinium from a phlox, or a carnation from a marigold, but he admired them all. He admired the old summerhouse, which was really, as Mr Martin could have told him, what used to be called a gazebo and was a good deal older than the house. In the days when Grove Hill was really a hill with wooded slopes it had been contrived to afford an agreeable view of fields going down to the river. Since it held some of Althea's most deeply hidden memories, she was glad to find that Mr Blount was not interested in it, passing it over with the remark that summerhouses were draughty, and that Mrs Blount had to be very careful about draughts.

When they were gone she went back up the garden and sat down in the gazebo.

4

Nicholas Carey came back to Grove Hill because he had left a lot of kit there and he supposed he had better go through it. If he had thought about it at all in the last few years, it was to imagine that Emmy Lester would have taken it with her when she moved, or failing that, would have thrown most of it away. But no, the letter which greeted him on arrival in England informed him that she had left the attic positively stuffed with his things. There was a good deal on the lines of· 'You know the Harrisons have bought the house – some distant cousins of mine – and Jack Harrison couldn't have been kinder about my leaving everything just as it was. But I don't know his wife Ella quite so well, and I think she would be glad if you could go down and just sort out what you want to keep. We haven't much room here, but anything we *can* take in . . .'

Emmy came up before him as he read the letter – a kind, vague creature with a heart as soft as butter. But no fool. . . . He fancied that in the reference to Ella Harrison the sense could be reversed. After meeting Ella he was to be quite sure of it. Emmy had seen right through her, and didn't like what she saw.

There is always something strange about the return to a

place which has once been very familiar. The you who lived there comes back out of the past. It is no longer you yourself, because you have gone on and left it behind. Its loves and likings, its sorrows and despairs, are no longer yours. The misty years have dimmed the memory of them and they can no longer give pleasure or pain. But when you go back in the flesh, walk the old streets, and see the old places, the mists have a tendency to wear thin. A snatch of verse came into his mind and whispered there:

> 'Grey, grey mist
>   Over the old grey town,
> A mist of years, a mist of tears,
>   Where ghosts go up and down –
> And the ghosts they whisper thus and thus
> Of the days when the world went well with us.'

The Harrisons had invited him to stay, and he had accepted. He told himself afterwards that Emmy's letter ought to have warned him. He should have made it his business to be much too busy to come down except for the day. Ella Harrison was everything he disliked most in a woman, and poor old Jack couldn't call his soul his own. He gathered that they had returned in the late spring from a cruise of the jazziest kind, and that every minute of it had been pure poison as far as Jack was concerned.

'We had the most marvellous time!' Ella said. 'Such a gay lot of people! Maria Pastorella – the film star, you know – eyelashes about a yard long, and the most marvellous figure! And her latest husband, an enormously rich South American with a name nobody could pronounce, so we all called him Dada! Really – these South American men! The things he said! He rather singled me out, and I don't think she liked it! We really had a wonderful time! I'm telling all our friends they ought to go!' She called across to her husband on the other side of the room.

'Jack, I believe the Grahams *are* going to sell their house and go off! Winifred is getting all excited! She says that man who came to see it has taken the biggest sort of fancy to it! He offered five thousand, and she turned it down, and now he says he'll go to six!' She came back to Nicholas.

'By the way you knew them, didn't you?' Her voice became rather arch. 'Rather *well* by all accounts!' She gave the laugh he disliked so much. 'There's nothing quite so dead as one's old affairs, is there? But the poor girl has just sat here gathering mould ever since! *Not* an attractive occupation! I expect she was quite good-looking when you knew her.'

Emboldened by a position behind the sheltering pages of *The Times*, and perhaps a little by the presence of another man, Jack Harrison said,

'She is very good-looking now.'

Ella's laugh was not quite as ringing as it had been a moment ago.

'Really, Jack! What extraordinary creatures men *are*! I should have said she had let herself go completely – but there's no accounting for tastes. Of course Winifred makes a perfect slave of her, but that's their look-out.'

Nicholas said that he thought he had better start in on his stuff in the attic.

He was astonished at his own anger. It might have broken out once, but five years of some very odd places had taught him self-control. His temper could still flare up at a spark, but he could keep the blinds drawn and the shutters barred whilst he dealt with it. In some of those places the merest momentary failure to control himself could have meant instant and imminent danger. He had walked strange paths, watched strange rites, kept strange company.

Ella Harrison, accompanying him to the foot of the attic stair, had no idea how much pleasure it would have given him to strangle her. He was better looking than in that old photograph that Emmy was so proud of. She admired slim, dark men, and naturally he would admire her. Just his type – bright hair, plenty of curves, plenty of colour. She felt very much pleased with herself and with him.

Up in the attic Nicholas was being appalled at the amount of stuff he had dumped there. There were three trunks full of things that had belonged to his mother. Some of them were valuable. All had been thought worth preserving. He had been going to go through them with Althea. There was an enormous blanket-box, the contents most carefully looked after and annually camphored by Emmy. Only last May she had made a special journey from Devonshire for the purpose. There was a linen-chest. There were stacks and stacks and stacks of books. There were pictures – portraits of grandparents and great-great-grandparents. He remembered an enchanting Regency lady in clinging muslin with a blue riband in her hair. What was he to do with her – what was he to do with any of them? Leave them to the dust of Ella Harrison's attic? He had a feeling that they would prefer it to her company downstairs.

He lifted the lid of yet another box and discovered photograph albums jammed down upon a mass of letters and papers. They would have to be gone through – but how and where? The idea of remaining with the Harrisons for more than the very briefest of visits filled him with horror. A dreadful woman and poor old Jack the completely trodden worm. Yet where if not here could he deal with such a mass of stuff? He couldn't drag it to an hotel, he couldn't cart it down to Devonshire, where Emmy would think him impious if he destroyed so much as a second-cousin's photograph. So what was he to do except stick it out here and get on with the job as fast as he could? He supposed that quite three-quarters of the letters and papers would be for the scrap-heap. He thought he had better get going on them.

There was an empty clothes-basket in the corner which would do nicely to hold the discards. He had it about a third full, when he picked up a battered book on engineering. He couldn't remember having ever possessed such a thing, but when he turned to the fly-leaf it had his grandfather's name in it. As he tossed it into the basket, half-a-dozen unmounted photographs fell out from between the pages and fluttered down upon the attic floor. They were at least seventy years younger than the book. They were, in fact, no more than six years old, and he had taken them himself. They were all photographs of Althea Graham, some of them taken in the garden here, and some of them in the Grahams' garden. There was a very bad one of her with Emmy's cat Ptolemy on her lap. Ptolemy was hating every moment of it, and when Ptolemy hated anything he made himself felt. The scene came flashing back. The photograph was a bad one, because Althea was trying not to laugh, Emmy kept saying 'Don't!', and just as he touched the camera off Ptolemy scratched and fled. The whole thing came back with extraordinary vividness – Emmy in her gardening clothes with earth on her hands and her hat falling over one ear, Allie in a green linen dress. Her eyes were a sort of mixture of brown and grey, but the dress and the garden setting had made them look almost as green as Ptolemy's. It was a very bad photograph, but it didn't go into the discard. None of the photographs were really good. Besides, what did a photograph ever do except set memory and imagination to conjure up a lost image?

He went on looking at the pictures for a long time. He had an impulse to tear them across. The conjuration of the dead is an unhallowed rite – he would have no part in it. But in the end he put them away in his pocket-book and tore up a number of letters from an uncle who had been his guardian and whom he had most particularly disliked. An irreverent satisfaction in being able to think of him as a scapegoat touched his mood and lightened it.

He went back to his sorting with a growing wonder as to why on earth one ever cluttered oneself up with all these lendings and leavings. After five years of being foot-loose it seemed to him to be pure insanity.

It was next day that he discovered he was expected to attend a cocktail party given by Mrs Justice. The Harrisons were not only going to it but had already told her that they were bringing him along, added to which she had rung him up, talked exuberantly about old times, about Sophy and Sophy's husband and children, with a special mention of the recent twins – about Emmy, and about how nice it would be to see him again. He had always liked Mrs Justice, one of those large rolling women who went her way like a benevolent juggernaut, flattening people with kindness, enthusiasm and good advice. The red-haired Sophy had been a friend of Allie's – a rollicking creature who always managed to keep one young man ahead of the gossip about her, and was now, he gathered, bringing up a family in the West Indies. Sophy and a tribe of children! It made him feel elderly.

5

Every returned wanderer is not greeted with enthusiasm. When you haven't seen a ne'er-do-weel stepbrother for several years you are not always disposed to order in even a portion of a fatted calf. Mr Martin had a rueful expression when Fred Worple walked into his office and shook him by the hand. He was fond of his stepmother – always had been. A good wife to his father and a good mother to himself and Louisa. But as to young Fred, the son of her first husband, well the less said about him the better. Up to every kind of trick at home and always in trouble at school. He was sharp enough, but you couldn't rely on him. Old Mr Martin took him into the office, but he wasn't any good there. He was invalided out after six months of his military service and went off into the blue. His mother worried herself sick about him, wanting to know where he was and why he didn't write, but Mr Martin had always had the feeling that the fewer inquiries you made about Fred the better. And now here he was, quite prosperous-looking, in one of those suits with a fancy cut and a handkerchief and tie which he wouldn't put up with in one of his clerks. He said, 'Well, Fred?' and then, 'Have you seen your mother?'

Mr Worple nodded.

'Staying with her. Come on Bert – aren't you going to say you're pleased to see me?'

Mr Martin said, 'That depends.'

'On what?'

'On whether you've come back to worry her.'

Fred laughed.

'You *are* pleased, aren't you! Well, I can tell you one thing, *she* is. Cried over me and kissed me as if I'd brought her the Crown jewels. And you needn't worry – I haven't come back to sponge on her or on you.'

'That is a good thing.'

Mr Worple altered his tone.

'Now, now, no need to be disagreeable. As a matter of fact I've done pretty well – been abroad and made a bit of a pile. Thought I'd like to come back to the old place and see my dear relations. You don't want to go on knocking about for ever, so I thought about settling down – buying a house, getting myself a wife, all that sort of thing. I suppose you wouldn't have anything to suit me?'

Mr Martin had a moment's indecision. He didn't know that he wanted to have anything to do with a business deal that had got Fred mixed up with it. He might have made money – though it would probably be better not to ask how – and he might have a fancy to settle down and get married and it would make his mother very happy if he did, but he didn't know that he wanted anything to do with it. He said in a noncommittal manner,

'Oh, well, you could look about a bit. But those small houses are fetching big prices nowadays, and the smaller they are the more they fetch, so to speak.'

Fred Worple laughed.

'Oh, I'm not set on anything as small as all that. Four or five bedrooms and a couple of sitting-rooms and a nice piece of garden – that's about the ticket. Used to be plenty of them knocking about in Grove Hill. Mum tells me you've moved right up on the top yourself – Hillcrest Road, isn't it? Nice and breezy up there. How would you like to have me for a neighbour?'

Mr Martin wouldn't like it at all. He kept his tongue quiet, but his face spoke plainly enough. There was nothing he would like less than to have a shady stepbrother round the corner.

Mr Worple had a hearty laugh at his expression.

'Not respectable enough for you? You just wait and see! Now what about one of those houses in Belview Road – nice gardens at the back they had. I'm a whale at gardening – you'd be surprised! Someone told me the corner house was going.'

'Who told you that?'

'Oh, just someone. I walked by and had a look at it from the road, but there isn't any board up.'

'Well, there's someone after it, but the people don't want to sell.'

Fred Worple whistled.

'What are they asking?'

'They don't want to sell.'

'Holding out for a bigger price?'

Mr Marton raised his eyebrows.

'They have had a very good offer, but they won't sell.'

'Like to tell me what the offer was?'

'No.'

'Would it be three thousand – four – five – six – you don't mean to say they've said no to seven!'

During the little pause after each of the figures he kept those sharp, rather near-set eyes of his watchfully fixed upon his stepbrother's face. When he reached the final sum, Mr Martin said firmly,

'I don't mean to say anything at all.'

'No, but look here, Bert, it's absurd. Why on earth would anyone be landing out seven thousand for a house like that? You're having me on. And as if anyone would refuse! They'd be crackers if they did! Now look here, if you're not telling me what this other chap has offered you're not. All I've got to say is, whatever it is I'll go a hundred pounds better. Now what about it?'

Mr Martin looked at him attentively. He hadn't been drinking, and he appeared to be in earnest. He spoke lightly – well, that had always been Fred's way, but the hand on his knee was clenched and the knuckles white. Fred was up to something, and whatever it was, the respectable firm of Martin and Steadman wasn't going to mix or meddle with it. He said so.

'Look here, Fred, I don't know what you're driving at, and I don't want to. I can't have two clients bidding against each other for the same house and one of them a family connexion. It's not the way we do business.' He didn't get any farther than that, because Fred had burst out laughing.

'All right, all right, keep your hair on! I just thought I'd give the old firm a chance, that's all. Jones down the street will do the job for me if I really want it done.' He pushed back his chair and got up. 'Well, it's been nice seeing you,

Bert. You'll like having me just round the corner, won't you? So long!' He went out whistling.

Mr Worple walked down the High Street. It hadn't really changed. There was a new cinema, and different names over one or two of the shops, but otherwise just the same old spot. A good respectable class of custom and a good respectable class of customer. Not the sort of place where you would expect anything much to happen. . .

It was at this point that he ran into Ella Harrison.

She was looking into a shop window, and when she turned round, there they were, face to face and near enough to have kissed without so much as taking a forward step. He thought of doing it, but only for a moment. Then he said 'Ella!' and she said 'Fred!', and there they were, looking at each other. He thought she hadn't worn at all badly. A fine woman, and one who knew how to make the most of herself. The touched-up hair and bright make-up, the extravagantly cut suit, were very much to his taste.

'Fred! Where on earth did you spring from?'

He gave her the smile which she had once admired so much. As a matter of fact she admired it still. He had a way of looking right into your eyes. . . . He said,

'That's telling!'

'What are you doing here?'

'Visiting my mum like a good boy.'

'Go on!'

'Believe it or not, that's just what I'm doing. Did I never tell you I came from these parts?'

'No, you didn't.'

'Well, maybe not, but it's true all the same. I'm respectably connected I am, and that's something you didn't know either. Martin & Steadman the house-agents half a dozen doors up – well, Bert Martin is my brother.'

'Your *brother!*' Her voice was shrill with disbelief.

'Well, step – my mum married his dad. And weren't we a happy family – I don't think! Why, I used to work in that dead-alive old office.'

Ella Harrison came to herself with a jerk. They couldn't stand here in the High Street with the chance of somebody who knew her bumping into them. One of the Miss Pimms for instance – help! And at that very moment whom should she see on the other side of the street and waiting to cross over but Mabel, the eldest and if possible the nosiest of the three. She said quickly,

'There's quite a good café at the corner of Sefton Street. Come along and we'll have a cup of coffee. We can't talk here.'

Since she had seen Miss Pimm, Miss Pimm had of course seen her. Practically all that the Miss Pimms went down into the High Street for was to see what there was to be seen. They kept an extremely sharp look-out for it and very little escaped them. Mabel's glance skimming across the road had already taken note of the fact that Mrs Harrison was wearing a new and expensive-looking suit, when she saw her turn round and greet a stranger. She was quite sure that he was a stranger, because nobody in Grove Hill wore the kind of clothes that he was wearing. But not a stranger to Mrs Harrison – oh, no! The way he was looking at her – well, she could only tell her sisters afterwards that she didn't think it was at all nice. Bold was the way that she would describe it – distinctly bold.

It was just as she had made up her mind on this point that Mabel Pimm had her view interrupted by what amounted to a traffic jam. The bus coming down the hill was discharging its passengers, and a furniture-van which had just turned out of Sefton Street took up nearly all the rest of the road. She couldn't see the opposite pavement at all. She had been most interested. That fast-looking Mrs Harrison – the Miss Pimms still employed the vocabulary of their youth – and a flashy-looking man standing very close together and engaged in what was obviously an *intimate* conversation! When she told Nettie and Lily about it afterwards, this was the term that she employed. 'They were standing much too close together – it really looked as if he might be going to kiss her! Not an *elderly* man at all, and I suppose some people would have called him good-looking, but not the sort of person one would meet socially! Of course one wouldn't expect Mrs Harrison to be *particular*, but there he was, smiling at her in the most intimate manner! And then that wretched van came along, and by the time the road was clear again they had completely disappeared. I thought they might have gone into the Sefton café, so I went in and bought half a dozen scones, but I couldn't see them. Of course there are those little screened alcoves ...'

Ella Harrison and Fred Worple sat in one of the alcoves and sipped their coffee. The Sefton had very good coffee. After the first shock – and frankly it had been a shock – Ella found herself astonishingly pleased to see him again. You don't always want bits of your past to come bobbing up so to speak out of nowhere, but she had had a bit of a soft spot for Fred. There was a time when she had gone right off the deep end about him, but that was all over and done with. It had been very uncomfortable while it lasted, because they had neither of them had a bean and they both had tempers. There were scenes and recriminations, and a furious parting. It was all a long time ago and the anger had faded out, but the soft spot remained. They were being very comfortable together. He told her she had better forget all about his having called himself Selby, because Worple was his real name – 'and don't you forget it, ducks.' And she told him about getting ill and losing her job in the chorus and running into Jack Harrison down at Brighton, where she was staying with her Aunt Annie.

'Mean wasn't the word for her! Kept everything locked up and measured it out! I wouldn't have stayed a day, only I hadn't anywhere else to go. And then, there was Jack Harrison coming up to me on the front and asking me if I remembered him. He'd been at a party Anna Kressler threw, so I said of course I remembered him, and he said he'd never forgotten me and perhaps I'd dine with him.' She laughed. 'I'd have dined with the devil and been glad to! It didn't take me long to see I could get him just where I wanted him. He'd come in for money from an old bachelor cousin, and – well, it was a chance I couldn't afford to let slip, so I took him and here we are.'

'All settled down and respectable?'

'Oh, I'm not chancing my luck.'

But even as she said it she knew that the luck had gone sour on her. When you were down and out, your looks all gone to bits through being ill and Aunt Annie getting the last ounce out of you, Jack Harrison might have seemed like a godsend. All very well to say he hadn't changed. That was just it – he *hadn't*. Day after day, week after week, year after year, he went on being the little dull, grey man whom she had married. There had been plenty of money until lately, but he had begun to talk about cutting down expenses – selling the house, finding somewhere cheaper. He spoke of losses, and the way he went on about the income tax was enough to feed any-one up. In the old days you were tired, you were hungry, you tramped your shoes out looking for jobs, but you didn't get bored.

She looked at Fred and thought about the times they had had together. There had been rows, but there had been other things as well. She thought about dancing all night, and the way men used to stare at her, and about making love and being made love to. And here was Fred looking at her the way he used to do. It didn't mean a thing, but – why shouldn't it? In the old days he never had a bean, but there seemed to be plenty of money in his pockets now, burning a hole there the way it does when you've never had much and it comes to you all of a sudden.

He laughed softly and said,

'Oh, I'm a good boy now – safe as houses. And look here, this is where you can help me. You'd like to help an old friend, wouldn't you, Ella?'

She flashed him a glance.

'Provided it's on the level.'

'Of course it's on the level! I want to settle down – buy a house and start a nice little business.'

'What kind of a business?'

'Haven't made up my mind yet. Partnership in a going concern, I think. I'll get the house first.'

'And the wife?' She looked at him between her darkened lashes.

He said lightly, 'They might go together.'

'And what do you mean by that?'

'Oh, just my joke. The fact is I've got my eye on a place already. Used to see it when I was a kid and thought I'd like to live there some day. Never thought it'd come off, but you never know your luck – someone tipped me a winner and I made a packet. So it's me for No. 1 Belview Road.'

Fancy his wanting to buy the Grahams' house and settle down in Grove Hill. She could think of a dozen better ways

36

of spending money than that. She could think of a dozen better ways of helping him to spend it.

She said with a dash of malice,

'Well, your luck is out. There's someone after it already.'

'How do you know?'

'The Grahams happen to be friends of mine. I don't know that they want to sell. They've been offered seven thousand, and they're not jumping at it.'

He gave an incredulous whistle.

'Seven thousand? You're kidding!'

'Well, I'm not.'

'Who's the sucker?'

'A man called Blount.'

His face changed so suddenly that she was startled. He said in a voice that was more like the snarling of an animal,

'The dirty double-crossing swine!'

6

Miss Madison was always extremely offended if anyone alluded to her establishment as a boarding-house. The word had drab associations. It suggested something inferior to an hotel. Miss Madison took Paying Guests. The term guest house was not unacceptable. It was her aim to provide cheerful surroundings, nourishing and appetizing food, and the amenities of home at a moderate charge. Since she was a very good cook, her rooms were seldom empty. Old Mr Peters had occupied one of them ever since his wife died ten years ago. He might be a disconsolate widower, but the Miss Pimms often remarked on how much younger and better he had looked since he had gone to live at Miss Madison's.

Each of the rooms was furnished in a distinctive colour and was known by that name. Mr Peter had the Red Room. Old Mrs Bottomley, who had been there nearly as long as he had, occupied the Blue Room. She was in her middle eighties, and she had one of those fair downy complexions which seem to get fairer and downier as time goes on. She was a very nice old lady. She had blue eyes and fluffy white hair, and she really looked charming in her pale blue room. Mr and Mrs Blount were in the Pink Room, which was a pity, because poor Mrs Blount had no complexion at all, and the flowered carpet, the pink walls and curtains, and the twin beds with their rose-coloured bed-spreads, only made her look paler and plainer than ever. The pink was also very unfortunate as a background for her rather sparse sandy hair. Not that she herself was in the way of noticing such things as colour effects, but it afflicted Miss Madison who was. If another double room had been vacant, she would have pressed the Blounts to take it, though really when she came to think it over she didn't know which of the other colours would have been any better. Yellow or green wouldn't have been too bad with the hair, but she felt shaken when she considered what they might do to that pale flat face, those dull pale eyes. Miss Madison decided that it wasn't worth worrying about. People who worried disseminated gloom. She considered cheerfulness to be a duty.

Mrs Blount sat in the easy chair in her pink bedroom with a gaily coloured magazine on her lap. It was one of those publications which announce themselves frankly as appealing to Woman with a capital W. It contained household hints, the kind of love story in which everything always comes right in the end, advice on dress, on health, on the conduct of your love-life, on how to manage your house, your children, your husband, together with answers to correspondents, and most important of all, how to be beautiful. Mrs Blount always read the love stories first. When the current serial left the heroine convinced that the tall fair man who had come into her life was unalterably attached to another, she could solace herself with the thought that if not next week, or the next, or the next after that, at any rate in the end it would all turn out to be a misunderstanding and the wedding-bells would ring. Sometimes the man was dark with flashing eyes. Sometimes instead of being handsome he had strong, rugged features. But it all came to the same in the end. He put his arms round the heroine and they kissed each other. Of course the people who wrote the story put it in much more complicated ways, but that was how Mrs Blount thought about it. She was a simple woman and a most unhappy one. It soothed this unhappiness to read about other people who were unhappy, and who got over it and lived happily ever after. It wasn't that she thought it would happen to her, she just liked to read about it happening to other people. It was for the same reason that she read every word of the advice on beauty culture – 'If your skin is inclined to be greasy – if you are getting a double chin – if there are any of those fine lines about your eyes – if you are inclined to lose weight, to put on weight – if your face is too long, too wide, too plump, too thin . . .' There were ways in which you could put everything right, and she never got tired of reading about them. She didn't get as far as imagining herself doing any of the things that were recommended. Never for an instant did she picture herself with wavy hair, a transfigured skin, eyebrows carefully shaped and darkened, eyeshadow, rouge, powder, and lipstick. She just liked to read about these things.

When she heard Mr Blount's step on the stairs she pushed the magazine behind a cushion. He laughed at the stories and made unkind remarks about the letters from correspondents. They were people who had their troubles, and it wasn't right to laugh at them. When he came into the room with a frown she knew at once that something had upset him. He shut the door behind him and said in an ugly voice,

'Fred's here.'

Mrs Blount's pale mouth fell open, and he swore at her.

'You needn't make yourself more of a damned idiot than you are! I said, "Fred's here!" You can understand as much as that, can't you?'

She said, 'Yes, Sid.'

He stared at her angrily.

'We've been too long about it, and that's a fact! Might have made a difference if you'd played up a bit! You're supposed to be dead set on the house, aren't you? But I take you to see it, and what do you do – just sit about like a bundle of old clothes and say, "Very nice!".'

'What did you want me to say?' The words came slow and dead.

He swore again.

'I ought to have left you at home, and that's the fact! I ought to have known it wasn't any good expecting you to play up! You are supposed to be so keen on that house that I shan't get any peace until I've bought it! You're supposed to want it so badly that I've got to go on raising the price until they are willing to sell, and when I take you there you sound just about as keen as a cat would be for a ducking! I tell you I could have twisted your neck! And what's the result – what's the result, I ask you! Fred, I tell you – Fred turning up here with money in his pocket and bidding me up! Fred who hadn't two sixpences to rub against each other and came to me to put up the money! And now what? He's had a lucky win, and here he is, in the market against me and bidding me up! In a wicked temper about it too, that's what he is! Says I double-crossed him! When he hadn't got twopence to put up him-self – not twopence! And now he says he'll blow the gaff if I don't take him in! After bidding me up too! The dirty spite of it!'

Mrs Blount sat on the chair and looked at him. She never knew anything about his business – he never told her any-thing. Only every now and then when something had put him out he would talk like he was doing now. He never explained anything, and she didn't want him to. She didn't want to know about his business. Sometimes at night when she couldn't sleep it would come to her that if she ever did get to know about it anything might happen. Anything dreadful. She just sat there and went on looking at him. When he used that voice to her she was too frightened to do anything else. She would have liked to look away, but she was afraid even to do that. He wasn't tall, but he was broad. He had a red face, and eyes that were too light for it. People thought him a jolly-looking man. There was a frightening strength in his arms and his big coarse hands. She had married him because nobody else had asked her, and it didn't take her long to find out that he had married her because of the house her Uncle George had left her and the thousand pounds in the post office savings bank.

He stumped over to the window and came back again.

'Now look here!' he said. 'If you run into Fred, you don't know anything – see? Not anything at all! If he asks you what I'm doing bidding for the house, *you don't know*! You can look as much like an idiot as you want to and you don't know anything at all! It would be just like Fred to catch you

40

alone and try and get things out of you! You just shake your head and say you don't know a thing! You can say I never talk to you about business, and that's gospel truth! Have you got that?'

She said, 'Yes, Sid.'

'All right, don't you forget it!'

He stumped out of the room and shut the door behind him carefully, not banging it, because he was the kind husband who was always so considerate to a trying wife.

Miss Moxon was coming out of the Green Room, followed by her friend, Mrs Doyle. She was tall and thin. Mrs Doyle was as round as a dumpling but full of energy. She undertook shopping for people who were abroad. She also met school-children and saw them across London. In the intervals she wrote innumerable letters to her married sons and daughters, who were scattered round the world in both directions from China to Peru. Miss Moxon only did cross-word puzzles, but she did them very slowly and they sufficed. They stopped and spoke to Mr Blount and asked him if Mrs Blount was feeling any better. When he shook his head regretfully, they com-miserated with him, and thought what a good husband he was.

On the other side of the door Mrs Blount heard their voices. She knew what they were saying, because it was just what everybody said. They were sorry for her because they were kind, but they were much more sorry for Sid having such a poor thing of a wife.

When the footsteps and the voices had quite gone away she got her magazine out from under the cushion and began to read about how to renovate a woollen dress which had got the moth in it. You did it by cutting the sleeves short and making patch-pockets out of the pieces you cut away. It didn't say what would happen if the mothholes were where they couldn't be covered by pockets. The moths had been terrible two years ago. She had forgotten to put moth-ball with her com-binations, and they had come out full of holes.

She passed to a recipe for getting stains out of marble.

7

Mrs Graham's state of mind was becoming very much confused. On the one hand it was desirable that Althea should be paying more attention to her appearance, having regard to the fact that no one is going to believe you are under forty yourself if you have a daughter who might be thirty-five. But on the other hand it was impossible to help connecting the change with Nicholas Carey's undesired return. When anyone had been away for five years you really don't expect them to turn up again. Not that he was likely to take the slightest interest in Thea after all this time. She had always thought that French proverb about coming back to your first loves very silly — just a jingle for the sake of the rhyme.

> 'On revient toujours
> A ses premiers amours!'

In her experience once a man went away he stayed away. All the same she hoped they wouldn't meet. Thea might be upset, and when she was upset it made a very depressing atmosphere in the house. Really the best thing would be to sell the house to this Mr Blount who seemed to want it so badly. They could store the furniture and be off on their cruise before the cold weather set in. She wondered whether he would rise beyond seven thousand. If he did, it would be madness to refuse, and Thea would be kept much too busy to have any time to spare for Nicholas Carey.

She continued in this frame of mind until the afternoon of Mrs Justice's cocktail party. By an irony of fate it was Ella Harrison who disturbed it. Making her way to the comfortable chair which Mrs Graham had managed to secure, she sat down on the arm of it and embarked upon a kind of running commentary.

42

'What a crowd! I see the three Miss Pimms are here. I thought they never went anywhere together, but as Sophy Justice married a connexion of theirs I suppose they felt bound to show up. Mabel's been wearing that blue dress ever since we came to Grove Hill, and whatever induced her to buy it in the first instance I can't imagine! But none of them have got any taste!'

'She had it for Sophy's wedding five years ago.'

Mrs Graham spoke with the complacency induced by the fact that her own dress was quite new. It was of a soft shade of blue with a matching coatee, and it had really cost her more than she was justified in spending, but if they sold the house she could take it off the price and it wouldn't be noticed. She would, in fact, have got it for practically nothing.

Mrs Harrison said,

'It looks like it! It must always have been pretty awful anyhow. Where's Thea? You don't mean to say she hasn't come! I've brought Nicholas Carey, you know. I wonder whether they will have anything to say to each other! He's staying with us to clear up all that mess in the attic. He left it with Emmy Lester, and she left it with us, and goodness knows I shall be glad to get rid of it! Why, there is Thea over there by the window talking to Nettie Pimm! My dear, what has she done to herself — I never saw such a change! If I hadn't known that green dress of hers I really don't suppose I should have recognized her! You know, Winifred, if you take her away on a cruise looking like that she'll be getting off with someone and you'll be left lamenting!' There was a certain edge on the words.

Mrs Graham's delicate eyebrows drew together in a frown.

'What a ridiculous thing to say!'

'Not at all! Of course I don't say the men you meet are always serious, but there would be plenty of fun and games. I know I'd go off again tomorrow if I could! But there isn't much chance of that the way Jack keeps harping on about how much it cost, and the losses he's been having. Why, to hear him you'd think he expected me to sit down in Grove Hill and economize for the rest of my life! What a hope! You know, I always say one might just as well be dead as dull. That cruise was fun. I haven't enjoyed anything so much for years.

I only wish I had your chance of doing it all over again!'

Mrs Graham looked away.

'I don't know that I should care about it.'

Ella Harrison had a moment of exasperation. What a weathercock Winifred Graham was! She had been keen enough to go on this cruise when she thought she might pick up a man for herself, but the minute anyone suggested that there might be a chance in it for Thea she was off again.

Ella took a look at her own interest in the matter. Fred wanted the house, and she would be doing him a good turn if she got the Grahams to sell. She couldn't think why he wanted it, but she meant to find out. She was seeing Fred every day – meeting him casually for coffee, going to the cinema with him in the evenings. If he wasn't falling for her all over again, he was putting on a pretty good act. She knew just what a piece of folly it would be if she let herself fall for him. He was up to something – she knew him well enough to know that. You couldn't trust him an inch – she knew that too. She oughtn't to have any truck with him, and that was a fact. Even as the thought was in her mind she knew that she was just as much of a fool about him as she had ever been in the past, and that if he wanted the Grahams off the map she would go all out to help him.

These thoughts were all in her mind as she answered Mrs Graham.

'My dear, you'd love it! And you'd have no end of admiration. Men always fall for the fragile type! And there'll be plenty of them! Why shouldn't Thea have her share? I'll say that for her, she pays for a bit of brightening up!'

As an exponent of the art of brightness Ella Harrison could certainly speak with authority. Everything about her appeared to glitter, from the brassy hair, the eyes set off by long black lashes, the teeth which were so much in evidence that she seemed to be advertising somebody's dentifrice, to the diamond studs in her ears, the dazzling sunburst at her shoulder, and the valuable rings which flashed with every movement of her hands.

The skilfully applied complexion and startling lipstick achieved emphasis from a clinging garment of royal blue, the colour being repeated by a twist of tulle and a jewelled clasp in the hair. She had felt a good deal pleased with herself when she came down the stairs at Grove Hill House to where Nicholas Carey was waiting in the hall. He stood and watched her, and seemed quite unable to look away. It gave her the feeling that she was on the stage again. There was nothing like a staircase for an entrance. She would have been gratified to know that a somewhat similar idea had presented itself to Nicholas, though she might have been offended if she had guessed that he was summing her up with stage directions: '*A Blare of Trumpets. Enter the Barbaric Queen!*'

Althea, looking across the intervening crowd, wondered for the hundredth time or so how her mother could stand the woman. She could put up with her being vulgar and over-dressed, but when it came to her pushing this frightful idea of a cruise and selling the house it was just too much. In the last resort, of course, she would be driven into playing her own trump card. The house was hers and it couldn't be sold without her consent, only she hoped – very much she hoped – that she wouldn't have to say so.

Nicholas Carey, in the far corner of the room where the massive figure of Mrs Justice practically screened him from view, saw Althea's face change. He had been watching her whilst Mrs Justice told him all about Sophy's wedding which he ought not to have missed and then went on to impart the latest particulars about her husband, her elder boy, her second boy, her girl, and last but most important of all, her twins. 'One of each, and regular little dumplings, she says. And oh, my dear boy, they've all got red hair and she glories in it – though between you and me, I do think there's some chance of its darkening as they get older. At present, she says, it's just pure carrots. Of course it's a cheerful colour, and they are a very cheerful family.'

He said, 'Sophy always was cheerful.'

She rolled on to speak to someone else, and he continued to look at Althea. She had on a green dress. Not linen like the one in the photograph, but it altered the colour of her eyes in the same way. Ella Harrison had tried to make him believe that she had changed, but what took hold of him now was a sense of how little five years had done to make any difference in the familiarity of her every movement, every look. He had shut her image away and locked the door on it and walked in strange exciting paths, and at the end of it all he had come home to find that nothing had changed. The locked place was open and empty. Althea was just across the room from him, and he might never have been away. She turned her head and their eyes met.

It was a most curious experience. It was like waking up and finding that something horrible had never happened. He saw a flush come to Althea's face quick and bright, and he saw it fade and leave a patch of colour on either cheek. She had put it on so carefully that no one could have told it was not her natural bloom until everything in her failed and left it visible. She began to make her way towards the door.

She had known all along that Nicholas might be there. And so would the Miss Pimms have known, and all the other people who knew about her and Nicholas, and who would all be deeply interested to see them meet again. It was going to be a really absorbing moment for Grove Hill, and there had been times when she felt as if she couldn't face it, but they passed, because there was something that she could face even less. If it came to seeing him in a crowd or not seeing him at all, there wasn't really any choice to be made. He wouldn't come and see her – not after the way they had parted five years ago. Now he was back for an hour or two, a day or two. If she didn't see him in this little space of time she would never see him again. She stopped reasoning about it. If you are very thirsty in a desert and there is water within your reach, you don't reason about it and say, 'It will be worse afterwards,' you snatch and drink.

But when she looked across the room and saw him and he looked at her, she couldn't go through with it. She didn't know what was happening, or what was going to happen. She only knew that it couldn't happen here under all these curious eyes. The long unnatural control of years was cracking, she must get out of the room before it broke. She threaded her way between people all shouting at each other without very much chance of making themselves heard. She didn't look at Nicholas again. She heard Ella Harrison's metallic laugh, and quite suddenly in a momentary lull a girl's voice said, 'and his nose was as cold as *ice*!' And then she was at the door.

There was a fat man leaning against it. He seemed to have had a good many cocktails and to need support. She was wondering how she was going to get past him, when she heard Nicholas say, 'Just a minute, old chap, we want to get out.' A hand came over her shoulder. The fat man was eased along the wall, the door opened, and she found herself in the passage. Nicholas said, 'Quick!' and ran her along with an arm about her shoulders to the little room which used to be Sophy's. With the door shut on them, he let go of her and stood back. They didn't speak, they looked at each other. In the end he said, 'Well?' and she said, 'Where have you been?'

8

Nicholas's laugh was not quite steady.

'Oh, just going to and fro in the earth and walking up and down in it, like my namesake in the book of Job.'

She said with a kind of soft irrelevance,

'Do you remember when you dressed up as the devil with horns and a tail and frightened Sophy's birthday party into fits by turning out the lights at the main and coming in all daubed with phosphorescent paint?'

He laughed again.

'It went with a bang!'

'Because you had a squib at the end of your tail and when you let if off everyone screamed.'

'*You* didn't.'

'I can't when things happen – I go stiff.'

'The trouble with you, darling, is that you're just a mass of inhibitions. You don't scream, and you don't cry, and you don't climb on a chair when you see a mouse.'

'I might if it was a spider.'

'Spiders can run up chairs, but it's only the little ones that have an urge that way. The large hairy ones are given over to sloth. They lurk and brood in baths and places where you want to wash. Let us return to your inhibitions. If you don't get the better of them, they'll end in turning you to stone. You know that, don't you?'

She said, 'Yes . . .' from the very bottom of her heart.

'What are we going to do about it, Allie?'

Her lips were stiff, but she made them move.

'I don't know . . .'

'Sure? What about this?' His arms came round her hard and strong. They held her up against him and she felt the beating of his heart. He didn't kiss her, just held her there and looked into her eyes. She didn't know what he saw in them, but she knew what she saw in his. It wasn't any of the things she expected to see. Anger, mockery, passion — he had looked at her with all of these in his time. This look was different, and she couldn't look away. He said,

'What are we going to do about it, Allie?'

There wasn't anything they could do about it. She said,

'Nothing.'

'It's very strong. I didn't know it was as strong as this. Did you?'

'Yes . . .'

'You ought to know. You did your best to kill it five years ago, and I've been having a go at it ever since. If it hadn't been practically indestructible we ought to have been able to polish it off. I've been telling it just how dead it was for the last five years, but it doesn't seem to have had the slightest effect.'

'No . . .'

'I only came down here because I had to. Emmy left all my things behind when she sold the house to Jack Harrison. I wasn't going to come and see you, because I was afraid. And do you know why? I kidded myself that it was because I didn't want to risk the whole thing starting again. But it wasn't that. I was afraid that I might find out how dead everything really was. And what do you do when you're left with a corpse on your hands? Very difficult things to get rid of corpses. I wasn't going to risk it! And I needn't have troubled, need I? The damned thing was not only alive, it was ramping. I had only got to see you across the room and there it was, shouting at the top of its voice and hurting like hell!'

He spoke with extraordinary velocity. The words drove,

and checked, and found their way again, his voice quite low, his clasp of her unbroken, and through it all the heavy beating of his heart. Something in her that had been slowly freezing to death began to thaw. She felt a warmth and a relaxing. She couldn't move away, she couldn't move at all – they were too close. She laid her head against his sleeve and felt the tears run down. It was all that there could ever be between them, tears and parting and pain, but at least they were shared, they hadn't to endure them alone.

He let go of her suddenly and stepped back.

'Allie, you're crying!'

No use to say she wasn't with her face wet and the tears still running. She said,

'Yes . . .'

'You never cry!'

'No . . .'

He broke into sudden shaken laughter.

'Well, you've made a proper job of it now! Here, have my handkerchief. I don't suppose you've got one – unless you've changed a lot.'

The linen was soft and cool. She held it to her face and said,

'That's just it, Nicky, I have changed – dreadfully . . .'

'And how?'

'I've got hard and cold – and – and resentful. I don't like people any more – I don't have friends. I'm not a bit the same as I used to be. You wouldn't like me a bit. I don't like myself.'

'And who is to blame for that? She's made a slave of you. Even Ella Harrison says so.'

She said, 'Yes . . .'

The barriers were all down and nothing was there but the truth. Her tears had even washed away the futile pretence of girlish bloom. He could see her as she was, too thin, too pale, too old for her years. He said in a laughing voice,

'Darling, some of the colour has got on to your nose. Here, you'd better let me have the handkerchief.'

All at once something happened. It was like a fresh wind blowing over her and carrying away all the morbid thoughts that had been crowding in her mind. She felt a thrusting impatience of them, she felt as if she couldn't do with them any more. Nicky was here, and he loved her, and the past was gone.

He finished drying her face and put the handkerchief back in his pocket.

'Or perhaps you had better keep it.'

'No, I've got one — I really have. Nicky, we ought to go back.'

'No — we're going to talk. You will sit and I will sit, and we'll get down to brass tacks. But you're not to cry any more, because it interferes with rational conversation. And just in case anyone comes you'd better powder your nose. I suppose you've got something in that bag of yours?'

She opened it and took out the compact he had given her for Christmas, a month before the crash. When she had finished with it he took it out of her hand.

'I've seen that before. Did I give it to you?'

She nodded, and he dropped it back into the bag with the comment, 'Quite a long time since I handled one of those. Joyous reunion!' His tone was light, with a tinge of malice.

She said quickly,

'Nicky, where have you been?'

'I told you.'

'Nicky . . .'

'Darling, we'll keep it for the winter evenings. A serial in umpteen instalments. You will be enthralled, enchanted, intimidated, and at times appalled. There really won't be a dull moment.'

'Nicky, I saw an article in the Janitor signed "Rolling Stone." Was that you?'

He nodded.

'I thought it was. I went on getting the paper, because I thought there might be some more. After the second one I was sure they were yours, but they didn't come out at all regularly.'

'Darling, the wonder is that they ever came out at all. My very best one never arrived. Of course I can't prove it, but I believe what happened to it was that my messenger took it to the local medicine man, who boiled it down for the use of some of his more exclusive patients. You see, my reputation was very high in those parts and anything I wrote was considered to be extremely strong magic. But we won't anticipate the winter evenings. What we've got to do now is to talk business. Now listen! When are you going to marry me?'

'Nicky . . .'

'No, you had better not say anything rash! Besides I've heard it all before, and it's damned nonsense! Five years ago you were an earnest young fool and I was a hotheaded one. And your mother put it across us good and proper! I must say, looking at it dispassionately, that she put up a very talented performance, ably assisted by Barrington, one of the most gullible old women in the medical profession.'

'*Nicky* . . .'

'Darling, it's not the slightest use your saying Nicky to me in that tone of voice. The gloves are off and the sword is out of the scabbard, and any other nice mixed metaphors you can think of. In other words, we're going to have the truth, the whole truth, and nothing but the truth. Your mother started trying to separate us seven years ago. She made you believe that she had only a short time to live, and that it was your duty to stay with her. After this had gone on for two years there was a final blow-up. I'd been worn down to the point of saying we would live at Grove Hill and I'd go up and down to my job on the *Janitor*. Right at the end I lost my head to the extent of suggesting we should take over the top floor of the house. I must have been crazy, but she wouldn't even have that. She threw a heart attack, and Barrington said she might die if she went on agitating herself about your getting married. Of course what he ought to have done was to tell us to get on with it and confront her with a *fait accompli*. She was, and is, much too fond of herself to take any serious risks once she knew the game was up.'

'Nicky . . . Nicky . . . what is the use . . .' She wasn't crying now, just sitting there, her hands slack in her lap, her eyes imploring him.

'Quite a lot. That is a statement of the situation up to date, just to make sure that we are both thinking on the same lines. Now we'll get down to what we are going to do about it.'

'There isn't anything we can do. Everything is just the same as it was five years ago. Mother hasn't changed, and she won't.'

He laughed.

'Don't be nonsensical! Five years – no, as much as seven years ago – she was supposed to be going to die at any moment. Well, she didn't, and she hasn't and she isn't going to. Ella says she takes a lot of care of herself and keeps you waiting on her hand and foot. She'll probably live to an ornamental ninety, with everyone running her errands and saying how wonderful she is. I don't want to say anything I oughtn't to, but if people can only prolong their lives by being vampires and sucking the last drop of blood out of everyone round them they would be a great deal better dead.'

'Nicky!'

'Well, they would! But you needn't worry – she'll live as long as she can! And what we're going to do is what we ought to have done five years ago – first find her a companion, next walk round the corner and get married. You can have three days to break the companion in, and then we go off on our honeymoon. If your mother behaves well, we'll find something here. I'm writing a book and going on contributing to the *Janitor*. If she doesn't behave well, we'll go and live on the other side of London, and Barrington and the companion can have her all to themselves. My own feeling is that once she knows it's no go she'll be all out to make the best terms she can. You see, it's really quite easy.'

She shook her head slowly.

'She wants to sell the house,' she said.

'And go on a cruise. I know – Ella told me.'

'We've had a very good offer. Mother seems to have told Mr Martin that she would like to go on a cruise, and he sent up a Mr and Mrs Blount with an order to view. Mr Blount says his wife has taken a fancy to the house, and every time I say we don't want to sell he offers more. He has got up to seven thousand.'

'That's fantastic!'

'I know. It worries me. There are two houses just round the corner in Linden Road, and they are practically the same as ours. Mr Martin says the Blounts won't even go and look at them. And this morning a man came round with an order from Jones, the other agent. I told him about the Linden Road houses, and he said he wasn't interested – what he

52

wanted was The Lodge. He said he used to pass it when he was a boy and think he would like to live there.'

'You don't want to sell?'

'No.'

'Why?'

She looked distressed.

'It would be so difficult. You see the house is mine, and that has always been a grievance. But as long as we're living in it the grievance is more or less in the background and she can pretend that it isn't there. But if the house was sold and the money was in the bank in my name it would be quite dreadful. She is already talking about using some of it for this cruise and saying of course the only thing to do with capital is to live on it.'

He said quickly, 'She can't do that if it's yours.'

She moved her hands as if she was pushing something away.

'If I once said that, it would be the end – it really would. There would be the most terrible scene. She would never forget it, and she would never forgive me. No, I shall just have to tell Mr Martin that I won't sell, no matter what they offer, and leave it at that. I shall have to remind him that the house is mine, and ask him not to talk to my mother any more.'

He leaned forward and took her hands.

'When will you marry me?'

'Nicky, I can't!'

'I wish you wouldn't talk nonsense! My Uncle Oswald has left me a competence. He is the one who was my guardian. I never liked him – nobody did. He used to quarrel with everyone and make a new will every six months or so. Owing to my being off the map I missed my turn in the quarrels, and the current will left me quite a lot of money. We can buy your mother a companion and be able to live very comfortably on what is left. We shall in fact be affluent, because everything has been piling up whilst I was away.'

Just for a moment it all seemed possible. She and Nicky would have their own house. She would have her own life. There would be children. Her mother would be reasonable – she might even go on a cruise with the companion. The prison doors were opening – Nicky was opening them, and she could walk out. And then she woke up and knew that it was a dream. People don't suddenly turn reasonable and unselfish. She had given way for too long to make a stand now. She said in an exhausted voice,

'She won't ever let me go.'

His grasp tightened until it hurt. He said in a vicious undertone,

'She isn't going to be asked. Five years ago I was a boy and a fool. This time it's going to be different. She can like it, or she can lump it. If she wants to destroy herself she can. I'm going to get you away if I've got to smash her and everything else in sight.'

He had his back to the door, but Althea was facing it. She saw it opening and she pulled on her hands to get them away, but she was too late. The door swung in and Myra Hutchinson stood there. She was more like a poster than ever – bronze hair, scarlet lipstick, and a dress with a halter-neck in a surprising shade of green. She had been laughing, but the laugh had stopped half way. It had stopped because of what she had just heard Nicholas say. She said 'Oh!' and he looked over his shoulder and grinned at her.

'See you later, darling. We're having a private conversation.'

She did finish her laugh then, but it wasn't quite as carefree as usual. She said, 'So I see,' and stepped back and shut the door again.

Nicholas laughed too. He hadn't let go of Althea. He laughed and he got up, pulling her with him.

'And now I'm going to kiss you,' he said.

9

Miss Maud Silver did not as a rule accept invitations to cocktail-parties, a modern innovation which in her opinion compared unfavourably with the now practically extinct tea-party or At Home. In pre-war days one sat at one's ease and conversed with one's friends. At a cocktail-party you were very lucky indeed if you got a chair, and it was quite impossible to converse, the competition in voices being such as to produce

54

a roar resembling that of a cataract or the passing of a procession of tanks. Yet she had come down by tube to Grove Hill in order to attend one of these disagreeable functions. She would not have done it for just anyone, but Mrs Justice was an old friend and her daughter had once had reason to be grateful for Miss Silver's professional help. She was now comfortably and happily married in Barbados, and had been more than kind to Miss Silver's niece by marriage, Dorothy Silver. There had been an emergency — Dorothy's husband away, Dorothy taken suddenly ill — and nothing could have exceeded Sophy Harding's kindness. It was now four years ago, but grateful recollection induced Miss Silver to take her way to Grove Hill. As was her wont, she dwelt upon the brighter side of the excursion. It would be pleasant to see Louisa Justice. They had not met for some little time, and she would be able to hear all about the latest addition to Sophy's family, the twins. There was something very attractive about twins.

Arriving a little early, she had a very pleasant talk with Louisa Justice before the room filled up. Presently she found herself on a sofa pushed well back into the deep bay-window — quite an agreeable position as not only was the noise considerably mitigated but it afforded a comfortable corner seat and gave her an excellent view of the room. She had an unflagging interest in people. Detective Inspector Frank Abbott of Scotland Yard was in the habit of remarking that as far as she was concerned the human race was glass-fronted. She looked not so much at them as through them, and whether they liked it or not, she saw whatever there was to see. Be that as it may, she found plenty to interest her and to occupy her thoughts as she watched Louisa's guests.

Presently she was aware that the sofa had another occupant, a lady in blue who leaned back in the opposite corner with a languid air. After a moment the lady spoke.

'So hot . . .' she said and drew a sighing breath.

Miss Silver turned a sympathetic gaze upon her. She appeared distressed, but was neither flushed nor pale. Her colour had indeed been augmented, but it was supported by the natural tint. She said,

'The room is certainly very hot.'

It is the climate,' said Mrs Graham. 'Never the same two days together. And I have to be so very careful about changes of temperature – I am so very far from strong.'

'That must be a great trial to you.'

'Oh, it *is*! I am so sensitive to anything like damp, and of course the English climate is never really dry. I had been thinking of going on one of those Mediterranean cruises so as to escape the worst of the winter, but I am afraid I shall not be able to manage it.'

'Indeed?'

Mrs Graham shook her head mournfully.

'I think it would be too much for me. And I hear that the company is really very mixed. One has to be so particular when one has a daughter.'

Miss Silver agreeing, Mrs Graham went on in a sighing voice.

'Girls are so headstrong. They think they know everything, and they resent the attempts we make to guard them. There – that is my daughter Althea over there.'

Miss Silver saw a tall slender girl in a green dress. She was bareheaded and she had pretty hair and good features. Her eyes were bright and she was looking about her as though there was someone she expected to see.

Miss Silver smiled indulgently and said,

'She is a pretty girl.'

Mrs Graham didn't know whether to be pleased or not. She said peevishly,

'Girls are a great anxiety. And of course they think of nobody but themselves. There was a most undesirable young man who used really to pester her with his attentions. Fortunately it all came to nothing and he went away, but he has come back and it really will be dreadful if it starts all over again. That is one reason why I thought about the cruise – it would get her away from him. But then on the other hand there might be someone even less desirable on the boat.'

Miss Silver said,

'Or someone desirable . . .'

Mrs Graham shook her head.

'I am afraid not. These cruises are so very mixed. Besides, the young man I was talking of came up and spoke to me a

56

little while ago. If I had known that he was to be here I would have persuaded Thea to stay away. Most unpleasant for her, and so disturbing. Because do you know what he said to me, and without the *least* encouragement? I shook hands with him of course – I had to do that – but when he said he would like to come and see us I said I was afraid we were going to be very busy as we were going off on this cruise, and he had the effrontery to ask when we were sailing, and to say that he felt very much tempted to come too!'

On the other side of the room Althea was making for the door. She reached it as Nicholas Carey reached it. They went out together and it shut behind them. Mrs Graham had missed the incident. She was looking at Miss Silver and warming to the theme of Nicholas's effrontery. But Miss Silver had seen the young couple go, and she had not missed the sudden glow on Althea's face as she turned and saw who it was behind her. She went on listening to Mrs Graham on the subject of ungrateful daughters and undesirable young men.

About twenty minutes later when she was alone again, Mrs Graham having drifted away, she saw the return of Althea and Nicholas. They came into the room and separated, the young man going off to the left and the girl coming straight across the room. It was perfectly plain to Miss Silver that something had occurred between them. The girl had been crying. Her lashes were still wet, but she had a softly radiant air and she looked as if she was walking in a dream. As to the young man, he looked as if he had just come into his heart's desire.

Althea spoke to no one. She threaded her way amongst the crowd and dropped down upon the sofa beside Miss Silver. She was indeed in a dream. It was the kind of dream in which impossible things become possible. You float easily over obstacles which have reared themselves like cliffs across the path. You climb the unscalable heights and there is no voice to call you back. She was only vaguely aware of Miss Silver's presence. This state of mind continued for no more than a few minutes. She began to realize that people would think it strange if she went on sitting here quite silently beside a stranger. She turned her head, and at the same time Miss Silver addressed her.

'Am I right in thinking that you are Miss Althea Graham?'
Althea was startled. She saw a little dowdy person who looked the governess in some old photographic group. She had on one of those patterned silk dresses which are thrust upon elderly ladies who have an insufficient sales-resistance. It had a small muddled pattern of green and blue and black on a grey ground, and it had been made high to the neck by the insertion of a net front with little whalebone supports. The hat that went with it was black like all Miss Silver's hats, but whereas they had up till now been made of black felt in the winter and black straw in the summer, this was the black velvet toque which she had bought for a wedding in the spring and upon which she had been complimented by an old pupil of hers, Randal March, now the Chief Constable of Ledshire. It was trimmed with three pompoms, one black, one grey, and one purple, and her niece Ethel Burkett considered that it became her very well. Althea being naturally in ignorance of these interesting particulars, it did not appear to her to be as dashing as it had to those conditioned to an unending sequence of felt and straw. She said a little vaguely,

'Oh, yes, I am.'

Miss Silver smiled.

'You will wonder why I ask, but Mrs Graham was sitting here a little while ago and she pointed you out to me across the room. Your name is an uncommon one, and when she spoke of you as Althea I could not help wondering whether you were the Althea Graham who was such a good friend to Sophy Justice.'

Althea was startled quite out of her dream, because six years ago cheerful, careless Sophy had got herself into a nasty jam. She had written some very silly letters to a man who was unscrupulous enough to blackmail her on the strength of them. Snatches of talk came up out of the past —

'Sophy how could you be so idiotic?'

'Darling, I just didn't think anyone could have such a foul sort of mind.'

'That's the sort of mind some people have.'

And in the end Sophy rescued by — 'Darling, an absolutely governessy-looking person, but marvellous just like Cynthia Urtingham said she was. She got back Lady Urtingham's *pearls for them when they all thought they were never going to see them again!'*

She found herself saying, 'Oh, is your name Silver — Miss Silver? Sophy told me you were marvellous.'

'I was very glad to be able to help her.'

Althea's voice and manner had gone back six years. She and Sophy were twenty again — up in the air one minute and down in the depths the next, walking on the edge of a precipice and half falling over it, panic-stricken when disaster loomed, and ringing all the bells when it was averted. Her colour was bright and high as she said,

'She was most frightfully grateful to you — we both were.'

Miss Silver coughed in a deprecating manner.

'When I left the scholastic profession in order to apply myself to private detection, it was in the hope and belief that it would put me in the way of helping those who were in trouble. And Mrs Justice is an old friend of mine.'

Althea said quickly, 'She never knew — about Sophy. You didn't tell her?'

Miss Silver said with gravity,

'The confidences of a client are naturally sacred.'

The Althea of today might have gone no farther. Habits of reticence and self-control had fastened themselves upon her during the passing of five slow years, but the meeting with Nicholas had swept those years away, and now, thinking and talking of Sophy, she went back to the old impulsive Althea who had not learned to put a bridle on her tongue. Something came surging up in her and was across her lips before she could stop it.

'Oh, I do wish you could help *me*!'

Miss Silver turned on her the smile which had won the hearts of so many of those who came to her. Althea was aware of a kindness, an understanding, and a reassurance, and she was aware of them in a measure which she had seldom experienced since her childhood. To a child there is nearly always some one person upon whom its sense of security is based. For Althea it had been her father. After he went she had never really felt as safe again. That Miss Silver should remind her of her father was fantastic, but after the lapse of years during which it was she who had to carry the family burdens, here was the old feeling of security back again. She leaned a little towards Miss Silver and said,

'It's a stupid thing, but just now when I was talking about it I had the feeling – well, it's difficult to put it into words and, as I said, stupid too, but . . .'

'Yes, my dear?'

Althea gave a little laugh.

'It does sound just plain stupid, but – it frightened me.'

'Would you like to tell me about it?'

'Yes, I would, and then you can laugh at me and tell me it's all nonsense and I shall have got it off my mind. It's like this. We have had an offer for our house . . .'

'You had put it up for sale?'

'No, that is just the thing – we hadn't. One of the local house-agents lives up our way. We've known him for years, because he is a sidesman in the church we go to. Well, he saw my mother in the front garden one evening when he was passing and he stopped to admire the begonias, which have been very fine. I don't know how they got on to talking about the house, but she seems to have given him the impression that it was too large for us. It is of course, but I've never thought about selling. Never. I told him so when he spoke to me about it, but he sent some people up with an order to view.'

She told Miss Silver about the Blounts.

'He was all over it, but all she did was to say "Very nice", as if it was something she had learnt like a parrot. Yet he goes on saying what an extraordinary fancy she has taken to the house and making out that she won't give him any peace unless he buys it for her, and he goes on making his offers higher and higher. It's a nice house and the garden is pretty, but it isn't worth seven thousand pounds, and that is what he is offering now.'

Miss Silver said, 'Dear me!' It was the strongest expression that she allowed herself, but Althea was not to know that. She nodded.

'And the extraordinary thing is that now the other agent, Mr Jones, has sent someone up too – a man who used to live here when he was a boy. He says he used to pass our house and think he would like to live there. He is the slick talkative kind and I didn't like him. I told him we didn't want to sell, and he said he knew there was someone else after the place, but whatever Mr Blount offered he was prepared to go one better. I really didn't like him at all.'

Miss Silver asked a few questions about the house — its age, the number of rooms, the extent of the garden, how long the Grahams had been there, and who were the previous owners. To the last of these questions Althea replied that she did not know. 'But we have been there for more than twenty years. I can't really remember being anywhere else.'

'It is an old house?'

'Oh, not really. Fifty or sixty years old, I should think — not more. I told you it was all very silly, didn't I? There isn't anything about the house to make two men start bidding against each other to get it, but they can't make us sell if we don't want to. The trouble is that my mother has some idea of going on a cruise . . .' She broke off and her voice changed. 'The only thing is just to keep on saying no. As I said, they can't make us sell.'

10

Mrs Graham was not feeling at all pleased. Half a dozen people had remarked upon the change in Althea's appearance. Three of them had said how pretty she was looking, and two of them had added, 'Just like her old self.' Myra Hutchinson swooped down and murmured in the husky voice which she had always so much disliked, 'Dear Mrs Graham, isn't it lovely to have Nicky back again! Althea looks like a million pounds!' It was really all extremely annoying. If she had known how it was going to be, she could have had a mild attack of palpitations and have stayed at home, and Thea would naturally have had to stay with her. But then she wouldn't have been able to wear her new dress. Ella Harrison had admired it very much, and even Mrs Justice had said, 'You are very smart, my dear.' It seemed very hard indeed that she could not go out to a party at an old friend's house without being annoyed by the presence of Nicholas Carey. And it was Ella

Harrison who had brought him. She should have known better – she did know better. She felt very much annoyed with Ella. She leaned back in her chair and told Nettie Pimm in a failing voice that she didn't feel very well and she thought she had better go home – 'If you wouldn't mind just finding Thea and telling her.'

Talking it over afterwards with Mabel and Lily, Nettie was of the opinion that Mrs Graham really didn't like to hear her daughter praised.

'I only said that Althea was looking sweet, and that Nicholas Carey seemed to think so, and she leaned back against the cushion with her eyes shut and said she didn't feel well. I don't believe she *wants* Althea to get married.'

Mabel and Lily agreed with her.

Althea took her mother home, got her out of the blue dress and into a comfortable house-coat, and administered sal volatile. To these accustomed tasks she brought a new equanimity. There was no impatience to be controlled, no resentment to be repressed. In the inner chambers of her mind there was happiness and freedom. What had been miraculously given back to her she would not throw away again. A line from an old song stayed with her – 'My true love has my heart, and I have his.' The light and warmth it gave her made it quite easy to be kind.

Mrs Graham lay on the sofa and made plans. They must go away, but not on a cruise which might give them Nicholas Carey as a fellow traveller. There was the private hotel where they had stayed two years ago. She hadn't liked it very much, but there were other places . . . She lay comfortably back on the cushions and went on thinking.

They had their supper on a tray in the drawing-room, and when Althea had finished clearing away and washing up she found her mother looking at her in an affectionate and smiling manner.

'It was a little too much for me, but it was a nice party, Thea.'

Althea said, 'Yes.'

'It does one good to get out of the rut and see fresh people.'

'Yes, it does.'

'I am so glad you agree with me, darling, because I was

62

thinking a little change would be good for both of us. You know that place we went to two years ago. I didn't care for the hotel, but there was one right on the front which I thought looked rather nice – The Avonmouth, I think it was called. We had tea there once or twice, if you remember, and the cakes were really good. We might try that.'

Althea looked at her with a faintly startled air. She was a long way off and she didn't want to come back. She said,

'Go away – *now*? But why?'

'Darling, you weren't really listening. Going out this evening made me feel that it would be good for us to get away for a change.'

This time it got home. Something spoke – 'She wants to get you away from Nicky.' Aloud she said,

'Mother, we couldn't afford it.'

Mrs Graham kept her smile.

'Now, darling, don't be hasty. We have got to be practical about this, and I have thought it all out. You know the Mediterranean cruise we were thinking about – well, I am afraid it might be too much for me, and I hear the society is really very *mixed*, so perhaps something quieter. And as to not being able to afford it' – she gave a little silvery laugh – 'why it wouldn't cost a quarter of what the cruise would have done. So you see, we should actually be saving money.'

Her speedwell-blue eyes looked up innocently. Althea could never remember when she had not known that look for what it was – a danger signal. Even as a child she had been able to recognize it as a warning that she was going to be asked to do something she didn't like. She stiffened herself to resist it now.

'We couldn't afford the cruise, and we can't afford to go away to an hotel like the Avonmouth. It's quite out of the question. We are overdrawn at the bank.'

Mrs Graham sighed.

'It sounds so sordid when you put it that way, I meant it to be a little pleasure for us both. And I am afraid it's my fault. I oughtn't to have got that blue dress, but it was so becoming and just right for the evening if we had gone on the cruise.'

Althea said slowly,

'I would rather not go away just now.'

'But I think you need the change, darling. I'm not thinking about myself of course, though Dr Barrington has been urging me to get away to the sea. I am just trying to think what is best for you. You know, people *will* talk, and you did make yourself rather conspicuous this evening. Nettie Pimm said you were out of the room for quite half an hour with Nicholas Carey. I didn't see you go, or I would have tried to stop you. Nettie didn't say it at all unkindly, but I could see that she thought it a pity you should give people the opportunity to say you were running after him.'

If Mrs Graham expected this to sting Althea's pride she was disappointed. She certainly flushed a little, but she smiled in a dreamy way which was very alarming, and she said in quite a soft kind of voice,

'Oh, I'm not running after Nicky.'

'People will say you are.'

'They will be wrong.'

'Thea, I don't understand you at all. You must realize that there's nothing quite so dead as an old flirtation. He flirted with you, and he went away for five years. Did he write even once – or so much as let us know whether he was alive or dead? He didn't, and you know it. But he has the impertinence to come back and make you conspicuous by flirting with you all over again! Can't you imagine what people must be saying? The least you can do is to show him that he can't just pick you up one minute and drop you the next! I should have thought you would have had more pride!'

Althea wasn't feeling proud, she was feeling safe. Her mother's words were like flies that buzz on the outside of a window-pane – the window is shut against them and they can't get in. They made a stupid noise a long way off. She was still smiling when she got to her feet. It was time to fill her mother's hot water-bottle and to get her to bed. At the door she turned and said,

'Please don't worry – there's no need. I don't want to flirt with Nicholas, and he doesn't want to flirt with me.'

11

'I can't think why you want it,' said Ella Harrison.

Fred Worple flashed his teeth in what he considered to be a fascinating smile.

'You don't have to think about it at all, ducks.'

They were lunching together in town. Since a crowd of people were doing the same thing and a jazz band was playing, it was as good a place for private conversation as anyone could wish. To both of them noise, glitter and plenty to drink were the essentials of enjoyment. Mr Worple's hint that she could mind her own business was not taken amiss. She said,

'You know, I could help you if I had any idea of what you were driving at.'

'I just want to buy that house – that's all.'

'Sure?'

'Certain.'

'It's too big for you.'

'Not when I get married and have half a dozen kids.'

There was a sharp anger in her. She spoke just a little too quickly.

'Who is the girl?'

'Nobody – anybody – what about Miss Althea Graham?'

She said, 'Nonsense!'

He laughed. He had better not laugh at her like that.

'Well, I don't know – she's not bad-looking. And I'll tell you something – the house is in her name.'

'What!'

He nodded.

'Bert Martin let it for them last year, and it was the girl who signed the agreement. He didn't mean to give anything away, but we were talking, and when I said, "Give me a chance and I'll get round the old lady," he came out with, "Well, the house belongs to Miss Graham — you'd be wasting your time." So I thought to myself, "Fred, my boy, what about it? If you can get round an old woman you can get round a young one. Marry the girl and you get the house, free, gratis and for nothing. Money in your pocket, and nothing to pay for except a wedding ring." What do you think of that for a bright idea?'

What Ella Harrison thought about it wouldn't bear saying. He was kidding of course, poking at her to see if he couldn't make her wild just like he used to do in the old days. She'd been fool enough to rise for it then, and she'd be a fool if she rose for it now. What did he want, stirring her up again like this? If she wasn't so bored with Jack, if everything wasn't so damned flat, she would tell him where he got off! Dangling another girl at her, even if he was only kidding! She said with an appearance of frankness,

'She wouldn't look at you.'

'That's all you know. There she is, a good-looking girl moped to death with an invalid mother, and I come along, take her out a bit, splash the money around and give her a good time — it stands to reason she'd jump at it.'

Ella shook her head. She wasn't going to let him get that rise.

'You're not her sort. Besides there's someone she was more or less engaged to, only her mother got it broken off and he went abroad, but he's come back and from what I can make out it's likely to be on again. Though what he sees in her ...'

He laughed.

'Oh, well, it was just a thought. I might think about cutting him out, or I mightn't. What's the odds so long as I get the house?'

She said, 'I don't know what you want it for.'

It was next day that Althea found Mr Worple at her elbow in the High Street. He said 'Good-morning,' and before she had any idea what he was going to do he took her shopping-bag out of her hand.

'It's much too heavy for you. I'll carry it.'

She stiffened.

'Thank you, but I'd rather ...'

He didn't give her time to finish her sentence. A smile was flashed at her.

'Now, now, you just leave it to me. You do the shopping, and I'll do the carrying. You don't want a heavy bag like this pulling you all down on one side. Mustn't spoil a figure like yours – wouldn't do at all.'

'Mr Worple, will you please give me back my bag.'

No one could have called Fred Worple a sensitive plant, but it was borne in upon him that he had given offence. With no more than a murmured protest he gave her the bag, but he continued to walk beside her undeterred by the fact that she neither looked at him nor spoke.

'You know, Miss Graham, I do hope you are thinking about my offer for your house.'

After some unsuccessful small talk this obtained a reply. Althea said,

'No, I am not thinking about it. We do not wish to sell.'

She was becoming very angry, not only with Mr Worple himself, but with Mr Jones the house-agent who had no excuse for inflicting him upon her. The house was not on his books – it was not on anybody's books – but whereas her mother had given Mr Martin a pretext for introducing the Blounts, nobody had given, or would give, Mr Jones any pretext at all. Her colour rose brightly and Mr Worple's next remark incurred the snub direct.

'I am really not prepared to discuss the matter, either now or at any other time. Good-morning!' She turned as if to enter the post office and almost ran into Nicholas Carey, who was coming out.

Mr Worple, observing the encounter, was not so much discouraged as annoyed. She would give him the brush-off, would she? Well, they would see about that. He had a comfortable theory that girls liked to play hard-to-get, and that rudeness was really an encouraging sign. They put it on to make you keener, and if they appeared to be friendly with somebody else it was just a stunt to play you up. He saw Nicholas Carey take over the shopping-bag which he himself had not been allowed to carry and watched them to the corner of Sefton Street, where they turned and went into the café.

Nicholas said,

'This is new since my time. Let's get one of the green rabbit-hutches right at the back – the end one if there isn't someone there already.'

The alcoves really were rather like hutches – something about the way the green draperies were arranged. The end one was vacant and they took possession of it. When Nicholas had ordered coffee he said,

'What was all the nice bright colour for, Allie? Was it for me – or had the character who looked as if he might be a spiv been annoying you?'

Even in the pale greenish light of the alcove the return of the nice bright colour was discernible.

'Nicky, he's dreadful! And he's the other person who wants to buy The Lodge – the one who says he will always go a hundred pounds better than Mr Blount. He doesn't look as if he's got a lot of money, does he?'

'Millionaires have been known to go about in rags.'

'But they're not rags – that's just it. They're quite new and quite dreadful.'

'He might have won a pile on the pools, or he might have put a possibly tattered shirt on a horse. Or he might be the enterprising type of footpad who rustles bullion on its way from post offices and banks – I gather there's quite an opening in that direction for a bright young man. Those are the only three ways I can think of in which you can put away any money nowadays – the Chancellor sees to that. I think there should be an Association for making burglars pay income tax. At present the harder you work, the less you earn and the more you pay. It's a fascinating topic, but as a matter of fact there's something else I want to talk about.'

A waitress brought their coffee and set it down on a shiny green table. When she had gone away again Nicholas Carey said,

'What I want to talk about is our getting married. What about it, Allie?'

She had known that it was coming. She hadn't known just how it would make her feel. She didn't know quite how she did feel, but you couldn't take the most important step of your life unless you did know how you felt about it. She looked at him in a soft, distressed kind of way and said,

'Oh, Nicky, I don't know – don't rush me . . .'

Those narrow dark eyebrows of his went up.

'Do you get the idea that we are rushing our affairs? After seven years? One can believe most things if one tries hard enough, but I can't manage that one.'

She went on looking at him without any change of expression.

'I feel as if we were on a hill – and it's steep. We've started to run down it and it keeps on getting steeper – we're running faster and faster and we can't see where we're going – we can't see the bottom of the hill.'

He said,

'Wake up, Allie! Don't you see the way you're feeling is just what everyone does feel when they've been bullied within an inch of their lives or in prison for years, and then quite suddenly there's an open door in front of them and they are free to walk out? They have only got to take that one step and shut the door behind them, and they are afraid to do it. It's the common reaction – they think it's a trap – they think they'll be caught and brought back again. And they've been conditioned to being at someone else's orders – they can't face having to take their own decisions and act on their own initiative. Wake up and realize that there's nothing on earth to stop you from walking out and marrying me!'

'Suppose I did, and suppose she died . . .'

'Suppose she didn't do anything of the sort.'

'She might . . .'

He said,

'Look here, Allie, you can't tell me anything about your mother that I don't know. She was much younger than your father, and she was pretty and he spoiled her. Incidentally, he knew perfectly well what she was like. He tied up the money so that she couldn't touch it and he left the house to you. Outside his job he let her have her own way. And when he died you took over, only you haven't got a job to escape into. There isn't one turn or twist in the game of getting her own way that she hasn't got at her fingertips, and as long as she has anything to gain by it she'll use them all.' He said the last words over again with a heavy emphasis on them – '*As long as she has anything to gain*. But once we are married, Allie, the game will be out of her hands and she'll know it. If

69

she goes on and throws fits she will only be hurting herself, and as I've said before, she is a great deal too fond of herself to do that.'

Althea listened. She hadn't looked away. He could see right down into her eyes. The green hangings made them look very green indeed, and the colour had gone out of her face and left her pale. They ought to have run away together seven years ago. They ought never to have let Winifred Graham drive them apart. It wasn't going to happen again. He laughed and said,

'I've got a present for you, my sweet. Wait a minute — it's in my wallet.'

He produced the leather case, opened it, took out a paper, and spread it in front of her on the shiny green table.

'Marriage licence.' He dipped into his waistcoat pocket. A screw of tissue paper came up and was unwrapped. A plain gold ring dropped down upon the licence. 'Wedding ring,' he said. 'Just try it on and see if it fits.'

12

Miss Silver put down the letter which she had been reading and turned to the telephone. Since she was sitting at her writing-table, the receiver was conveniently to her hand. She lifted it and heard her own name spoken.

'Is that Miss Maud Silver?'

'Miss Silver speaking.'

The voice said in rather a hesitating manner,

'I wonder if I could come and see you. Perhaps you will remember talking to me at the Justices' the other day. I am Sophy's friend, Althea Graham. You gave me one of your cards . . .'

'Oh, yes. What can I do to help you?'

Althea said, 'I don't know.' And then, 'At least — I hope you don't mind my troubling you, but would you let me come and see you?'

Miss Silver said, 'Certainly.'

'At once – today? I – I'm in town – just round the corner. Would it be all right for me to come now?'

'It would be quite all right.'

Miss Silver resumed the letter which she had put down in order to answer the telephone. By one of those coincidences which really do happen, it was from her nephew Jim Silver's wife Dorothy – the same Dorothy Silver whom Sophy Justice had befriended four years ago in Barbados. Jim Silver's work as an engineer had taken him to the island, and his wife had accompanied him, taking with her what was then her only child, a little boy born after ten years of marriage. Her illness in Barbados had fortunately proved of short duration, and on her return a few months later a little girl was added to the family. Since then there had been twins, a boy and a girl, just as in Sophy's case.

Dorothy's letter was full of what were to Miss Silver the most interesting particulars about all these children. Jamie was growing so very like his father. Jenny knew all her letters though she wouldn't be four until after Christmas. Teddy and Tina were like a couple of puppies – under your feet all the time, but so sweet. It was really delightful to get such a happy letter. She placed it on the left of her blotting-pad to be answered at leisure and rose to greet Althea Graham.

If she had not already committed herself on the telephone Althea might have reached Montague Mansions, but she would probably not have gone up in the small self-operated lift or have rung the bell of No. 15. Even as she stood with her finger on the button it was all she could do not to turn and run away down the stairs. That isn't the sort of thing you do of course – not if you have been nicely brought up, so she didn't do it.

The door opened and Miss Silver's invaluable Hannah Meadows stood there, a comfortable rosy person with a country air about her. Althea was not the first of Miss Silver's clients to find reassurance in her aspect, and she would not be the last.

Althea came into Miss Silver's room with its workmanlike table, its carpet and curtains in the shade which used to be called peacock-blue and which is now rather oddly known as petrol. There were chairs with curly walnut frames and the spreading laps designed to accommodate skirts of the crinoline period and upholstered in the same material as the curtains. There was a yellow walnut bookcase, there were little tables. There was a perfect host of photographs on the tables, on the bookcase, on the mantelpiece, framed in leather, in silver, in silver filigree on plush. A great many of them were pictures of young men and girls, and of the children who might never have been born if Miss Silver had not stepped in to disentangle the net in which innocent feet had been caught. From three of the walls, framed in yellow maple, reproductions of famous Victorian pictures, *Hope*, *The Black Brunswicker*, and *The Stag at Bay*, looked down upon the scene.

A small cheerful fire burned on the hearth. Althea sat down on one side of it. Miss Silver, taking the opposite chair, lifted a gaily flowered knitting-bag from the low table beside her and took out a pair of knitting-needles upon one of which some rows of ribbing stood up like a frill. The colour was a pleasing shade of pink, and the completed garment would be one of a set of vests for Dorothy Silver's little Tina, about two years old. There was something very soothing about this domestic occupation. Althea watched whilst Miss Silver inserted the second needle and began to knit, her hands held low in her lap after the continental manner.

Althea leaned forward and said,

'I don't know that way of knitting.'

Miss Silver smiled.

'It was taught me when I was at school by a foreign governess. It is much easier and better than the English way. You do not have to loop the wool over the needle, and it is practically impossible to drop a stitch.'

'I see.' There was a pause before she said, 'I mustn't take up your time – but I don't know how to begin. You see, if I talk to people I know, they will either be on one side or the other. They will have known all about it for years and their minds will be made up.'

The small nondescript coloured eyes out of which Miss Silver was regarding her were full of intelligence. She said, 'Yes?'

'But someone who hears about it for the first time...' She broke off and her colour rose. 'You do see what I mean, don't you? It's so difficult for anyone to be impartial when they have known you for years and years and years.'

Miss Silver continued to knit. The needles moved with incredible speed, but her voice did not hurry as she said,

'Perhaps if you will tell me what is troubling you . . .'

Althea bit her lip.

'Yes, I will. And I will try very hard to be fair. It isn't easy when you are in a thing up to your neck, but I will try.'

Althea Graham was twenty-seven, but for the moment Miss Silver was reminded of the child who says, 'I *will* be good.' She smiled her reassuring smile.

'Do not think too much of what you are going to say and of how you are going to say it. I shall get a clearer impression of the facts if you will allow yourself to be natural.'

Althea gripped the arms of her chair. They were not very comfortable to grip, because the yellow walnut of which they were made was carved with acanthus leaves. The edges of the leaves were quite sharp, and the one on the right cut into her palm and left a deep scored line there. She began to tell Miss Silver about Nicholas Carey.

'He used to spend the holidays with an aunt who lived quite near. He is two years older than I am. I used to go round to their house a lot, and we went on bicycle rides together. It was like having a brother. Then we began to grow up. He had his military service to do, and he was abroad for two years. When he came back he got on to the staff of a weekly paper, the *Janitor*. He writes well, you know – differently. We went on going about together. He has some money of his own, and he had a car. We used to go out into the country – quite long runs. My mother was an invalid then, but she began not to like our going off together.'

Miss Silver looked across her busy needles and said,

'Why?'

'It took me away. She has always liked to have someone to do things for her.' It was said simply and without bitterness. 'When Nicholas wanted us to be engaged it upset her dreadfully, but we thought she would come round.' There was quite a long pause before she went on to say, 'She didn't.'

Miss Silver said, 'Dear me!'

Althea's colour, which had faded, came up momentarily. She kept her voice steady with an effort.

'We planned a cottage in the country. There was an old cousin who would have been glad to come and keep my mother company, but she wouldn't even listen to our plans. She just cried until she made herself ill, and Dr Barrington said to give her time and she would come round. He said her heart wasn't strong and if she went on as she was doing it would be very bad for her. We waited six months, and then we tried again, but the same thing happened. We said then that we would get a flat in Grove Hill – Nicholas would go up and down to town. But it wasn't any use. Every time we brought the subject up she had a heart attack. Nicholas asked Dr Barrington what would happen if we just went ahead and got married, and he said he couldn't answer for the consequences. Well, after two years we got to the point where we offered to take over the top floor of the house. Of course it wouldn't have answered, but we were desperate. We – we – both cared a great deal.' She jerked her head back and bit her lip again hard. 'Of course I can see how it looked to her. She had got used to my being there to do all the odd jobs, and even if I had still been in the house it wouldn't have been the same thing – there would have been Nicky to think of. But in the end he said he couldn't go on.' The familiar name slipped out on a failing breath. It was some time before she said, 'There were the sort of scenes that tear you to bits – I don't wonder my mother was ill. I said I would try to be fair. I think she really did believe that she hadn't got long to live. She kept on saying couldn't I stay with her for just the very little time that she had left. She used to cry, and hold my hand, and beg me not to leave her. I told Nicky I couldn't marry him, and he went away.' She stopped there and drew a long breath.

Miss Silver said,

'And now he has come back again?'

Althea looked at her with a heartbreak in her eyes.

'After five years. He said he wouldn't write, and he didn't. He said I would have to choose between him and my mother, and I had chosen. He went to all sorts of wild places. I didn't know where he was, or what he was doing. His aunt sold her house and went down to Devonshire to live with a sister. After that I didn't even know whether he was alive or dead. Then one day I picked up a copy of the *Janitor* on the railway bookstall. There was an article in it signed "Rolling Stone", and I was sure that it was Nicholas who had written it. There were more articles – at irregular intervals. They were about the sort of places that are right off the map. They were odd and exciting, and brilliant. People began to talk about them and look out for them. When I read one I did know at least that he was alive when it was written. And then after five years he came back.'

Miss Silver's gaze rested upon her compassionately. Althea said,

'Five years is a long time. I didn't know whether he would be the same person. I knew that I wasn't. Being unhappy does things to you – it makes you dull. He never could do with people being dull. I didn't feel as if there was anything left that he could possibly care about. But I did feel I had got to put up as good a show as I could.' She took her hands off the arms of the chair. They were numb with the pressure that she had put on them. She folded them in her lap and felt the blood come tingling back. She said, 'His aunt Emmy Lester had left a lot of his things in the attic of her house when she sold it to a cousin. Nicholas had to come down to sort them out. I didn't think I should see him – I didn't think he would want to see me. But he was at Mrs Justice's cocktail party, and the minute we saw each other across the room it was just as if he hadn't ever been away. I went out into the hall – I couldn't trust myself. He came after me, and we went into Sophy's little room and talked . . .' Her voice stopped, her eyes remembered.

Miss Silver pulled on the pale pink ball in her knitting-bag. The silence had lasted quite a long time before she broke it.

'And now?'

'He wants me to marry him at once without saying anything to my mother. He has got a licence. I think we ought to tell her. But it will be the same thing all over again if we do.'

'Miss Graham, what is the real state of your mother's health?'

Althea lifted a hand and let it fall again. The acanthus leaf had marked the palm. She said,

'I don't know. If she upsets herself she has an attack. Dr Barrington says she mustn't be allowed to upset herself.'

Miss Silver said gravely,

'It is a doubtful kindness to encourage a selfish course of action. May I inquire whether the cousin you spoke of would still be available as a companion for your mother?'

'I should think she would. I know that she has had losses and is finding things difficult. She has a couple of rooms in a friend's house, but I don't think the arrangement is being a great success. The friend has recently taken up table-turning and automatic writing, and my cousin doesn't approve of it. We could pay her a salary, and I think she would be quite good with my mother. The trouble is that if I write to her and wait for her to make up her mind and let me know, it will get round the family and come back to my mother. Cousin Bertha writes reams to all the relations every week. None of them could keep a secret if they tried, and of course they don't try.'

Miss Silver found her sympathies warmly engaged. She stopped knitting, rested the now considerably lengthened pink frill upon her lap, and said,

'Emily Chapell!'

Althea repeated the name in an inquiring voice.

'Emily Chapell?'

Miss Silver beamed.

'She would be extremely suitable.'

'I don't think . . . .'

The knitting was resumed. Miss Silver inclined her head.

'She is not a trained nurse, but she has had a good deal of nursing experience. A very dependable person and, most fortunately, disengaged. If you decided on an immediate marriage, she would be able to move in as soon as you had broken the news to Mrs Graham.'

Althea could say nothing but 'Oh . . .'

Miss Silver's needles clicked.

'I have known her for twenty years, and I have never known her to fail in tact and good temper.'

Althea had a picture of Miss Silver and Emily Chapell as twin angels shooting back the bolts of her prison doors and throwing them wide. She heard Miss Silver say,

'Your cousin would naturally require a little time to consider your offer and to give notice to her friend. Miss Chapell would, I am sure, be prepared to remain with Mrs Graham until her arrangements had been made.'

Althea leaned forward. The doors were opening, but could she – might she step across the threshold? She looked at Miss Silver with piteous intensity and said,

'Oh, do you really think I could do it?'

13

Althea returned home to find Mrs Graham in an extremely fretful mood. She held forth for some time on the congenial theme of selfishness in the young, with particular application to a daughter who left her mother alone whilst she wasted time and money on going to town.

'And if it was to shop, I am sure there are very good shops here in the High Street.'

'I didn't go up to shop.'

Mrs Graham looked at her suspiciously.

'Then what did you go up for?'

'To see a friend of Sophy's.'

'A friend of Sophy Justice's – of course she's Sophy Harding now, but it seems so much easier to say Sophy Justice – why on earth should you go and see a friend of Sophy's?'

'I thought I should like to see her again.'

'Oh, you've met her before?'

Althea said, 'Yes, I've met her,' and then hurried on with, 'I thought Nettie Pimm was lunching with you. You told me she was, and I left everything ready.'

'She rang up at the last moment and said she couldn't come. She said she wasn't feeling well.' A delicate sniff expressed Mrs Graham's opinion of Nettie's ailment. 'Most inconsiderate I call it, and I let her see I wasn't pleased. And then on the top of that Mr Jones rang up again about the house. He said Mr Worple had withdrawn his offer of seven thousand five hundred. You know, there's something about Mr Jones that

I don't like at all. He sounded quite pleased about the price having come down. And I told him that it wasn't any good his going on worrying us, because I didn't like Mr Worple and I didn't feel at all inclined to sell to him. He reminds me of someone we saw in a film. I can't remember who he was, but Mr Worple reminds me of him, and in the film he really wasn't at all the sort of person I should care to sell a house to. After all, one does owe a certain duty to the neighbourhood, and we have been here for more than twenty years. And with my health what it is, I shouldn't like to feel that I hadn't got a home to come back to. I did think the cruise we were planning might be good for us both, but one couldn't be sure of congenial companionship, so I have really given up the idea. A few weeks in a nice hotel by the sea would be quite a different thing. One would have one's own comfortable home to come back to at any time. I really think that is a necessity. I am sorry that you should be disappointed about the trip, but my mind is quite made up. For one thing I shouldn't care to have to call in a strange doctor. Dr Barrington understands me, and that is everything. So I told Mr Jones it wasn't any good thinking I would sell, and I rang up Mr Martin and told him too.'

She had talked herself into a better humour, and Althea left it at that.

At a little after nine o'clock Nicholas Carey rang up. The telephone was in the dining-room, with an extension in Mrs Graham's bedroom. On the not infrequent occasions when she felt a disposition to rest she was thus able to enjoy long gossipy conversations with her friends. She could also listen in to anything Althea said when using the instrument in the dining-room. With this in mind Althea, lifting the receiver and hearing Nicholas Carey's voice, had to consider what chances there were of being overheard. Mrs Graham was in the bathroom. If the taps had been running when the bell rang, she probably wouldn't have heard it. If her mother was already in her bath she wouldn't get out of it to answer the telephone. The chances were that it would be safe enough to talk to Nicky, but prudent to keep the conversation on noncommittal lines. She began with a quick,

'I told you not to ring me up.'

His voice came back, lazy and teasing.

'Counsel of perfection, darling. I want to see you. No don't say you won't, or you can't, or you don't want to.'

'I wasn't going to.'

He went on as if she had not spoken.

'Because it's perfectly easy – you let the cat out and come out with it.'

She could not help her voice laughing a little as she said, 'We haven't got a cat.'

'Very remiss of you! But the principle remains the same. The operative words are "You come out".'

'Oh, Nicky, I can't.'

'Darling, I warned you about saying that. If you don't come out, I shall come in.'

'You can't do that!'

He said, 'Watch me!'

She had a perfectly clear picture of what he was looking like at the other end of the line – frowning brows, eyes with a spark of malice, lips just curling into a grin. When Nicky was in that sort of mood he didn't really care a damn. He was perfectly capable of marching into the house and saying what he wanted to say. If she didn't open the door, he was capable of breaking a window. She would have to slip out. She said in a hurry,

'Well, just for a moment.'

'Me come in, or you come out?'

'I'll come out.'

'Good girl! Half past ten. In the gazebo.' He rang off.

The hand with which she put the receiver back was not quite steady. Half past ten was too early – her mother might not be asleep. She had her bath at nine, her cup of hot Ovaltine between a quarter to ten and ten o'clock, and as a rule she would be fast asleep before the quarter past. No – half past ten ought to be all right. But suppose it wasn't – suppose her mother was still awake. Part of the picture of herself as an invalid was the belief that she lay awake for hours, suffering but unwilling to disturb Althea. Suppose that for once she really did lie awake, not for hours, but even for one half hour. Althea turned quite cold at the thought. She wanted to see Nicky every bit as much as he wanted to see her,

79

but they oughtn't to risk it. A scene or an upset now would be a danger which mustn't be risked – not now, at the very minute when the prison doors were opening to let her through. She had meant to ring Nicky up from the call-box at the corner as soon as her mother was in bed. She had meant to ring him up and to tell him that she would marry him at once – tomorrow if he wanted her to. Then they could get Emily Chapell down and have her handy and choose their time for breaking the news. It was all beautifully planned in her mind. She had a perfectly clear picture of it with everything going smoothly to a beautiful climax in which her mother resigned herself to the inevitable and gave them her blessing. It hadn't seemed incredible when she planned it, but it did seem incredible now. If only Nicky hadn't rung op . . .

Something in her which would always take his part began to defend him. It was her own fault. She ought to have said, 'I can't talk now – I'll ring you up at ten o'clock,' and just put the receiver back. Even Nicky couldn't have come banging at doors and bursting in after that. He would have waited half an hour, and she could have slipped out to the call-box after washing out the empty Ovaltine cup. She would have to meet him at the gazebo now. It was where they always used to meet. It was where they had met five years ago to say good-bye. Tonight would blot that parting out. She wouldn't stay a moment, but it would be a wonderful moment for them both. She would say, 'I'll marry you tomorrow,' and they would kiss, and she would send him away for the last time.

She went out into the hall and up the stairs. When she came to the bathroom door she stood there for a moment, listening. When she could hear nothing, she knocked gently.

'Are you all right, Mother?'

There was a slight splashing sound. Mrs Graham said fretfully,

'Of course I am all right! What is it?'

'I couldn't hear anything.'

'Really, Thea! Am I a noisy person? I am enjoying my bath, which is making me feel sleepy. I should like my Ovaltine a little earlier than usual tonight. I really feel as if I might drop off.'

She repeated the words later on when she had drunk the Ovaltine and was handing the cup to Althea.

'Be as quiet as you can. I really do feel as if I might drop off.'

Althea said, 'I hope you will.' She had a guilty feeling as she said it.

She put out the bedside light, felt her way to the door, and turned on the threshold to say good-night. Her mother's voice sounded quite sleepy as she answered her.

14

All the events of that evening were to be gone over with a microscope. The slightest word, the most unconsidered action, the time at which Nicholas Carey had left the Harrison's house, the time at which he returned to it, the time at which young Mr Burford rang up Miss Cotton from the call-box at the corner of Lowton Street, the time that Miss Cotton left her cottage in Deepcut Lane, the time that it would take her to arrive at that point on Hill Rise where it skirted the back garden of No. 2 Belview Road, the movements of Mrs Traill who had been baby-sitting for Mr and Mrs Nokes at 28 Hill Rise – all these were to be worked out and compared. All that was spoken and overheard, all that the people concerned had seen or done, was to have a bright and terrifying search-light turned upon it. But from Althea, letting herself out softly by the back door and leaving it ajar so that there should be no click of the latch to betray her, these things were hidden. It was not the thought of the future that came to her as she went softly up the garden in the kindly dark. It was the past which came back with every step she took. This meeting might be any one of the many meetings which she and Nicky had snatched five, six, seven years ago. Her foot trod the same paved pathway. The same scent came up from the thyme which she bruised as she went. There was night-scented stock in the right-hand border. It liked the place and seeded there, to come up every year and fill the dark with fragrance.

There were three steps up to the gazebo. She took them. Someone stirred in the black shadowy place and she was in Nicky's arms.

Mrs Graham was not asleep. She hadn't intended to go to sleep. She was much too angry to feel sleepy. But she had been clever – she hadn't let Althea see that she was angry. When she was a girl she had had quite a taste for private theatricals. They were enjoyable, and everyone said she ought to go on the stage. She had even toyed with the idea herself, but she had got married instead. She felt a good deal of complacency in thinking that she could still act well enough to prevent Althea knowing how angry she had been. And still was. She wasn't in her bath when the telephone bell rang. She was still in her dressing-gown, and she had slipped across to her bedroom and lifted the receiver just as Althea lifted the one in the room below. If you used both hands and moved the receiver very gently, the other person who was telephoning would have no idea that you were listening in. She heard everything that Nicholas and Althea said, and she laid her plans accordingly. She would have her bath and she would have her Ovaltine, and she would say how sleepy she was, and she would beg Althea not to make any noise. She wasn't afraid of going to sleep – she was much too excited and angry for that. She would just stay propped up amongst her pillows and wait until it was half past ten.

She must have dozed a little, because she was suddenly aware of the wall-clock striking in the hall below. There was a stroke that had waked her, and a second which came as she listened for it. She glanced sideways at the table by her bed and saw that the luminous hands on the small ornamental clock were pointing to half past ten. She counted up to twenty before she got out of bed and felt her way to the door. There was always a light on the landing. She couldn't sleep with one in her room, but she liked to feel that it was just outside the door. Standing there listening, she was aware of the silence and emptiness of the house. Thea had already gone to her meeting with Nicholas Carey. She had gone out, leaving the house unlocked and her invalid mother alone in it. A drenching wave of self-pity broke over Winifred Graham. Anything may happen to a woman alone in a house with an open door –

anything may happen to an invalid in a delicate state of health. Thea didn't care what happened to her. All she cared for was slipping out to meet her lover like any girl who has not been brought up to behave herself. It was not only callous and heartless, but exceedingly ill-bred.

She went back into her room, turned on the bedside light, and dressed as she had planned to do. Stockings and outdoor shoes – gardens are always damp at night. A pair of warm knickers pulled right up over her filmy nightdress, a fleecy vest, a cardigan which buttoned up to the neck, a skirt and a long black coat. She tied a chiffon square over her head and wound a fleecy woollen scarf about her throat. Then she went into the bathroom without putting on the light, drew back the curtains, and looked out of the window. The bathroom was at the back of the house. If they had a light in the gazebo, she would be able to see it from here. Her eyes searched the shadowy darkness. There wasn't any light. She listened with all her ears, but there wasn't any sound. Everything in the garden was dim and quiet under the arch of a windless sky.

She went down the stairs and through the house without putting on any of the lights. The backdoor was ajar. Her anger flamed afresh, her self-pity deepened. It was wicked of Thea – wicked, wicked, wicked.

Her eyes had become accustomed to the darkness. Once she was clear of the house she could see well enough. She passed between the two cut hollies, each screening a dustbin, and made her way as Althea had done along the paved walk and up the slope to the gazebo. It was not until she came to the foot of the steps that the murmur of voices reached her. That was really all it was – a murmur. The sound had no words for her. If words there were, they passed from lip to ear, or between lips that met. She was filled with an anger which stopped her breath. She had to gasp for it, stumbling up the steps of the gazebo, catching at the jamb of the door.

It stood open. The sound of those stumbling feet and that catching breath came into the dream in which Althea and Nicholas stood and startled them apart.

'Mother!'

'Mrs Graham!'

Winifred Graham found breath for her anger. Her voice came high and shrill.

'How dare you, Nicholas Carey – how dare you!'

'Mother – *please!* You'll make yourself ill!'

'You wouldn't care if I died! You wouldn't care if you killed me! You only think about yourself!'

Nicholas said in a controlled voice,

'I'm sorry, Mrs Graham, but you wouldn't let me come to the house, and I had to see Allie. I'll go away now and come back and talk to you tomorrow.'

She was clutching at Althea and sobbing.

'No – no – you mustn't come – I won't see you! Send him away, Thea! I can't stand it – he'll kill me! Send him away!'

Althea was having to hold her up. She said,

'Yes, he'll go. Nicky, you'd better. It's no good trying to talk to her now, but I think you'll have to help me get her back to the house.'

Nicholas took a step towards them and Mrs Graham cried out,

'No – no! Don't dare to touch me! Don't dare!'

Althea spoke only just above her breath.

'You'd better go – I'll manage. Mother, you really will make yourself ill. If you won't let Nicholas help you, just lean on me and come back to the house. You don't want to stay here, do you? Let me get you to bed and make you comfortable.'

Nicholas stood where he was. If she wouldn't let him help her she wouldn't, and that was that. It wasn't the slightest use talking to her. It never had been, and it never would be. The only argument to be used against her was the argument of the accomplished fact. Once Althea was his wife she would have to give in. And they were to be married tomorrow. There was a cold fury in his heart as he wondered just what chance there was of that plan being carried out. Mrs Graham would certainly not stick at making herself ill if that was the only way she could keep them apart. Well, if she could fight, he could fight too. He wasn't going to stand for it – not a second time. Not, as he had said when they had met in Sophy's little room, not if he had to smash everything in sight! Not if he had to snatch Althea away by force! At this moment he felt capable

84

of anything. He felt as if he could pick her up in his arms and walk away with her over the rim of the world. He was hers, and she was his, and nobody was going to part them again.

15

Althea took her mother in and got her to bed. To a constant stream of reproaches, strictures and dismal prognostications she opposed a silence which was neither wounded nor stubborn but quietly impervious. She administered sal volatile and filled a second hot-water-bottle with careful efficiency, but she did not speak except to say such thing as, 'Are you warm enough?' 'Are you comfortable?' 'Can I get you anything else?' And finally, 'Good night, Mother.' It was as if a sheet of sound-proof glass had shut her in. She and Nicky were on one side of it, her mother with her petty tyranny, her self-assertion, and her reproaches on the other. She was aware of her there, of her gestures, of her efforts to control, to wound, but it was like seeing something a long way off – the sound and the fury did not reach her. There was a barrier which they could not pass. She stood behind it and was safe. There was nothing now that would make her change her settled mind. She would marry Nicky in the morning, and she would send for Emily Chapell. There were no barriers any more and the prison doors were wide. She lay down in her bed and was asleep almost as soon as her head touched the pillow.

Mrs Graham lay awake and added this wakefulness to her other grievances against Althea. She wasn't going to be able to sleep, and it was very bad for her not to be able to sleep. Sensitive people need a great deal of rest, and she was a highly sensitive person. She had often told Dr Barrington how sensitive she was, and he had not failed to agree with her. She had been subjected to an intolerable ordeal, and it would take time for her to get over it. Even if she hadn't caught her death of cold – the night air, so treacherous – she had been obliged to go to the top of the sloping garden and mount the steps of the gazebo. It was true that she did not feel any ill effects as yet, but they might be all the worse for being delayed. At the moment she did not really feel ill at all, only restless and as if she would not be able to sleep. Actually, she did not want to sleep. She was very comfortable and warm. She wanted to lie here and think what a bad daughter Thea was and how underhand she had been – taking up with Nicholas Carey again and slipping out to meet him in the middle of the night! It came to her suddenly and with intolerable force that she might have slipped out to meet him again.

Disgraceful behaviour! Really disgraceful behaviour!

Suppose Nicholas had not gone away when he was told to go. Suppose he had waited in the gazebo. Suppose he had waited for Thea. Suppose they were there together now. She really couldn't endure the thought. She got out of bed, slipped on her black coat and went across the landing to the bathroom. She wouldn't have worn a coat instead of a dressing-gown if there had been anyone to see her. She considered it a most slatternly habit. She had a very pretty pale blue quilted dressing-gown, but the colour was so pale that it might be seen if she leaned out of the bathroom window. There mightn't be anyone in the gazebo to see her, but if there were, the black coat would be safer.

The curtains were still pulled back as she had left them. She came up close to the window and as she lifted the latch of the left-hand casement and pushed it wide she thought she saw a light in the gazebo.

She thought she saw it, and she thought that she had seen it – but when she leaned right out she could not see it at all. There was only the shadowy insubstantial darkness with nothing to break it. She stayed where she was and did not move. The darkness remained unbroken. And then just as she was beginning to feel the chill of the outer air she saw the light again. It came and went in the space of a moment, but this time she was certain that she had seen it. There was someone in the gazebo. The light just showing and fading again could be a signal. Thea's windows looked this way. Mrs Graham craned sideways until she could see them. They stood wide as they always did, but there was no light in the room behind them and no one moved there.

She turned and went back to her room and put on the

shoes which she had taken off. She did not stay to dress herself or to put on her stockings. She had on her black coat and skirt, and she took the two scarves which she had worn before, the chiffon one for her head, and the gauzy woollen one for her neck. Since there was a light in the gazebo, it meant that Nicholas had not gone away and Thea had either joined him already or would do so at any moment. Mrs Graham shook with anger. They thought they could make a fool of her, but she would show them! Thea putting her to bed with a hot water-bottle, giving her sal volatile, saying good night in a soothing voice as if she was a child – she would show her! She was so angry that she didn't feel as if she would ever want a hot-water-bottle again. The front door was, of course, locked and bolted. She took the key and dropped it into the pocket of her coat. Then she picked up Thea's flashlight from the hall table and went out of the back door, locking that too and taking the key. Now if Thea wanted to leave the house she would have to get out of a window!

She came up the paved path to the steps which led to the gazebo and stood there listening. There was someone there. Her hearing was very acute – she could hear that this some-one moved. And then, screened by a man's body, she saw the light again. It would be Nicholas Carey waiting here in the dark – waiting for Thea to come to him! She went noise-lessly up the steps and stood on the threshold. He had his back to her – he hadn't heard anything. Well, she would give him a fright! She said in a high clear voice, 'How dare you, Nicholas Carey!'

It was her last conscious action.

16

Althea woke from a dreamless sleep. She felt rested. Yester-day seemed far away. It didn't seem to matter. She looked at her watch and saw that it was half past six. There was a lot to be done – Emily Chapell's room to be got ready, and some-thing prepared that could be quickly cooked for lunch. It was their wedding day, hers and Nicky's. Everything must go smoothly.

She went to the window and looked out. There was one of those weeping mists. Sometimes they turn into rain, but more often they lift and give place to a cloudless day. She stood for a moment listening to the drip from the leaves, from the trees, from the plants in the border. Then she went into the bathroom, found the water hot enough to take a bath, and dressed herself. She put on an old brown skirt and a yellow jumper. The Sungleam certainly had brought out the lights in her hair. She thought it looked nice, and hoped that Nicky would think so too. Then she went downstairs and unbolted the front door. She was about to unlock it, when she found that the key was gone.

It couldn't be gone. It must have fallen out of the lock, only she didn't see how it could have done that either. If it had, it would be on the polished floor or under the mat. She took up the mat and shook it, and she looked in every possible and impossible place on the floor. As she moved the two hall chairs and the table and lifted the mat at the foot of the stairs, she was expecting every moment to hear her mother's voice calling out to know why she was making so much noise. The key wasn't anywhere, and no voice called from Mrs Graham's room.

Suddenly and sharply it came to Althea that her mother had taken the key. With her lips pressed together and a heightened colour she went through the house and found the back door locked and its key gone missing too. What a silly trick to play — what a silly childish trick. She turned, ran quickly up the stairs and, coming to her mother's door, noticed for the first time that it was only closed, not shut. There was no chink between door and jamb, but the catch was not engaged. At a touch of her hand the door swung in and she saw the empty bed.

It did not occur to her to be alarmed. It wasn't until she turned and saw the bathroom door wide open as she herself had left it that the first faint stirrings of fear began. She stood in the middle of the landing and called,

'Mother – where are you?'

There wasn't any answer. The house had an empty feeling.

She called again, and her voice came back to her with a shaken sound. She ran downstairs to look in the dining-room, the drawing room, the downstairs cloak-room, the kitchen, pantry, larder, and then ran up again to search the bedroom floor. By the time the postman's knock sounded on the front door she knew that there was no one in the house but herself.

She went back to her mother's room and opened wardrobe and shoe-cupboard. The black coat and the skirt which she had hung up herself at something short of midnight were gone. The shoes which she had put away with her own hands were gone.

Her mother had gone out.

For a moment Althea felt perfectly stupefied with surprise. That her mother should have risen before seven o'clock on a foggy morning and have gone out, locking both doors behind her and taking the keys, was perfectly incredible. It became not only incredible but alarming when she discovered that, though the shoes had been taken, the stockings and under-clothes still lay on the chair at the foot of the bed neatly covered by a spread of blue silk brocaded with mauve and silver. A further search disclosed the fact that no dress or suit was missing from the wardrobe, but the vest and night-gown which Mrs Graham had been wearing, her fleecy blue bed-jacket and the two scarves, were gone. They were gone, and she was gone. Impossible to escape the conclusion that she had left the house with bare feet thrust into outdoor shoes and a skirt and coat pulled on over the things she had been wearing in bed. Only an emergency could account for such a course of action, but for twenty years it had been Althea to whom the task of dealing with emergencies had been delegated. It came home to her with terrifying force that in this emergency her mother had turned away from her. She had not rung her bell, she had not called out, she had not come to her. She had put on a coat and a pair of shoes and hurried out of the house, leaving it locked up behind her.

Just for a moment the room swung round. Althea caught at the foot-rail of the bed and held on to it till everything was steady again. She could think of only one thing which would have taken her mother out – one thing, or one person. She must have thought or supposed that Nicholas was still in the garden or the gazebo. She might have thought that Althea would slip out — that they meant to meet again. But if that was what had taken her out, it must have all happened hours ago. She would not, she could not, have supposed that Nicky would return between six and seven in the morning. No, she had gone in the dark and she had gone in haste. But she had not returned. More than seven hours had passed since midnight, but she had not come back.

Althea ran down the stairs and got out of the kitchen window. The mist lay heavy on the garden. She couldn't even see the gazebo until she was half-way up the path. She couldn't see it clearly then. It was just a shadow against the shadowy hedge. It was in her mind that her mother had come out to make sure that Nicholas had gone. She had come out in a hurry, and than she had had an attack of some kind and fainted and not been able to get back to the house. This was the worst thing that came to her. She went up the steps into the gazebo and saw her mother's body flung down on the right-hand side of the door.

There was a solid oak table in the middle of the room. There was a wooden bench, and some deck-chairs stacked against the wall. The floor boards were dusty and in the corners there were cobwebs. There was the body of Winifred Graham. It lay on its face, bare ankles showing beneath the black cloth coat. From the very first moment Althea had no doubt that her mother was dead, but she knelt down, found an ice-cold hand and wrist, and felt for a pulse that wasn't there.

It wasn't there. It hadn't been there for hours. She went on kneeling on the floor of the gazebo whilst the intolerable certainty of this made its way along the channels of thought until everything else was blotted out. She got to her feet with just one instinctive feeling. She must have someone to help her. She must call Dr Barrington.

When she looked back on it afterwards there was a dull background of fear and confusion like a sea under fog, and rising out of it, strangely and horribly distinct, the things she would never be able to forget. Her hand in the pocket of the black coat, feeling for the keys. Her own voice without any expression speaking to Dr Barrington on the telephone — 'Will you come at once? My mother is dead,' and the surprised protest in his voice when he said, 'No!' Something moved dully behind the numbness in her mind. He hadn't expected her mother to die. Did that make it more her fault, or less?

When he came into the house it was she who was calm. She could move about but she didn't seem able to feel anything. Dr Barrington was a big man, and he had been in practice for thirty years. It was he who ought to have been calm, but he wasn't, he was very definitely upset. She thought, as she had sometimes thought before, that he was very fond of her mother, even perhaps a little in love with her. He was going towards the stairs, when she stopped him.

'She isn't up there,' she said.

He turned.

'Down here? You haven't told me what happened.'

'I don't know. I found her in the gazebo at the top of the garden.'

He said in a stupefied voice,

'In the garden? What do you mean?'

'I found her there. She was dead. I called you up.'

His face worked angrily.

'You ask me to believe that she went out into the garden at this hour and in this weather?'

'I think she went out in the night. She – isn't – dressed . . .'

He stared, as if she had said something monstrous, then turned and led the way through the house to the back door. They went up the path without a spoken word. When they came to the gazebo she put her foot on the bottom step and drew it back again. He went past her, and she stood there waiting for what he would say – for what she knew he must be going to say. She knew what it would be, but to hear it said aloud would be like a blow, and just for a moment she held back from it. But when the words came they were not what she expected. They were quite dreadfully and incomprehensibly worse. He stood in the doorway and said in a terrible voice,

'It's murder – she has been murdered! Who did it?'

17

Miss Maud Silver had finished her breakfast, but there was a second cup of tea on the table beside her and she was taking a little longer than usual over the more frivolous of the two newspapers for which she subscribed. She was reflecting on the rapidity with which news is transmitted, and wondering what prompted the selection of such items as 'Film Star Weds Fifth Husband,' and, 'Mother Says I Love My Baby Son,' when the telephone bell rang from the next room. She put down the paper and, neglecting her cup of tea, went through to answer the call. A voice which she did not recognize spoke her name. She did not recognize the voice, but she was immediately aware that its owner was quite desperately afraid. There is the fear that makes the voice tremble, and there is the fear which makes it rigid. The voice which said, 'Miss Silver . . .' was stiff with fear. When she said, 'Who is speaking?' there was a pause before it said,

'Althea Graham. I saw you yesterday. Something dreadful has happened. My mother is dead.'

Miss Silver was aware of the force which controlled the words. She said,

'If there is anything I can do to help you . . .'

Althea said in that unnatural voice,

'They say she was murdered. Will you come?' The line went dead.

Miss Silver did not attempt to recover the connexion. She congratulated herself on having taken Althea Graham's address, and she went into her bedroom and packed a suit-case. She might be required to stay, or she might not. Certainly that poor girl must not be left alone. Having just completed a most exciting case, she had been hoping for an interval in which to catch up with her correspondence, but this was not an appeal she could neglect. Within twenty minutes of the time when she had taken up the receiver she was seeing her suit-case into a taxi at the Marsham Street entrance to Montague Mansions and saying good-bye to Hannah Meadows who had come down to see her off.

The case already referred to having been of an extremely lucrative nature, she decided to drive the whole way to Grove Hill.

She arrived to find Dr Barrington gone and the police in possession. The local Detective Inspector informed her that a couple of officers would be coming down from Scotland Yard, beyond which he had nothing to say, except that Miss Graham would be wanted for questioning when they arrived, and that she ought not to leave the house. She was in the drawing-room, he added, and stood aside for Miss Silver to pass.

Althea turned round from the window, her face white and strained. It was hard to recognize her as the girl who had left Montague Mansions yesterday, her eyes bright with hope. She said,

'You've come . . .'

'Yes, my dear. I told you that I would come.'

Althea said in a dazed voice,

'Nothing happens the way you think it is going to . . .'

Miss Silver looked at her very kindly indeed.

'You have had a great shock. Let us sit down and see what can be done to help you. Do you feel able to tell me what has happened?'

Althea did not look at Miss Silver. She stared down at her straining hands.

'I don't know what did happen – nobody does. I'll tell you as much as I can. She went to have her bath about nine. Then Nicky rang up. I think she must have gone across to her bedroom and listened in on the extension. He said he wanted to see me, and I said he couldn't. There is one of those old-fashioned summerhouse places which they used to call gazebos at the top of the garden. We used to meet there – long ago . . .' Her voice failed. After a little she went on again. 'He said he would be there at half past ten, and if I didn't come out he would come in. He is like that – you can't stop him if there's something he wants to do.'

A feeling of apprehension was growing in Miss Silver's mind.

The word murder had been used, and the police were in the house. Scotland Yard was taking over, and Nicholas Carey was a young man who would stick at nothing to get his own way. She said,

'You went to meet him?'

The hands in Althea's lap strained more tightly.

'If I hadn't gone he would have come in. If I had locked the door he would have broken a window. He is like that. It wouldn't have been any use saying no, and I wanted to see him. My mother would be asleep by half past ten. I took up her Ovaltine before ten, and I waited until the half hour had struck, but I am afraid that she waited too. I met Nicky and we talked. I told him about your Miss Chapell, and I said we could be married today. And then – she came . . .'

'Your mother?'

Althea made a very slight movement and said,

'Yes. She was angry – very, very angry. I was afraid she would make herself ill. She said I wouldn't care if I killed her – she said I only thought about myself. Nicky did his best, but it wasn't any good. He didn't lose his temper – he didn't really. He said he was sorry he had to see me like that, but she wouldn't let him come to the house. He said he would come round and see her in the morning, and she said he wanted to kill her and he wasn't to come. So I made him go, and I got her back to the house and put her to bed. I wouldn't talk about it. When I had settled her down I went to bed myself. I didn't think I should sleep, but I slept like a log. And then when I woke up she wasn't in her room. She wasn't in the house.'

'What time was it when you waked?'

'It was half past six.'

'What did you do?'

'When I had looked everywhere in the house I went up the garden to the gazebo.'

'Why did you do that?'

For the first time Althea looked at her. Her eyes had a puzzled expression.

'I don't know. I thought she might have gone back to see if Nicky had really gone. She liked – to make sure. I thought she might have gone back to make sure about Nicky and –

and fainted. I thought she must have been in a hurry. She hadn't put on her stockings or underclothes like she had the first time — only a skirt and a coat over her night things.'

'Could she see the gazebo from her window?'

'No, but she could see it from the bathroom. She must have seen something to make her go out like that. And she had locked the front door and the back door and taken the keys — they were in the pocket of the coat. I had to get out of the kitchen window.'

She looked away again. They had come to the part which had got to be told, and she didn't know how to find words for the telling. It was like digging in the ground for something very hard and heavy and pushing it up a hill. It was the sort of thing you cannot do unless it has got to be done.

It had got to be done. She said,

'She was in the gazebo. Lying on the floor. She was dead. I thought it was her heart, but Dr Barrington said she had been murdered. He said — someone had — strangled her.'

She had got the words out. Even the last and the worst of them. There was no more strength in her. No more strength at all. She lifted her eyes to Miss Silver's face and said in an exhausted voice,

'It couldn't be Nicky. It couldn't, couldn't, *couldn't* be Nicky.'

Miss Silver was very grave indeed. She said,

'How much of this have you told to the police?'

'I told them . . .'

'Have they seen Mr Carey yet?'

'No. I rang up. He had gone out. He was going to arrange — about — our getting married.' A little more life came into her voice. 'You won't — you won't let them think he did it. He was keeping his temper — he had promised me he would keep his temper. He couldn't have done a thing like that! Oh, you will help us, won't you?'

Miss Silver took the hand that was suddenly and impulsively held out to her.

'My dear, I will do all that I can to help you. But there is no help in anything except the truth. I must say to you what I say to every client. I cannot take a case in order to prove this person innocent or that person guilty. I can only do my best to arrive at the truth. If Mr Carey is innocent, the truth will clear him. I cannot undertake to prove either innocence or guilt. I can only serve the ends of justice and say, what I most earnestly believe, that in the end mercy and justice are the same.'

Althea drew her hands away. They were so numb that she could not feel them. For a moment her startled glance remained fixed upon Miss Silver, then it turned towards the door. From beyond it the front door banged. There was a sound of voices raised and a rapid step in the hall. The drawing-room door was flung open and Nicholas Carey strode into the room. He did not trouble to shut the door. The local Inspector stood there watching him.

Althea got to her feet. They moved together. She put her head down on his shoulder and he held her close. Detective Inspector Sharp and the Detective Sergeant behind him both heard her say,

'Oh, Nicky, tell them you didn't do it – you *didn't!*'

18

Detective Inspector Frank Abbott was of the opinion that the Yard had got the dirty end of the stick again. You expected it when you were brought in on a country job, but as near in as Grove Hill you might with a bit of luck have hoped to be on the spot in time to get the first reactions of at least the principal suspect. What annoyed him most was that he would have been in time if the Chief, otherwise Chief Superintendent Lamb, had not delayed him over some inquiries as to the winding up of the case against the Callaghan gang, which could perfectly well have waited for a more convenient occasion. Added to which the Chief's rather bulging brown eyes, sometimes irreverently compared with the smaller kind of peppermint bullseye, having discerned a certain impatience to be off with the old case and on with the new, he was treated to one of Lamb's well known homilies on the duty of junior officers to behave themselves lowly and reverently to their betters, and to bear in mind the proverb that more haste made worse speed. Ensuing upon which, he arrived at No. 1 Belview Road about ten minutes after Nicholas Carey had made his dramatic entrance.

He had with him Detective Sergeant Hubbard, a young man whose ambition it was to mould himself in every way upon Inspector Abbott – this becoming so evident in the course of the case that the goaded Frank was driven to remark to Miss Silver that if there was going to be a second murder she wouldn't have far to look for either the victim or the assassin. But all that lay in the future. He knew Detective Inspector Sharp, and had nothing but praise for what had been done up to date. When he had put him in possession of the facts as he knew them Sharp said,

'It's an odd story – a very odd story. Here's a woman who is supposed to be an invalid, and she goes out not once but twice in the night to see if her daughter isn't meeting a chap in the garden.'

'They will do it.'

'Well, there's rather more to it in this case. This fellow Carey and Miss Graham were going together – oh, it must be the best part of seven years ago. He had a shocking old car, and I've seen them out in it myself. Everyone said they were engaged. Then about five years ago it was all off and he went abroad. The mother played up being an invalid – I don't think there was much the matter with her, but she made the most of what there was. Selfish old woman by all accounts. Didn't want her daughter to marry and worked her to the bone. A pretty clear case of slave-driving, if you ask me.'

'You say she went out twice?'

'If the daughter is telling the truth. She says she went out to meet Carey because her mother wouldn't let him come to the house and he said if she didn't come out, he was going to come in. He has the name of being a determined sort of chap. She says they were going to be married, and they wanted to discuss the arrangements. He had come back after five years, and I gather they were going to get on with it and not tell her mother until it was too late for her to do anything to stop them. There's a sort of summerhouse at the top of the garden. That's where they met, and that's where Mrs Graham was murdered. Miss Graham says her mother came out and found them there and made a scene, but she sticks to it that she sent Carey away and took her mother in and put her to bed. If that is true, Mrs Graham must have gone out again. She may have thought Carey was still hanging about and wanted to make sure her daughter didn't meet him. If it isn't true and she only went out once, then she was killed when she surprised them, and they are both in it up to the neck. However it was, she was choked by a pair of strong hands and the scarf she was wearing twisted round her neck to make sure.'

'Was the daughter alone in the house with her?'

'She is as a rule – she was last night.'

'And what do you mean by that?'

Sharp pulled rather an odd kind of face.

'Your Miss Silver arrived about half an hour ago, and Nicholas Carey walked in about ten minutes before you did. He banged past young Hammet who opened the door for him, and was in the drawing-room before anyone could stop him. I came up with him just in time to see the girl fling herself into his arms, and to hear her say, "Oh, Nicky, tell them you didn't do it!" '

Frank Abbott whistled.

'Well, that's straight to the point at any rate. I suppose you didn't leave them to put their heads together?'

'What do you take me for? He's in the dining-room – you had better come in and see him. Perhaps you had better look at Miss Graham's statement first.'

Nicholas Carey was walking up and down with a good deal of vigour and impatience. He wanted to get on with making a statement, and he wanted to get back to Althea. She was looking all in, and what she wanted was a shoulder to cry on. What he wanted was to know what had been happening, and how it could possibly have happened. He stopped his pacing when the two police officers came in, and said abruptly:

'What's been going on here?'

Frank Abbott's colourless eyebrows rose. He had the type of looks which lends itself without effort to an appearance of being supercilious. A long nose, a long pale face, fair hair slicked back into mirror smoothness, eyes of the palest shade of a bluish grey, a tall light figure, a certain elegance of dress, a certain fastidiousness as to detail, added up to something

98

as unlike the popular idea of a police inspector as possible. He might have been any young man in any rather exclusive club. The light eyes focused themselves upon Nicholas in a daunting manner as he said,

'Don't you know?'

Nicholas had stopped pacing. He stood between the dining-table and the window, his face pale and frowning.

'I heard that Mrs Graham was dead. I came to find out if it was true. Miss Graham and I are engaged. I asked you what has been happening. I'm still asking.'

Frank said without any expression at all,

'Mrs Graham was murdered last night.'

Nicholas exclaimed, 'Murdered!'

'Some hours ago.' He turned to Inspector Sharp. 'Did the police surgeon hazard any guess as to the time?'

'Somewhere round about midnight.'

Frank Abbott resumed.

'Perhaps you can help us. What time was it when you left?' Then, as everything in Nicholas tautened, 'Oh, we know you were here – Miss Graham has been quite frank about that. By the way my name is Abbott – Detective Inspector Abbott from Scotland Yard. I have only just arrived, and I haven't seen Miss Graham myself. I shall be interested to have your account of what happened. You had an appointment with her. How was it made?'

'I telephoned. I said I would come round and see her at half past ten.'

'Mrs Graham went to bed early?'

'Yes – about nine.'

'She did not welcome your visits?'

'You might put it that way.'

'Which is why you arranged to meet Miss Graham in the summerhouse at the top of the garden?'

'Yes.'

'And you kept this appointment?'

'I did.'

Frank Abbott said,

'Well, Mr Carey, are you going to tell us what happened after that? You are not obliged to do so of course. On the other hand, if you haven't got anything to hide . . .'

99

'I certainly haven't got anything to hide.'

'Then I think we might just as well sit down.' He turned one of the chairs which stood in to the dining-table and sat down on it. Inspector Sharp followed his example.

Nicholas Carey jerked back the chair for himself. It went through his mind that it must be all of six years since he had broken bread in this house. Yet it was Allie's house and always had been – an added irony! He took his seat and waited for one of the policemen to begin. It was the Scotland Yard man who led off.

'Well, you got here at half past ten. Did you come into the house?'

'No, I waited in the gazebo.'

The word rang a bell in Frank Abbott's mind. His grandmother, the formidable Lady Evelyn Abbott, had possessed a gazebo in the old-fashioned garden at Deeping. It had been Abbott property for three hundred years, and it belonged now to his uncle, Colonel Abbott. The gazebo looked down a yew walk which Monica Abbott kept planted with lilies in their season. But Lady Evelyn's money had gone past them to their daughter Cicely, the only one of her relations with whom she had not managed to quarrel.* All of which was ancient history and did not weigh on Frank at all. Only the gazebo came into his mind in a familiar manner and remained there.

Nicholas Carey went on with his statement.

'Miss Graham met me as we had arranged, and we were discussing plans when Mrs Graham interrupted us.'

Frank Abbott said, 'There was a scene?'

Nicholas looked darkly in front of him.

'She made one. Miss Graham told her she would make herself ill, and I said I would come round and see her in the morning.'

'Why?'

'We were discussing arrangements about our marriage. Mrs Graham had put a stop to it five years ago, and she wanted to put a stop to it now.'

Curiously enough, at that moment Frank Abbott and Nicholas Carey entertained the same thought – on Frank's side 'He was a fool to say that'; on Nicholas' side, 'I suppose

* Eternity Ring

100

that was a stupid thing to say.' He followed it up by going on aloud,

'She wouldn't listen, so Miss Graham told me I had better go away, and she took her mother back to the house.'

Frank's cool gaze narrowed a little.

'And then?'

'I went.'

'Straight back to — by the way, where are you living?'

'I'm staying at Grove Hill House with Mr and Mrs Harrison.'

'And you went back to Grove Hill House?'

'No — I went for a walk.'

'When did you return?'

'I don't know — pretty late. I was disturbed and I wanted to walk it off. I didn't notice the time.'

'I see. And this morning you heard that Mrs Graham was dead. Who told you?'

'I went out directly after breakfast. We had planned to be married today. Miss Graham wanted a church wedding, and I had to see the parson — I thought I'd catch him before he got going. He used to be rather a friend of mine. I didn't want to use the telephone. Well, he had had a call to someone who was ill, so I went back to Grove Hill House. Mrs Harrison said her daily maid had just come in to say Mrs Graham had died in the night.'

'And who had told the daily maid?'

'She said the milkman told her. I came round straight away.'

The questioning went on. In the end Nicholas Carey had said nothing that did not agree with the statement already made by Althea Graham. When he had signed his own statement they let him go.

As he walked into the drawing-room, Miss Silver emerged from it. She was still in her outdoor things — the black cloth coat with many years service behind it and the prospect of more to come, the black felt hat which was not her best but had been done up for the autumn with some of those ruchings of black and purple ribbon so unbecoming to elderly ladies but so constantly pressed upon them by the hat trade. The weather being mild, she was not wearing the archaic fur tippet, so warm, so cosy, which could be called upon to supplement the coat on colder days, but having regard to the changeable nature of the English climate, it reposed in the suit-case which had not yet been unpacked. She greeted Frank Abbott with the formality which she was always so careful to observe before strangers. In private she might, and did, address him as Frank and permit him the affectionate and familiar behaviour which she would have accorded to a relation, but in public there would be no lapse from the conventions. She said,

'How do you do, Inspector Abbott?' and received his entirely proper and respectful reply. After which, Inspector Sharp and the other local detective having departed, Frank took her into the dining-room and shut the door.

'Well, ma'am?' he said when they were seated. 'And how did you get here, may I ask? The Chief will certainly suspect a lurking broomstick. Even I can't help wondering how you beat us to it.'

Miss Silver smiled indulgently.

'Miss Graham consulted me yesterday.'

'And pray, what did she consult you about?'

She was silent for a moment. Then she said,

'She tells me that she has made a statement. I suppose that you have seen it?'

He nodded.

'Sharp showed it to me. What did she want to consult you about?'

'Whether she would be justified in marrying against her mother's wishes.'

'And you said . . .'

She gave the slight cough with which she would sometimes introduce an important remark.

'Considering the extremely selfish nature of those wishes and the fact that they had stood as a barrier between her and Mr Carey for the last seven years, I was of the opinion that a sufficient sacrifice had been made, and that they should now be disregarded. Mr Carey had secured a marriage licence. He was anxious that the marriage should take place immediately without consulting Mrs Graham any further. Since she has in the past invariably produced a heart attack whenever the subject came up, it seemed desirable to confront her with a *fait accompli*, and I was able to recommend a retired nurse who would be prepared to take over as her companion. It was therefore natural that Miss Graham should at once acquaint me with the present tragic development and ask me to come to her.'

Frank Abbott had taken up as easy a position as a dining-room chair allows. One long leg was crossed over the other, displaying an inch or two of discreet sock and the polish of a well-cut shoe. One of his very pale eyebrows lifted as he said,

'Having gone to you in the first place, she would naturally call you in, but I should like to know how she came to go to you at all.'

Miss Silver smiled.

'It is extremely simple. I was able to help a friend of hers some years ago. She talked about it, and about me. The other day I came down to a cocktail-party at the house of an old friend who lives at Grove Hill, and there I met Mrs Graham.'

'Oh, you did, did you?'

'She was the kind of woman who will talk to a stranger about her private affairs.'

He laughed.

'People do talk to you, you know! What did the late Mrs Graham talk about?'

'She talked about herself, and about an undesirable young man who was pestering her daughter, and about going away on a cruise in order to separate them. She pointed her daughter out to me and indicated Mr Carey as the undesirable young man. She appeared agitated at discovering that he was present and said that fortunately it had all come to nothing and he had been away, but that it really would be dreadful if it started all over again. Whilst Mrs Graham was speaking to me Miss Graham was making her way across the crowded room and out at the door. Mr Carey followed her. I was in a position to see this, but Mrs Graham was not. It was, I understand, their first meeting for five years. I saw them go, and I saw them return about half an hour later. It was perfectly plain that they had come to an understanding. Miss Graham looked as if she was in a dream. I was sitting on a sofa in a retired position. She came over to it and sat down. After a

103

little while I spoke to her, mentioning her friend's name and my own. We talked for a little, chiefly about some rather curious offers that were being made for the purchase of this house.'

'Curious? In what way?'

'In this way, Frank. The house was not up for sale, yet two would-be purchasers, each introduced by a different agent, had arrived with an order to view and were competing with offers which were proving a serious temptation to Mrs Graham. I gathered that what made this very awkward for Miss Graham was that the house is hers. From what I had seen of Mrs Graham I could imagine that she would find it convenient to forget this or any other fact which did not suit her. I really have very seldom encountered so self-centred a person. Miss Graham was quite restrained in what she said, but I discerned that the situation was weighing upon her. I was therefore not very much surprised when she rang me up and asked if she could come and see me. Now before we go any further, I should like to suggest an inquiry into the antecedents of these would-be purchasers.'

'My dear ma'am!'

Her look reproved him.

'I am sure I need not remind you that anything in the least abnormal should be investigated.'

'Naturally. But I don't quite see . . .'

'The situation as regards the house was abnormal. You have to remember that it was not being offered for sale. Nevertheless two prospective buyers appear. They bid the property up to a price quite beyond its value. Then two things happen. One of them, Mr Worple, suddenly withdraws. Mrs Graham is murdered. The two events may have nothing to do with one another, or there may be some connexion. Even if remote, this would bear looking into. I have made a few notes on what little is known about Mr Blount and Mr Worple. I think that it would be wise to add to it.'

She passed over a neatly written sheet which contained no more about Mr Blount than his address and the fact that he was married to an invalid wife, but furnished particulars of Mr Worple's previous connexion with Grove Hill and his relationship to Mr Martin of Martin and Steadman, the house-agents, who were, however, sponsoring, not him, but Mr Blount.

Frank put the sheet away in his pocket-book. He was not much interested in Mr Blount or Mr Worple, whose connexion with the case he regarded as hypothetical, and he was very much interested in Nicholas Carey. He said,

'Suppose we get back to Carey. Mrs Graham described him as an undesirable young man. Any support for this point of view?'

'I do not think so. He seems to have spent his holidays here with an aunt. Miss Graham had known him since she was a child. They were companions and friends before they fell in love. He is on the staff of the *Janitor,* and he has comfortable private means. He seems to have made every possible concession to Mrs Graham, even going to the length of suggesting that he and Althea should take over the top floor of this house, an arrangement which would certainly have proved unsatisfactory in the extreme. If Mrs Graham had had anything against his character she would, I feel sure, have produced it for my benefit. She was prepared to use any weapon to prevent her daughter from marrying. In the end the situation became too much for Mr Carey. Miss Graham was afraid to leave her mother. She feared a heart attack which might prove fatal. Mr Carey could no longer bear the strain. He has been abroad for the last five years, travelling in the wilds and supplying the *Janitor* with articles which have been a good deal talked about.'

'He's not "Rolling Stone"!'

'I believe that is the name under which he writes.'

Frank whistled.

'His stuff is good, there's no doubt about that, but – he has certainly been in the wilds. The question is how much of their manners and customs might he have assimilated – enough to make him take an easy step over on to the wrong side of the law and choke an old woman who was standing between him and the girl he wanted? It's quite a motive, you know.'

Miss Silver shook her head.

'I do not think such a motive existed. Miss Graham had consented to marry him. The meeting last night was to arrange the details. They were, in fact, to have been married today.'

Frank Abbott's eyes took on a bleak expression.

'*Were* to have been,' he said. 'Do you suppose there was any chance that they *would* have been, after Mrs Graham had walked in on them and their arrangements? If heart attacks were her long suit, do you suppose she hadn't got all the cards she wanted up her sleeve, or that she would have hesitated to play them? Motive? I should say Carey had a whale of a motive! And quite a lot of inhibitions could have disappeared after five years amongst people who probably hadn't got any — at least not the sort that would prevent you from bumping off anyone who stood in your way.'

Miss Silver said with the mildness which did not for a moment deceive him,

'If, my dear Frank, you are asking me to believe that Miss Graham stood by whilst a murderous attack was being made upon her mother, and that she afterwards made a completely false statement and was prepared to swear to it, I feel obliged to tell you that it would be completely out of her character, and that I am unable to entertain the idea for a moment.'

19

In every murder case there are a number of scattered threads to be picked up and woven together. Some appear to be more important than others, but none can be neglected. Sometimes a chance word or an accidental happening may lead in the direction of an important clue. In the work of the police there must be a continual search for and sorting and arranging of even the slightest and least significant of these threads.

Nothing could appear to have less connexion with Mrs Graham's death than the fact that Mrs Sharp, the young wife of Detective Inspector Sharp, chose the following afternoon to visit her aunt Miss Agnes Cotton, the Grove Hill district nurse, yet it was to have a definite bearing on the course of events. Miss Cotton had very little interest in the daily press. Foreign affairs were a long way off and there wasn't anything you could do about them. And so far as domestic problems were concerned she had her hands quite full enough with confinements, accidents and other local emergencies, without wanting to read about them in the papers. What was the good of being told that a woman had had quads in Japan or that a man had stabbed his wife in Marseilles, when her hands were full enough with the Thomas twins and one of them all set to die only she had no intention of allowing it, or when Bill Jones just round the corner from her had knocked Mrs Jones about to such an extent that it didn't look as if they were going to get out of it without having a police-court case. When she did have time for reading, what she liked was one of the women's magazines with a nice love story where everything came right in the end, and some good recipes and knitting patterns. Sooner or later she would certainly have heard about a local murder, but she might not have connected it with Mrs Burford's false alarm and Mr Burford's call on Tuesday night. Young married people and jumpy, that's what they were. A first baby took them that way as often as not. Hilda Burford was a nervous little thing, and John one of those long pale lads for all the world like a piece of string dipped in tallow.

Miss Cotton was very pleased to see her niece. It was over the home-made scones and currant cake that Mary Sharp said how busy Ted was, and what a dreadful thing, someone being murdered in her own back garden! Miss Cotton poured a good strong cup of tea for herself, put in three lumps of sugar and about four drops of milk, and inquired who had been murdered.

Mary Sharp had come over quite flushed and excited.

'That Mrs Graham that's got the corner house between Hill Rise and Belview Road! They say she caught her daughter in the garden with her boy friend in the middle of the night, and in the morning there she was dead in a sort of summer-house place they've got!'

Miss Cotton's cup was half way to her lips. She set it down again. She was a comfortable rosy person with a smiling look about her, but she didn't smile as she said,

'When did it happen?'

Mary stared.

'Last night, Auntie. Ted is all taken up with it − too busy to know whether I'm out or in, so I thought it would be a good idea to come along to you and cheer myself up. I'm sure he hadn't a word to say dinner-time, and if I said anything all I got was a "What?" '

Miss Cotton separated the chaff from the wheat in this pronouncement.

'Then it wasn't Ted who told you about the murder?'

Mary tossed her head.

'Mentioned it, and then not a word more to say, except that he'd be busy on account of somebody coming down from Scotland Yard. No, it was that Mrs Stokes that works for the Grahams. I met her when I was out doing my shopping and – it wasn't her day with them, they only have her once a week, but she seemed to know all about it. She's one of those talkers – makes it her business to know everything. And there I was with Ted on the job and I didn't know the first thing about it except that it had happened. I'm sure I don't know what she thought – *nor* what I felt like.'

Miss Cotton administered a lecture. Mary was a good girl, but she was new to being a policeman's wife. If Ted Sharp didn't talk about his business it was no more than what was expected of him, and she ought to be proud of him and not go about pulling a long face. Tittle-tattling and talking to gossips like Mrs Stokes wasn't at all the way to help him to get on – 'And don't you forget it, my dear.'

When Mary left, Miss Cotton walked back with her, said good-bye at the corner of the road, and then instead of return-ing along the way that they had come, she took the bus down into the town and got out at the police station.

20

Ted Sharp and the Scotland Yard Inspector came knocking at Miss Cotton's door next day. They had rung up, and she was fitting them in between the Thomas twins and old Mrs French's back. Her cottage really was a cottage, standing much farther back from the road than the new council houses on either side of it, with a long narrow garden full of autumn flowers in front, and cabbages, Brussels sprouts and artichokes behind. There was a living-room and a kitchen on the ground floor, and two bedrooms above. Between the two wars a bathroom and a lavatory had been built up at the back. The front door opened directly into the living-room, which had a round table in the middle, an easy chair on either side of the fireplace, a corner-cupboard, and four chairs with their backs against the wall. There was a teapot and sugar basin, four cups and saucers and a milk-jug in copper lustre with a bright blue band and a pattern of raised fruits, in the corner-cupboard. And there was a vase with 'A present from Margate' on it in the middle of the mantelpiece. It was full of bronze and yellow chrysanthemums, and so was the blue and white ginger jar on the table. The other things on the mantelpiece were a framed photograph of Mary Sharp in her wedding dress balanced on the other side by a snapshot of her at her christening, and at one corner one of those large shells flushed with pink, and at the other the reproduction of a woman's hand in brass. It was about three inches long, and extremely elegant, with a ring on the third finger, and it was polished to the colour of pale gold. Everything in the room was as neat as a new pin, including Miss Cotton herself in a cheerful blue uniform with a white collar. She had a lot of grey hair, very blue eyes, and a hat worn rather on the back of her head.

She received them with composure, told them she was fitting them in, and came straight to the point with,

'You've come about a statement I made last night.'

Ted Sharp said yes, they had. After which he said, 'This is Detective Inspector Abbott from the Yard,' and left it to him.

They sat round the table. Frank Abbott took out the paper which was Miss Cotton's signed statement and laid it down in front of him. Then he said in his leisurely cultured voice,

'I believe you made this statement last night, Miss Cotton.'

She sat there very composed with her grey hair, her blue eyes, and her cheeks like rosy apples. She said,

'My niece was here to tea with me. She told me Mrs Graham had been murdered in the night at No. 1 Belview Road and I thought it was my duty to call in at the station and say what I knew about it.' Then, as the colour came flooding up under Ted Sharp's brown skin, she made haste to add, 'My niece is Mrs Sharp, as I suppose Ted here has told you, but it wasn't from him that she got anything she could tell me about the murder, it was from that Mrs Stokes that works at the Grahams'. And a real busy talker she is!'

Ted Sharp's colour subsided. He didn't look at her, but he was grateful in his heart. If he had ever thought that Mary ran round too much to her Auntie Ag, he took it back.

Frank Abbott went on.

'Well, Miss Cotton, we are grateful to you. Now will you just forget about this statement and tell me the whole thing all over again in your own words?'

She gave him a quick appreciative nod.

'They change things a bit when they write them down, don't they? I told the young man that was writing it, and he didn't like me saying what I did — said I needn't sign it if I didn't want to. But there wasn't anything exactly wrong if you know what I mean, only it wasn't just the way I'd have put it myself, so I signed it and came away.'

His smile had a humanizing effect upon the inherited features.

'I know. Well now, suppose we have it just the way it comes.'

'It began with Mr Burford calling me up. It's a first baby and I thought it would be a false alarm, but of course you never can tell. I wasn't undressed, which was a bit of luck, so I just had to get into my out-of-door shoes and put on my coat and hat and come away. I got my bicycle out of the shed and rode it until I came to the steep part of Hill Rise. It's not worth riding to the top — takes more out of you than it saves you — so I got off and walked. Being a stranger, I don't know if you know how the roads go, but Hill Rise runs into Belview Road just beyond the top of the hill, and No. 1 Belview Road is the corner house. The garden runs back along Hill Rise right to the top, and that's where I was just going to get on to my bicycle again, when someone called out on the other side of the hedge.'

'Man, or woman?'

'It was Miss Graham. She called out, "Mother!" '

'How do you know it was Miss Graham?'

110

Miss Cotton maintained her composure.

'Oh, I've nursed there more than once when Mrs Graham took a notion that she was going to die and they couldn't get anyone else.'

'All right, go on.'

'There's a sort of summerhouse at the top of the garden not so far from the hedge, and that's where they were. There was a man's voice that said, "Mrs Graham . . ." and I could hear her catching her breath. There's quite a slope on that garden, and she never would walk up it, so I wondered what she was doing there. She got her breath and called out, "How dare you, Nicholas Carey — how dare you!" Miss Graham was trying to quiet her down. She told her she would make herself ill, and Mrs Graham called out, "You wouldn't care if I died! You wouldn't care if you killed me! You only think about yourself!" Mr Carey said he was sorry but she wouldn't let him come to the house, and he had to see Miss Graham. He called her Allie — her name is Althea, you know. He said he would go away and come back and talk to her in the morning. Mrs Graham was properly worked up, crying and carrying on. She said he mustn't come and she wouldn't see him if he did. She told Miss Graham to send him away — said she couldn't stand it — "He'll kill me — send him away!" ' She paused and said with a shade of embarrassment, 'It doesn't sound very good me standing and listening like that, but it all seemed to happen so quickly, and if she had worked herself into an attack they might have been glad of my help. I didn't feel I could just ride on and leave them.'

'No, of course not, Miss Cotton. Please go on.'

'Miss Graham said something about getting her back to the house. I didn't catch it all, but I think she was asking Mr Carey to help her, because Mrs Graham called out, "No — no! Don't dare to touch me — don't dare!" After that I could just hear Miss Graham's voice, but I couldn't hear what she said, only at the end there was something about getting her mother to bed and making her comfortable. And that was all, except that I heard them going off down the garden together, and Miss Graham was having her work cut out.'

'In what way?'

'Oh, every way. Mrs Graham was crying and catching her

breath, and by the sound of it I should say Miss Graham was three parts carrying her. So I waited to see if she could get her into the house, and when I heard the door shut I got on my bicycle and went on to the Burford's, and it was a false alarm, just as I thought it would be, so I made her a cup of tea and had one myself and came along home.'

Frank Abbott was reflecting a little sardonically upon the difference between the living spoken word and the stiff dead stuff to which the average police statement reduced it. There was no actual discrepancy between what Miss Cotton had just been saying and what she had signed at the police station last night, but there was exactly the same difference between them as there is between a living person and a corpse. The paper lay on the table before him. His eye picked out a sentence – 'As I was proceeding along Hill Rise upon my bicycle ...' He was prepared to bet that Miss Cotton had never proceeded anywhere in her life. He said,

'Did you come back the same way as you went?'

'Well, I did.'

'You passed along the garden of No. 1 Belview Road – were you bicycling or walking?'

'I got off my bicycle and walked. There's quite a bit of a rise there.'

'See anything – hear anything?'

'No, I didn't.'

'Any lights on in the house?'

'Not that I could see. There would be one on the upstair landing – they used to keep it on all night.'

There was a pause. Then he said,

'I take it you know that Mrs Graham was found dead in that summerhouse you spoke of, and that she had been strangled.'

'That was what I heard.'

'Miss Graham found her, but not until something after seven in the morning. She says she left her comfortably in bed, and that she had no idea she had gone out again. She searched the house, and when she found that her mother's outdoor coat and shoes were missing she searched the garden. She discovered her mother's body in the summerhouse and rang up Dr Barrington. That is her story. Now what I want

112

to know is this – what sort of terms was Mrs Graham on with her daughter?'

Miss Cotton looked at him out of those very blue eyes.

'Miss Graham did everything she could for her.'

'Mrs Graham was trying?'

Miss Cotton nodded.

'She was just about the most selfish person I've ever known. It was Thea do this and Thea do that, from the first thing in the morning till the last thing at night. I don't know how the poor girl stood it, I'm sure. And it was common talk that Mrs Graham had got her engagement broken off.'

'To Mr Nicholas Carey?'

'That's right – and a real shame too. Always about together from the time they were in school, and fond of each other – well, it stuck out all over them.'

'So you would say that Miss Graham was a good daughter. Was she fond of her mother?'

'It was a miracle if she was.'

'Oh, well, miracles happen. The question is, was she?'

'She did everything she could for her.'

'I see. Now tell me – you say you heard Mrs Graham say a number of things like "You wouldn't care if I died – you wouldn't care if you killed me!" That was talking to her daughter. Did you hear Miss Graham say anything to account for that?'

'No, I didn't. She was telling her mother that she would make herself ill.'

'It wasn't said in any threatening way?'

'Of course it wasn't! She was doing her best to soothe her down like she always did.'

'She always tried to soothe her mother?'

'Yes, she did. Anyone will tell you that.'

'I just wanted to know. Now with regard to Mr Carey. Speaking of him to her daughter, she said, "He'll kill me – send him away!" And, speaking to him, "Don't dare to touch me – don't dare!" Did you hear him say anything that would account for her speaking to him like that?'

'No, I didn't. Mr Carey is a gentleman and he spoke like one – kept his temper and said he was sorry but she wouldn't let him come to the house and he had to see Allie, meaning

Miss Graham, and he would come back and talk to her to-morrow. There wasn't anything to make Mrs Graham say what she did. She was right down hysterical, that's all.'

'And you are sure that Miss Graham took her mother back to the house?'

'I heard them all the way down the garden, and I heard them go in and shut the door. When I got to the corner I looked down Belview Road and I saw the light go on in Mrs Graham's bedroom.'

'Then it seems as if Mrs Graham must have gone back to the summerhouse later on. Are you quite sure you didn't see or hear anything on your return journey when you walked the length of the garden as far as the crest of the hill?'

'I didn't see anything or hear anything.'

'And there was no light on in the house?'

She stopped for a moment before she answered that — looking back — trying to remember. Then she said,

'If the landing light was on, I wouldn't see it — there's a thick curtain there. The house looked dark.'

21

'What are we going to do, Nicky?'

They sat close together on the deep sofa in the drawing-room. They were not leaning back. Althea's left hand rested palm downwards on the stuff of the seat. Nicky's right hand covered it. He said,

'There isn't anything very much that we can do.'

He didn't like to say, 'It will pass,' but the thought was in his mind. They would have to get through the inquest and the funeral, and then they could get married and he would take her away. He wondered if she would want to sell the house, and whether the two lots of people who were after it would still be so anxious to buy now that there had been a murder there. The sooner he could get Allie away the better — right away. These things filled his mind, but it was a bit soon to start talk-ing about them to Allie, so he just said there wasn't much they could do and left it at that.

He wasn't so stupid as to think they were clear out of the wood either. Miss Cotton's statement was all right in a way and as far as it went. Fortunately, it did go far enough to make it clear that Allie had taken her mother back into the house and shut the door. It also made it perfectly clear that there had been a frightful row. He had an unpleasantly sharp impression in his mind of Mrs Graham screaming out that he wanted to kill her, and a few other helpful things like that. There really wasn't any way out of the police having their eye on him as suspect number one. And he couldn't blame them, since look where he would, he couldn't for the life of him think of reasons why Nicholas Carey should want Mrs Graham out of the way, but as far as he could see, no reason at all why anyone else should.

He said abruptly,

'It's frightful for you, but it won't go on being so bad. We've just got to go through with it – the police and everything. They'll either find out who did it, or they won't. Whether they do or not, there will be a lot of talk, and then there won't be so much, and presently something else will happen and everyone will switch on to that. Miss Silver is staying on with you for a bit?'

'Yes.' Her voice became suddenly warmer. 'Nicky, do you know, Mrs Justice rang up and said would I come to them. I do think it was terribly kind of her. Only when she heard I'd got Miss Silver here she said I couldn't have anyone better, and I think she actually was a little bit relieved.'

'You'd rather be here?'

'*Much* rather. Mrs Justice is so kind, but she talks all the time, and she would keep wanting me to have cups of Ovaltine and things like that. It used to drive Sophy crazy.'

A shudder went over her. Mrs Graham was devoted to Ovaltine. She had it in the middle of the morning, and she had it the last thing at night in bed. She was very particular indeed about the way it was made. Althea had had to make it twice a day for years. She would never have to make it again.

This train of thought was broken in upon by Nicholas. He said in what seemed to be an entirely irrelevant manner,

'I had better clear out of the Harrisons'.'

Althea's hand jerked under his.

'Why?'

He had several reasons, but he only gave her one of them.

'Well, it's involving them in what isn't any affair of theirs. I expect the police will want me to be somewhere handy whilst they are clearing things up, and I can get a room at the George.'

An hour or two later Ella Harrison looked round an open bedroom door and found him packing. She came in and said 'Hullo, what's all this?' A suit-case was open on the bed, right on one of the new covers. Really men were the limit! He pushed a pair of socks into a corner and turned round.

'Oh, I was coming down to see you ... I thought I had better clear out.'

Eye-shadow, mascara, powder, lipstick, she had them all on. The reinforced eyebrows rose.

'What on earth for?'

'Well, I'm a bit conspicuous, don't you think? I don't think it's quite fair to you and Jack.'

'My dear Nicky – what nonsense! We won't hear of your going! Besides the police will expect you to hang around until after the inquest.'

'I could get a room at the George.'

'We wouldn't hear of it! Jack would be furious. Besides it would look so bad – as if we had turned you out. It might do you quite a lot of harm – as if we believed the kind of talk that's going round. That's what I really came up to see you about.' She went back a step, pushed the door so that it shut and latched, and came back again. 'You see, Nicky, you could be in a bit of a spot, couldn't you?'

She was being kind, and the trouble was that he couldn't take it. He disliked her too much – the brassy hair and all that make-up, her laugh, the way she picked on Allie, the way she treated poor old Jack. She was a handsome woman. The eyes that were smiling at him were undeniably fine. He didn't dislike people as a rule, but he disliked Ella Harrison.

She was saying in a voice as brassy as the hair,

'Lucky for you and for Thea that Nurse Cotton should have been passing after you'd had that dust-up in – what do you call the place – the gazebo. A bit of nonsense giving it an outlandish name like that, but that was just Winifred Graham all over!'

He shook his head.

'The name is much older than Mrs Graham — eighteenth — nineteenth century — at least a hundred years before her time.'

She laughed.

'Well, that's not what we were talking about anyhow. I said it was lucky Nurse Cotton could swear that Thea took her mother into the house and left you there in the garden. What the police are going to want to know is why did she come out again.'

He said,

'You seem to know a lot about it all.'

She made an impatient movement.

'Do you suppose that people don't talk? Nurse Cotton made a statement to the police, didn't she? She's friendly with a Miss Sanders who teaches at that little preparatory school in Down Road. Miss Sanders has an aunt who used to be governess to the Miss Pimms. I met Lily Pimm this morning, and she told me all about it. *And* all about what Miss Cotton said to the police. And as I said, it's a good thing for you that Nurse Cotton says Thea went into the house with her mother and left you there in the garden. She says she came back the same way about half an hour or three quarters of an hour later, which is about the time the murder must have been done, and she says she didn't see anything or hear anyone then. It gives one a creep to think poor Winifred Graham may have been lying there dead just the other side of the hedge in that — what did you call it — gazebo, when Nurse Cotton went by. Of course what puzzles everyone is, why should Winifred have gone into the house with Thea and then come out again as I suppose she must have done.'

She had come up close to him. He could smell the heavy scent she used. He loathed women who scented themselves. He made an excuse to go over to the washstand and collect toothbrush, nailbrush, a tube of toothpaste, and a face-cloth. He was rolling them up in paper, when Ella Harrison exclaimed,

'You ought to have a case for those! You can't pack them like that! I'll get you one next time I'm in the High Street! Men really do want looking after!' Then, breaking off, 'Of course what the police will want to know is, what did you do after Thea took her mother away.'

He was irritated every time she said Thea. For one thing it reminded him of Mrs Graham, and for another it wasn't for her to play tricks with Allie's name. The thought went through his mind and stiffened it against her as he said,

'I told the police what I did. I went for a walk.'

He tossed his parcel into the suit-case from the other side of the bed, but she was edging round it towards him again.

'Nicky, that is no good. You went for a walk! At that hour! It's too thin! What you want is someone to say what time you got back here! It would probably take Thea half an hour to get her mother back to bed and settled down after the upset she had had — at least she can always say it did. Nurse Cotton is supposed to have left her cottage at half past ten, and it would take her until about a quarter to eleven to get to the top of Hill Rise and start listening in to the row that was going on in the gazebo. Well, it wouldn't be a lot short of eleven by the time Thea got her mother indoors and up into her room, and it would be a good deal after that before she got her to bed and was able to leave her. So if someone could say that you were back in this house by eleven — well, that would let you out, wouldn't it?'

'And who is supposed to be going to say that?'

She had been moving along past the foot of the bed. Now she turned the corner and was on the same side as he was. She said,

'Suppose I was to say it . . .'

She looked at him between the long mascaraed lashes. It made her angry too. The pleasure and the anger were stimulating.

He said,

'You certainly couldn't do anything of the sort! I didn't look at the time, but it must have been all of twelve o'clock before I came back here.'

She laughed.

'Well, I shouldn't tell that to the police, darling!' Then, with a change of manner, 'Nicky, you know you might be in quite a tight place over this. There's Nurse Cotton to say you had a row with Winifred Graham, and that she said things like you wanting to kill her. And then later on she's found dead in that damned gazebo — well, there you are! There wasn't

118

anyone else who had quarrelled with her. There wasn't anyone else who had a motive for killing her, unless it was Thea – and that doesn't let you out, because if Thea was in it you would be bound to be in it too.'

'We weren't either of us in it.'

She stood there smiling.

'Well, that's what you say, but no one is going to believe it – unless you can prove that you just weren't there. It all turns on that. And when you say there isn't anything I could do about it, that's just where you're wrong, because I could. Look here, Nicky, why won't you be friends with me? I could help you a lot, you know – and I would if you'd stop glaring at me and looking as if you'd like to murder me too.'

He was so angry that he couldn't trust himself to speak. Instead he went over to the walnut chest on the other side of the room, opened the top long drawer, and came back with a pile of underclothes, which he dumped in the suitcase on the bed. By this time he was able to manage a tone of deadly politeness.

'It is very kind of you, but I am afraid there isn't anything you can do.'

It wasn't Ella's way to beat about the bush. She never had and she never would. She came right out into the open with a frank,

'I can say you got back here by eleven o'clock, and that you couldn't have gone out again because you were with me. Come along, Nicky, isn't that worth being nice to me for? Or isn't it? But you can't expect me to do it if you keep on looking at me as if I could go to hell and be damned to me!'

He restrained himself. When he had fetched half a dozen shirts and packed them, he was able to achieve a conversational tone.

'It's a kind thought, but I'm afraid I've already told the police that I went for quite a long walk and didn't get in until fairly late.'

'That, darling, was only because of your being Jack's cousin and a perfect gentleman and not wanting to give me away. Quite good reasons for saying you took that walk. Nobody will believe in it anyhow. It's just a question of whether you would rather they believed you were waiting in Winifred

Graham's garden to lure her out and murder her, or that you were here having fun and games with me. People always like to believe the worst, you know, and there's quite a good chance they could be got to believe it about you and me.'

'And what are Jack and Althea supposed to think about it?'

She shrugged her shoulders.

'I don't give a damn!'

'Perhaps I do.'

She sat down on the end of the bed. Her voice dropped.

'I meant that, you know – all of it! I suppose you haven't been here all this week without tumbling to it that Jack bores me stiff? Well, *you don't*. We could have a good time together, you know. I like travelling – going places. We'd get on like a house on fire if you'd only let yourself go. And you needn't bother about Jack – all he really wants is what he calls a quiet life. But I haven't got any use for being poor. If I swear you were with me on Tuesday night it'll clear you, but Jack will probably divorce me – and I should have to reckon on that. If I don't do it, you'll probably hang, and it would be up to you to see I didn't suffer for saving your neck, wouldn't it? We could go abroad till it all blew over – travel and have a good time.'

Oh, they could travel, could they? He found his thought straying to some of the places to which he might conduct Ella Harrison and dump her. There was an Asian desert scourged by Polar winds. There were leech-infested swamps. There was a tribe of head-hunters. He said in a perfectly civilized voice,

'I'm afraid there's nothing doing, Ella. You see, if it hadn't been for Mrs Graham's death Althea and I would be married by now.'

22

As has already been said, the Miss Pimms were in the habit of spreading their net as widely as possible. Even if they caught the same bus down into the High Street and took the same bus back, they would after alighting each take her separate way, dividing the errands between them and neglecting no chance of conversation. Lily, who was the middle Miss Pimm, was as a rule the least enterprising and successful of the three. She had neither Miss Mabel's keen nose for a scandal nor Nettie's passionate and persistent attention to detail. Her only gift was, in fact, one which seldom survives the impact of education. She could reproduce word for word a conversation which she had overheard, or a communication which had been made to her. It is to this faculty that we owe the great traditional tales and ballads which have been handed down by word of mouth through countless generations. Most literates have lost it, most children possess it. Miss Lily Pimm, distressingly impervious to the efforts of the excellent Miss Sanders, their onetime governess, had retained it.

She entered a greengrocer's shop, where she bought apples and a cauliflower. She met the youngest Miss Ashington and inquired solicitously after her mother, to which Louisa replied that she was very well, thank you. She seemed in a hurry to get away, so Miss Lily let her go, a thing which neither of her sisters would have done. Mabel's louder voice and dominant manner would have compelled a more satisfying answer, Nettie's bright darting questions would have extracted one, but Lily Pimm, though quite as well aware that Mrs Ashington was now practically off her head, could manage nothing better in the way of delaying tactics than a word and a smile which had no effect at all.

She bought soap in a packet at a grocery store, and toilet soap from the old-fashioned chemist's shop at which her parents had always dealt. She met Mrs William Thorpe who wanted to find homes for three female kittens of uncertain looks and ancestry, Miss Brazier who was earnestly trying to collect enough money to provide somebody's eleventh child with a school outfit, and old Mr Crawley who was telling everyone he met what his newspaper had that morning told him about foreign affairs. Since this was not the sort of gossip which interested the Pimm family, she got away from him as soon as she could and went to stand in the fish queue, where she was overtaken by a horrid uncertainty as to whether Mabel had told her to get fresh haddock or finnan. If she had been listening at the time she would have remembered, but that was the trouble — she had allowed her thoughts to wander, and if she bought the wrong sort Mabel wouldn't be pleased.

And then, there in the fish queue, a bare-headed woman in a shabby coat said to the woman in front of her, 'I don't rightly know what to do about it, and that's a fact.' The other woman had on slacks and a headscarf and she was smoking a cigarette. She said, 'Fancy that, Mrs Traill!'

Lily Pimm's memory began to record what they were saying. By the time she had reached the head of the queue and bought fresh haddock and got half way to the bus stop and then remembered that Mabel really had said finnan and gone back and changed it, Mabel and Nettie were waiting for her and not too pleased about it. Each had already asked the other more than once how on earth Lily managed to take so much longer over her shopping than they did. Her arrival almost at a run and with flushed cheeks did nothing to placate them. If they had missed the bus it would have meant another half hour's wait.

Fortunately they had not missed the bus. All the way up the hill Lily Pimm sat hugging herself with pleasure. What she had got to tell her sisters as soon as they got home really was news, and the woman in the fish shop had been able to give her Mrs Traill's address. She hoped Mabel would realize how clever it was of her to have thought of getting it. Mabel and Nettie always treated her as if they didn't think she was clever at all. Everyone always treated her like that, but this time she had been very clever indeed, and they would have to admit it.

She didn't say anything as long as they were on the bus, just sat there and hugged herself. They got off at the end of Warren Crescent as they always did, but she hadn't a chance of beginning about the fish queue then, because Nettie was telling Mabel about seeing Mrs Stock at the butcher's. 'And do you know, the meat she was getting was the very cheapest they had — and if she meant to make it do the four of them for even one day, no wonder they always looked half starved!'

Lily offered the suggestion that there might have been something left over from the Sunday joint, to which Nettie replied, 'Rubbish!' but without any rancour, and went on talking about

122

the Stocks. Lily had to wait until they were inside their own hall door before she got a chance to say,

'I heard the most dreadful thing in the fish queue.'

'About Mr Browning breaking his leg? I always did say he would have an accident if he went on climbing up ladders at his age!'

Lily shook her head.

'Oh, no, it was something much worse than that — something about Mrs Graham being murdered — something *dreadful*!'

Mabel opened the drawing-room door and beckoned the others in. As she shut it behind them she said in a cautionary tone,

'Doris Wills listens! I've always been sure she did. If she wasn't such a good worker . . .' She broke off and came directly to the point. 'What did you hear in the fish queue?'

This was Lily's moment of triumph. They were both waiting for her to speak — listening with all their ears. She felt warm and pleased like a purring cat.

'Well, there was a woman in front of me. I know her by sight, but I didn't know her name until the other woman said it. She is quite an elderly person and rather untidy. She had a very shabby old coat on with a worn place on the elbow. She was talking to the woman in front of her, that Mrs Rigg who goes about everywhere in trousers and never has a cigarette out of her mouth. The first thing I heard, Mrs Traill was saying, "I don't rightly know what to do about it and that's a fact," and Mrs Rigg said, "Fancy that!" Mrs Traill sounded quite cross. She said "No fancy about it, it's what I heard — I know that! What I don't know is what I ought to do, and when I asked my husband all he could say was not to let myself get drawn in to things that weren't any business of mine." That Mrs Rigg laughed — she's got a silly sort of laugh, like a child that's showing off — and she said, "That's all men ever do say, isn't it — keep your own side of the fence — don't get mixed up in things — mind your own business! And what I say is you might as well be dead!" Mrs Traill said, "Yes, you might." And then she dropped her voice right down and I shouldn't have heard what she said only for leaning forward as far as I could without touching her and then

123

it was all I could do, but I heard her say, "I just can't get it out of my mind, Mrs Rigg, and that's the fact. First thing in the morning and last thing at night it comes back to me, that poor thing calling out like she did, and me hearing her and not doing anything about it." '

Nettie Pimm said, 'Oh, Lily!' her voice twittering. But Mabel said, 'Go on!'

Lily Pimm went on.

'Mrs Rigg said, "Gosh! Whatever do you mean, Mrs Traill?" And Mrs Traill told her she was baby-sitting for that Mr and Mrs Nokes on the top of Hill Rise. She expected to be there until twelve o'clock because the Nokes were going to the cinema and supper with a friend afterwards. But it seems Mrs Nokes had a headache coming on, so they cried off the supper and came along home. There wasn't anything for Mrs Traill to stay for after that, so she got her money and came away down Hill Rise. It was twenty past eleven when she came out of the front door, because she looked at the clock in the hall and made out she would catch the bus at the corner of Belview Road. But just as she came to where the path runs along by the Grahams' garden she heard someone call out from the other side of the hedge.'

Lily Pimm looked first at one of her sisters and then at the other. She looked first at Mabel, because Mabel was the eldest and she always came first in everything. Mabel's bony nose jutted out from her long thin face, her eyes were avid and her mouth was tight. She looked at Nettie, the smallest and youngest of the three. Nettie's head was cocked a little on one side and her eyes were bright, like a bird that is just about to peck at a worm. For once in a way it was Lily who had something worth the telling, and she couldn't tell it fast enough to please them. They urged her, and she went on.

'Mrs Traill said it was Mrs Graham she heard calling out, and then she stopped and said she didn't know that she ought to say any more. Mrs Rigg said, "Oh, but you can't stop here. Come on, Mrs Traill, be a sport!" and she went on in a kind of whisper and said what she heard was Mrs Graham calling out, "Nicholas Carey – how dare you!" '

Mabel Pimm repeated the name.

'Nicholas Carey!'

Nettie said 'Oh!' in a frightened voice. And then, 'She didn't say that right out in the fish queue!'

Lily nodded. She was the plump one of the family. She had a round pale face and round pale eyes and a little button nose like a baby.

'Yes, she did! And there wasn't anyone to hear her except Mrs Rigg and me, because the next one beyond Mrs Rigg in the queue was old Mr Jackson, and he is as deaf as a post. And she wouldn't know I was listening, because I don't think she as much as knew I was there, and she was whispering, so she wouldn't think anyone would hear what she said, only you know how quick I am that way. And what she said was that she heard Mrs Graham calling out and saying, "Nicholas Carey – how dare you!" Mrs Rigg gave a sort of scream and said, "Oh, she never!" And Mrs Traill said, "Oh yes, she did, poor thing, and I can't get it out of my mind do what I will. It gave me a real start, and what with that and hearing the bus coming, I took and ran and caught it by the skin of my teeth. But I just can't get it off my mind. That poor thing calling out and me only the other side of the hedge! And when I seen in the paper what's happened to her it come over me if I'd called out something it might have saved her." And Mrs Rigg said, talking back over her shoulder, "More likely he'd have murdered you too, Mrs Traill." And just then Mr Jackson had got to being served by the young man in the shop, and the woman came over to Mrs Rigg, so she started buying kippers and Mrs Traill didn't talk to her any more. She waited outside the shop though, and they went away together, but I don't suppose there was anything much more for Mrs Traill to tell.'

Her voice fell to a deprecating tone. She didn't see how she could have managed to find out any more than she had. She was used to being blamed by Mabel and Nettie when things went wrong, but in this case she really had felt sure of being praised. She looked at Nettie, and Nettie shook her head. She looked at Mabel, and Mabel said in her firmest voice,

'You should have followed them.'

It was early the same afternoon that Miss Silver looked across the second of the vests she was knitting for Dorothy Silver's little Tina and said,

'My dear, I think you will just have to make it a duty to eat.'

Her mind had been on her knitting and upon the pretty fair-haired child who was to wear the vest. Pinks vary a good deal, but this was really a particularly pleasing shade. She looked up from it now and saw Althea Graham in profile. She had a book upon her knee, but it was a long time since she had turned a page. Her face was colourless and there were dark smudges under her eyes. The eyes themselves looked as if she had not slept. In reply to Miss Silver's remark she said in a soft, indifferent voice,

'Oh, I'm all right, thank you.'

The needles clicked briskly.

'It is possible to starve for quite a long time without being aware that one is doing so. The mind is occupied, food has become distasteful, there is a complete loss of appetite. It all happens unnoticeably. And then suddenly when one is called upon to confront an emergency one finds oneself at a loss. The mind is not active, and the judgement not to be depended upon. I should like you to promise me that you will eat an egg with your tea.'

Althea looked up with the ghost of a smile.

'How very, very kind you are. But you needn't worry about me – I am really very strong.'

Miss Silver produced what Frank Abbott would have acclaimed as one of her Moralities.

'Strength is given to us when we are trying to do what is right, but we are better able to avail ourselves of it if we do not neglect a proper allowance of food and sleep. You have eaten nothing all day. If I make a nice cup of tea, will you not please me by drinking it – perhaps with a beaten-up egg?'

'Oh, I couldn't. I don't like them raw.'

Miss Silver beamed.

'Then I will boil it lightly and cut a little thin bread and butter. I assure you that you will feel a great deal better when you have taken it.'

All at once it had become too much trouble to go on saying no. Miss Silver produced the egg, the tea, the thin bread and butter with the minimum of fuss, and when Althea had taken the first mouthful she found herself suddenly hungry. She ate the egg, the bread and butter, and some cold milk pudding pleasantly sprinkled with brown sugar, and whilst she ate Miss Silver conversed in a manner which somehow managed to be soothing without being dull. She seemed to be interested about Grove Hill.

'It is not of any very great age as a suburb, I believe?'

'No, I don't think it is.'

'These houses would be – about how old?'

'I think they began to be built about 1890. This is one of the older ones.'

'Before 1890?'

'Oh, no, I didn't mean that. But I think it was the first house built on what used to be called the Grove Hill Estate. Grove Hill House just above here, where the Harrisons are, was really an old country house. It was built somewhere about 1750. Our gazebo was in the grounds. It must have had a lovely view before everything was so built over. The house was wrecked and partly burned down in the Gordon Riots. It belonged to a Mr Warren who was a Roman Catholic, and the rioters were looting and burning all the Catholic houses. Mr Warren was a wealthy brewer. He had a fine collection of pictures and a lot of beautiful furniture and things. He was warned about the rioters but he wouldn't go away. He tried to save what he could, but I think nearly everything was burned, and some of the masonry fell in on him and killed him. Nicky's great-great-grandfather bought the estate from Mr Warren's grand-daughters.'

Miss Silver was gazing at her with rapt attention.

'How extremely interesting! Mob violence is a terrible thing. We now hardly know what it is in this country. Charles

Dickens has left a very vivid picture of the Gordon Riots in his novel *Barnaby Rudge*. It is extraordinary to reflect that the rioters attacked the Bank of England, burned down the prison of Newgate, and destroyed and pillaged at will, practically without a hand being raised to stop them.'

As she spoke she noticed with approbation that Althea was making good progress with the egg and bread and butter. Having contributed a Morality on the subject of religious intolerance, she said,

'This is all most interesting. Pray continue.'

'I don't think there is very much more to tell. My father liked going into the history of the place. There are some books of his up in the attic – there is one about Grove Hill. I think the High Street and the shops and the railway station were built somewhere between 1850 and the end of the century. The houses came farther and farther up the hill. Nicky's great-grandfather began to sell some of the land on the Grove Hill Estate. His grandfather sold everything except Grove Hill House and the garden round it. Nicky used to spend his holidays there with his aunt, Miss Lester. While he was away in the East she sold the house to the Harrisons who are cousins and went to live with a sister in Devonshire. That is why Nicky came here – the attic was full of his things and he had to sort them. It is Jack Harrison who is the cousin, not Ella.'

She spoke in a gentle, colourless manner, as if she were reciting a lesson so often repeated as to have lost its meaning. She had finished the bread and butter, and in the same almost mechanical manner she was now helping herself to the cold rice pudding. Miss Silver noticed the improvement in her colour with satisfaction and continued to talk upon such harmless and improving topics as the tendency of towns to expand and absorb the villages of an earlier day, with especial reference to London.

It was while she was so engaged that two of the Miss Pimms came out of Warren Crescent into Belview Road, which it joins no more than a hundred yards down the slope. They stood at the corner for a moment looking up and across in the direction of the lodge. After exchanging a few words they were about to cross the road, when the green bus came up the hill from the town. It stopped at the corner of Belview Road and

Hill Rise and Frank Abbott got off. Lily Pimm had a second moment of triumph, since she knew who he was and her sister Mabel did not. She was quite beaming as she told Mabel that that was the inspector from Scotland Yard.

Mabel Pimm was justly annoyed. It wasn't often that Lily could tell her something she didn't know, but this was the second time it had happened today, and her instinct was to reject it. She said in a deep, vibrant voice,

'Nonsense, Lily — he doesn't look in the least like a policeman!'

'I know he doesn't but he is. Mrs Justice told me all about him. His grandmother was Lady Evelyn Abbott, and she had one of these big shipping fortunes and she left it past all the rest of the family to a grand-daughter who was a schoolgirl of fifteen. This man's name is Abbott too — Frank Abbott.'

Mabel Pimm made the small explosive sound which is sometimes written 'Tchah!' When and how had Lily elicited this information from Louisa Justice, and why had she failed to pass it on? Lily was getting above herself. Lily would have to be snubbed. She snubbed her sharply.

'Frank indeed! Really, Lily, what has the man's name got to do with either of us, or why should you suppose it would be of the least interest to me? I can only repeat that if he is a police officer he doesn't look like one!'

Lily was unabashed.

'You hardly ever hear of anyone called Frank nowadays, do you? Look Mabel — he's going into The Lodge! I suppose we shall have to put off our visit now.'

'And why should we? We are calling upon Althea to condole with her upon the death of her mother. I can see no reason at all why we should alter our plan. I am merely waiting for the bus to go on.'

The bus moved. They crossed the road and were knocking at the front door of The Lodge just as Miss Silver preceded Frank Abbott into the dining-room. She had not expected him, and was wondering whether it was Althea or herself whom he wished to see, when he settled the matter by asking whether he could have a few words with her. There were times when she would have welcomed him more warmly. She intimated as much now.

'I have just got that poor girl to eat something. I have been trying to take her mind off the case. I am really very much afraid of the strain proving too much for her. I hope that you have not brought any bad news?'

He looked at her with affection.

'Well, I haven't come here with a warrant in my pocket, if that is what you mean by bad news. I don't think there's very much doubt about Carey's guilt, but up to date there isn't any evidence to show that he came back to the gazebo after Mrs Graham had gone into the house. Of course there isn't any evidence that he ever left the gazebo. He may have gone for a walk as he says he did and have come back again, or he may just have hung about in the gazebo and waited for Althea Graham to return. Her windows look that way, you know, and Mrs Graham's don't. He could have reckoned on her looking out of her window the last thing when she put out her light and drew back the curtains. Most people do that, you know. And he could have signalled to her with a torch. Suppose he did, and suppose it was Mrs Graham who got the signal. Her windows don't look that way but the bathroom window does. On Miss Cotton's evidence she was a hysterical woman, and she was in a very angry and suspicious frame of mind. I think she might easily have expected Carey to make some further effort to see her daughter. If she looked out of the bathroom window she could see the gazebo. She would see the least flicker of a torch. I think we've got to believe that she did see something, and that what she saw took her up the garden to the gazebo, where she was murdered. What we haven't got at present is a single scrap of evidence after Althea Graham took her mother in and Miss Cotton looked back at the corner of the road and saw Mrs Graham's bedroom light go on. From that moment there is a complete stalemate. Carey can't prove that he didn't just stay where he was, and we can't prove that he did. He may have gone away as he says he did. If he did, he can't produce anyone to prove it any more than we can prove that he came back and strangled Mrs Graham. He certainly had a motive, and he could as certainly have made the opportunity. As far as we've got there's nothing in it either way.'

The two Miss Pimms stood on the doorstep without either

lifting the knocker or ringing the bell. As they had walked up the flagged path there was a drawing-room window to their right and a dining-room window to their left. The drawing-room window was a square bay, and there would have been quite a good view of the interior if a completely opaque curtain had not been drawn across the side which was next the porch. The dining-room had a bay too but no curtain drawn, and the nearest window stood a handsbreadth open. Lily Pimm was looking to her right, but Mabel was more fortunate. She actually saw Miss Silver and Detective Inspector Abbott come into the room behind the open window. Most fortunately, they did not look in her direction. She touched Lily on the arm, put a finger on her lips, and rapidly gained the shelter of the porch. When Lily on a singularly foolish impulse opened her lips to speak, the touch on her arm became so painful a pinch that the water rushed into her eyes and she immediately desisted. Mabel removed her finger from her lips and pointed with it, and they both heard the Detective Inspector say, 'I don't think there is very much doubt about Carey's guilt.' After that even Lily did not need to be pinched.

They stood out of sight as if riveted to the doorstep, Mabel tall and thin, Lily round and plump. Her nickname as a child had been Podge, and it still suited her. They could hear everything that was said. But when Detective Inspector Abbott reached the point of asserting that Nicholas Carey certainly had a motive and could as certainly have made an opportunity, and went on to say, 'As far as we've got there's nothing in it either way,' he began to walk round the dining-table in the direction of the window. They heard him say, 'I don't know why we shouldn't sit down.' And then quite suddenly he turned towards the side window of the bay and saw them standing in the porch.

Mabel Pimm behaved with the greatest presence of mind. She had hardly glimpsed the movement of a coat sleeve on the other side of the casement, when her hand was on the knocker. Her vigorous knock practically coincided with Frank Abbott's 'There's someone at the door.' As a second knock followed he stepped back and said only just above his breath, 'Is there anyone to answer it, or shall I go?'

Althea was already in the hall. She did not show her dismay

at the sight of the Miss Pimms, but it came in on her like a fog. Having known them since she was six, she was under no illusion as to the rigorous cross-examination to which Miss Mabel would subject her. It was therefore with feelings of considerable relief that she saw the dining-room door open and Miss Silver and Frank Abbott emerge. The ceremonial kiss which Mabel Pimm was about to bestow was checked, and with no more than a subdued murmur of condolence they proceeded to the drawing-room. Frank Abbott was in two minds whether to stay or go. In the end he found himself being introduced to the Miss Pimms and decided to stay.

The interrogatory note in Miss Mabel's voice was very decided as she addressed Miss Silver.

'I do not think I have heard your name before. You are a relative?'

They were seating themselves, Miss Silver and Mabel Pimm upon the sofa, Frank Abbott in a fireside chair a little small for his elegant length, Althea on one of those square upholstered dumps a good deal in vogue at the time of Mrs Graham's marriage, and on the opposite side of the hearth to the sofa Lily Pimm, rather isolated in a big armchair. Her feet only just touched the floor. She wore her skirts as long as possible in order to add to her height, but the attempt was a failure. Her black kid gloves were too tight for her plump hands, and both she and Mabel had put on black coats and hats in order to visit a house of mourning. The garments were those usually reserved for funerals. They had the air of never having been in fashion, and they smelled powerfully of moth-ball.

Miss Silver picked up her knitting and replied to Miss Mabel's question.

'Oh, no, I am not a relation.'

'A friend then?'

'I hope so.'

Miss Pimm unfastened the top button of her coat. It was one of her characteristics that she never found any room to be at quite the right temperature. If she felt it too warm she unbuttoned her coat. If she did not feel it warm enough she buttoned it up. In either case she said just what she thought. She said it now.

'Warm rooms are enervating. This room is a good deal too warm. Are you an old friend? It don't remember having heard your name before.'

Miss Silver pulled on the ball of pale pink wool. She said, 'Indeed?' in so mild a tone that Frank Abbott cocked an eye brow.

Mabel Pimm turned a shoulder and addressed Althea.

'Lily and I have come here because we feel it to be our duty. We would in any case wish to express our condolences, but there was also something we felt we ought to let you know without delay. It is perhaps fortunate that the Detective Inspector is here, as he would certainly have to be informed about it.' She sat stiffly upright, her eyes small and bright, her nose jutting, her gloved hands folded in her lap. Then, as Althea turned a pale look in her direction, she continued. 'It is something which I feel may be of the greatest importance — something which my sister Lily happened to overhear.'

Lily Pimm nodded her head in the shapeless black hat.

'In the fish queue,' she said.

Frank's lips twitched. His sense of humour was sometimes a trouble to him, but he had it under control. Miss Silver sent him a glance.

'Perhaps if Miss Graham and I were to leave you ...' she said.

Even before his slight shake of the head Althea was speaking.

'No, it's very kind of you, but I'd rather stay.' She turned away from Mabel Pimm. 'What is it, Miss Lily?'

It really was a wonderful day for Lily. She was quite sorry for Althea Graham, quite kindly disposed towards her, but it was wonderful to have such an interesting story to tell. It wasn't very often that anyone listened to her with attention — it wasn't very often that anyone listened to her at all. But today everyone was listening. First Mabel and Nettie at home, and now Althea and the friend who was staying with her, and the police officer, and Mabel. They were all listening with the greatest interest and attention. Agog — that was what they were — agog. Such a curious word! She couldn't think why it should come into her mind, but it did. There they all sat, looking at her and waiting for her to speak.

She began to tell them what Mrs Traill had said to Mrs Rigg, and what Mrs Rigg had said to Mrs Traill, going right through the conversation and not missing a word, and finishing up with,

'And I asked Mrs Jones in the fish shop where Mrs Traill lived, and she said with her daughter-in-law at No. 4 Holbrook Cottages.'

She looked round the circle, as an actor for applause, and was disappointed to find that no one seemed to realize how clever she had been.

Miss Silver had laid her knitting down upon her knee. Mabel of course, had heard the story before. The Scotland Yard Inspector was looking her way, but there was something about his expression which she didn't care about at all, something that reminded her of a cold draught and getting her feet wet. And Althea Graham looked dreadful. Of course she had been engaged to Nicholas Carey, and people were saying perhaps they would make it up again now he had come home, only they couldn't possibly get married if he had murdered her mother. No, no – of course they couldn't! It shocked her very much to think of it.

The Inspector's voice broke in upon these thoughts. It surprised her a good deal, because it wasn't at all the sort of voice you would expect a policeman to have. It reminded her of a B.B.C. announcer, only not so friendly. He said,

'Are you sure Mrs Traill mentioned the time at which she left this house on Hill Rise?'

Mabel Pimm answered for her sister.

'It is No. 28, and Mr and Mrs Nokes live there. He is in a shipping office and goes up to town every day. And they have a young baby, so that if they want to go out in the evening they have to employ a babysitter, though I shouldn't myself have described Mrs Traill as at all suitable – a most untidy person.'

The Inspector looked her way.

'You know her?'

Mabel Pimm showed offence.

'Certainly not! I should not dream of employing a person like that. I was going by what my sister said.'

He turned back again to Lily.

'I just wanted to know whether you heard Mrs Traill say at what time she left the house on Hill Rise.'

'No. 28,' said Mabel Pimm.

Lily was not at all flustered. She said,

'Oh, yes, I did. Mrs Nokes had a headache, so they came straight back from the cinema instead of going out to supper. There wasn't anything for Mrs Traill to stay for after that so she got her money and came away, and it was twenty past eleven when she came out of the front door, because she looked at the clock in the hall and made out she could just catch the bus at the corner of Belview Road.'

He had begun to wonder whether it was going to be possible to stop or deflect her until she had gone through the whole story again. He struck in with a 'Thank you, Miss Pimm,' and from behind him on his right heard the sister say with an edge on her voice,

'Miss Lily, if you please, Inspector. *I* am Miss Pimm.'

Althea had neither spoken nor moved. The dump on which she was sitting afforded no back against which she could lean. She sat in what had been an easy attitude but which had gone on stiffening until all its grace was lost. She wore no make-up, and the black dress dictated by custom robbed her skin of its last vestige of colour. The eyes which could take the sea tints, brightening into green or softening from it, were now a frozen grey. They stared before her as if the people and the room were not really there at all. They had gone away into a mist like the one through which she had passed to find her mother dead. Her mind struggled with what Lily Pimm had been saying. She tried to fit it in with the things which were already there. Nicky ringing her up and saying she must meet him at half past ten. It was half past ten when she slipped out of the back door and went up the garden to the gazebo. And then her mother had come. She had come, and she had called out, 'How dare you, Nicholas Carey!' and there was a scene and they had gone back into the house together. But Lily Pimm said that this Mrs Traill had come out of the Nokes's house at twenty past eleven and when she was passing on the other side of the hedge from the gazebo she had heard her mother call out those very same words. She had heard her say, 'How dare you, Nicholas Carey!' None of these things seemed

135

to fit in at all, and the mist in the room got thicker. She knew Mrs Nokes quite well by sight. The baby had fair hair sticking up all over his head, and a jolly grin. Something said to her, 'You weren't any time in the gazebo – hardly any time at all. You were back in the house making Ovaltine and putting your mother to bed long before eleven. Mrs Traill couldn't have heard her in the gazebo at twenty past – she couldn't possibly have heard her say "How dare you, Nicholas Carey!" '

Miss Silver put down her knitting on the sofa beside her and got up. She addressed Frank Abbot formally.

'I think this is too much for Miss Graham, Inspector. Perhaps you will take the Miss Pimms into the dining-room.'

24

Althea did not quite lose consciousness but she came very near it. She lay on the sofa and felt vaguely how strange it was that she should be lying there with a soft rug over her and a cushion beneath her head. A small firm hand lifted the rug and felt her wrist. She opened her eyes a little way and said, 'I'm all right.' There was still a lot of mist in the room. Miss Silver's voice came through it.

'Yes, you are quite all right. Just lie still and rest.'

It would be lovely to let go of everything and slip into a dream. But there was something she had to do first. No, it was something she had to say, only she couldn't quite get hold of it – it seemed to be just out of her reach. And there was an urgency about it – she couldn't let it go. She had to think what it was – she had to say it. Her hand caught at Miss Silver's.

'There was something – I had to say.'

'Don't trouble yourself now, my dear.'

She began to say, 'I can't remember . . .' and then it came to her. It was about Nicky – there was something she must tell them about Nicky. She tried to lift her head, but the giddy feeling was too strong. She said in an exhausted voice,

'It was about Nicky — you must tell them. He didn't do it — he *really* didn't. You will tell them, won't you?'

Miss Silver did not take her hand away. She said,

'I will tell them just what you say, my dear.'

Althea drew a long breath. She had done what she had to do. The hand that was holding Miss Silver's relaxed. She drifted into sleep.

When Frank Abbott returned to the house she was still sleeping. Miss Silver took him into the dining-room, where he drew the curtain across that side of the bay which faced the porch, coming back to pull out one of the chairs and sit down across the corner from Miss Silver. He looked at her with affection. The neatly netted hair with its Alexandra fringe in front and its plaits behind, the little vest of tucked net with the boned collar, the grey dress with its faint black and mauve pattern, the brooch of bog-oak in the form af a rose with an Irish pearl at its heart, the grey thread stockings, and the neat black glacé shoes with little ribbon bows on them, made up a picture which delighted him. She had brought her knitting with her. A small pale pink garment depended from the plastic needles.

He said in a lazy voice,

'You are really a very demoralizing associate for a police officer, you know.'

She gave him a half smile and continued to knit.

'In what way do I demoralize you?'

'My dear ma'am! I find it impossible to look at you and to remember that there is such a thing as crime. You diffuse an atmosphere of security which forbids it.'

'My dear Frank!'

'I know, I know — crime exists, and we are here on a murder case. Let's get down to it. I have been interviewing the untidy Mrs Traill, and you may take it from me untidy she is. And so is No. 4 Holbrook Cottages, and her daughter-in-law, and the three little Traills under school age. But quite respectable and cooperative. I give the Miss Pimms top marks. Lily appears to be the human phonograph. Mrs Traill as reported by her being if anything rather more accurate than Mrs Traill as reported by Mrs Traill.'

Miss Silver gave the slight cough with which she was wont

to draw attention to an inaccurate or exaggerated statement.

'My dear Frank . . .'

He put up a hand.

'No – pause before you accuse me. I am prepared to prove the point. There were two occasions when Mrs Traill's version of what happened on Tuesday night differed slightly from Lily Pimm's account of the conversation in the fish queue. Pressed by me, Mrs Traill immediately discarded her own version and agreed that what she had said to Mrs Rigg outside the fish shop was the right one. Her own expression, I may say, and very handsomely conceded, was "That's right!" I felt that for tuppence she would have called me "ducks". It was all very matey.'

Miss Silver pulled on the pale pink ball.

'I have no doubt as to the accuracy of Lily Pimm's account. I do not believe her capable of inventing anything.'

He nodded.

'Well, she didn't in this case. So there we are with the missing link we were talking about when I looked out of the window and saw Mabel and Lily on the step. As far as I remember, I was saying that the chances were about fifty-fifty as regards Nicholas Carey. He couldn't prove that he didn't come back and murder Mrs Graham, and we couldn't prove that he did. Well, Mrs Traill's evidence alters all that, doesn't it? As reported by Lily and confirmed by herself, Mrs Traill states that she came out of 28 Hill Rise at twenty past eleven, walked approximately a hundred and twenty feet along the pavement until she was level with the gazebo, and then heard Mrs Graham call out, "How dare you, Nicholas Carey!" He is not going to find it easy to explain that away, is he? Miss Graham took her mother into the house at, shall we say, a quarter to eleven. She and Carey had an assignation for half past ten. They had to meet. Her mother had to get up, put something on, and come and find them. After which there had to be time for a row, persuasions, and getting Mrs Graham back into the house. Say a quarter of an hour or twenty minutes – but we should still be well this side of eleven o'clock. Carey says he went off at once, walked for a long time, and got back to Grove Hill House he can't say when. Mrs Traill, who can't have any axe to grind, is prepared to swear that she heard

Mrs Graham call out to him in an angry voice at somewhere between twenty and twenty-five past eleven. So one of them is lying, and only Carey has a motive for that particular lie.'

Miss Silver gave a gentle cough.

'I think that you are assuming more than is warranted by Mrs Traill's statement. Mrs Traill heard a voice say, "How dare you, Nicholas Carey!" and in view of the other evidence we are, I suppose, justified in assuming that it was Mrs Graham who was speaking. The words are the same as those heard half an hour previously by Nurse Cotton. But whereas Nurse Cotton was able to identify the voice as that of Mrs Graham, Mrs Traill is in no position to do so. Still it is a fair assumption that the speaker was the same in both cases. What I do not feel we are entitled to assume is that the person she addressed was necessarily the same.'

'She used his name!'

Miss Silver knitted briskly.

'It was about half an hour since she had gone into the house, leaving Nicholas Carey in the gazebo. Miss Graham had put her to bed and retired to her own room, where, as she tells me, she fell instantly and deeply asleep. We do not know what it was that took Mrs Graham back to the gazebo. There must have been some evidence of an intruder – probably the flash of a torch. There seems to be no doubt that what she saw convinced her of Mr Carey's continued presence in the garden, and she could place only one construction on it, that he was waiting there to see her daughter. Hurrying out, she reaches the gazebo, is aware of the intruder, and calls out, using the words overheard by Mrs Traill, "How dare you, Nicholas Carey!" But do you suppose that she really saw and recognized him? I think the most she would see would be an impression that there was someone moving there. I went up the garden last night just after eleven o'clock. The weather was very much the same as it was on Tuesday. There was no moon, and there are overhanging trees at the top of the garden. As I came up to the gazebo it was very dark indeed. The interior was like a black cave.'

He said,

'There was a flashlight in the pocket of Mrs Graham's coat.'

Miss Silver's voice reproved him.

'If she had been using it, it would not have been found in her pocket. It was probably her sense of hearing which told her there was someone in the gazebo, and I maintain there is no proof that it was Nicholas Carey.'

There was a pause before he said,

'I shall have to go up and report to the Chief. I think he will say that the evidence must go to the Public Prosecutor. You are predisposed in Carey's favour, but you don't need me to tell you that Mrs Traill's evidence looks bad for him. On the other hand no one will want to be in too much of a hurry. Those "Rolling Stone" articles of his made a big splash. But they are pretty tough, you know, and life in the sort of places they describe would be calculated to rub off some of the finer scruples. I think it might be just as well if you didn't give Althea Graham too much encouragement to expect a happy ending.'

25

Frank Abbott had been gone about half an hour when a knock upon the front door took Miss Silver into the hall to open it. There was a young man standing in the porch with a bunch of pink carnations in his hand. He was good-looking in rather an obtrusive sort of way, and he had the air of being very well pleased with himself. He was in fact Mr Fred Worple, and he had called to see Miss Althea Graham. He imparted these facts in a negligent manner and advanced a step as if he had no doubt that he would be admitted.

Miss Silver stood where she was.

'I am afraid Miss Graham is not able to see visitors.'

'It's been a shock,' said Mr Worple. 'Well, of course it would be, wouldn't it? But not a bit of good shutting herself up, is it? She wants to see her friends and get brightened up a bit. You just go and ask her whether she won't see me.'

Miss Silver looked at him in a thoughtful manner. Then she said,

'Miss Graham is resting. You are a friend of the family?'

'I'll say I am – and a very good friend too. Come, it'll do her good to see me.'

Miss Silver stepped back.

'I am afraid that you will not be able to do that. But if you would care to come in for a moment . . .' She led the way to the dining-room.

When the door was shut upon them she moved in the direction of the hearth and remained there standing.

'Miss Graham has mentioned your name, Mr Worple. She tells me that you wish to settle in Grove Hill, and that you had made Mrs Graham an offer for this house.'

'That's right. And a very good offer it was. Here, are you a relation?'

It would be difficult to find anyone more competent than Miss Silver to check a tone of impertinent familiarity. It was, in fact, an art in which she might be said to excel. Chief Inspector Lamb himself, though never a willing offender, had been known to blench. Yet for the moment Mr Fred Worple was spared. She replied quietly,

'I am staying with Miss Graham as a friend. Does Mrs Graham's death alter your plans with regard to the house?'

He had followed her to the hearth and was now lounging against the mantelpiece, the pink carnations dangling from his hand.

'Oh, well, I don't know. As a matter of fact there was someone else after it, and I had rather given up the idea. Murder – well, it does rather put you off, doesn't it? Of course it ought to bring down the price a good bit. I shouldn't think the girl would want to stay on here – not after what has happened.'

'I do not know at all what Miss Graham's plans may be.'

Fred Worple laughed.

'If she knows what's good for her she'll take what she can get for the place and clear out!'

The fire in the grate had been laid but not lighted. Miss Silver looked down in a thoughtful manner at the paper, the sticks, and the coal.

'I suppose these houses are not very old?' she said.

'Oh, about fifty years or so. My old dad – stepfather he was really – he used to say he remembered all this part before it was built over. Part of the old Grove Hill Estate it was.'

'There must have been quite a good view from the top of the garden then. I suppose that is why the summerhouse was built there. Miss Graham calls it a gazebo. She seems to think it might be older than the house.'

His foot slipped from the kerb.

'Oh, I don't know – I never took that much interest. I used to think I'd like to live in a house like this – used to pass it coming out this way and think, "Well, I'd like to live there," the way kids do. But I'm not so sure now – not after what has happened. Not unless it was going for a song.' He straightened up. 'Look here, be a sport and tell Miss Graham I'm here. Tell her it'll do her good to see someone who isn't mixed up in all this, and say I brought her these flowers.'

Miss Silver shook her head.

'I am afraid it is no good, Mr Worple. Miss Graham is asleep, and I could not possibly wake her.'

Althea woke refreshed. Her reactions on being shown the pink carnations sent by Mr Worple were very much what Miss Silver had expected.

'He's a dreadful person – he really is. He just pushed himself in with his offer for the house. Mr Jones – he is the other house-agent – hadn't any business to let him come up here. We hadn't put the house in his hands – we have always dealt with Mr Martin. Mr Blount, the other man who wanted to buy it, came up from him. Mr Martin shouldn't really have sent him either, but he did have some excuse, because I'm afraid my mother let him think we'd be open to a really good offer.'

Miss Silver appeared to be very much interested.

'It seemed to me that Mr Worple wished to find out whether you would now be prepared to sell the house. He wished to make me believe that he was no longer interested from a personal point of view, but I did not find his manner at all convincing. He is a forward and pushing person, but he appeared to be ill at ease.'

Althea said, 'He is quite dreadful!'

They were having tea when Nicholas Carey rang the front door bell. Rightly considering that her presence could now

142

be dispensed with, Miss Silver put on her coat and hat and went out. Arriving at Warren Crescent, she turned off there and proceeded along it into Warren Road. The houses here stood in gardens of between three-quarters of an acre and an acre and a half. The Hollies, which as the telephone-book informed her had the privilege of sheltering the Miss Pimms, occupied one of the larger plots. It had three storeys and a large Victorian conservatory. The holly bushes from which it took its name had been cut into the shapes of birds and beasts, but with time and diminishing care they had become less and less agreeable to the eye. Miss Silver regarded them with distaste as she turned in at the gate and ascended four wide steps to the porch. She rang the bell, and the door was presently opened by Lily Pimm. That was of course the drawback about having only a daily maid. The Miss Pimms could remember the time when The Hollies was served by a resident cook, parlourmaid, and housemaid, not to mention a woman once a week to scrub the floors and a boy for the boots and knives and to help in the garden, where there was of course a whole-time gardener. Now there was only Doris Wills, and Doris left at half past two. The Miss Pimms greatly disliked opening their own front door, and Mabel and Nettie combining in the matter, it had become one of the tasks allotted to Lily, the only drawback being that if it was a pedlar or someone collecting for a charity she was quite unable to say no.

She now stood gazing blankly at Miss Silver with the door in her hand. Miss Silver smiled.

'Miss Lily Pimm? We met a few hours ago at The Lodge, where I am staying with Miss Althea Graham. My name is Silver — Miss Maud Silver.'

Lily brightened.

'Oh, yes — but you've got a hat on now.'

Mabel Pimm appeared in the drawing-room doorway. She directed a caustic look at Lily, and changed it quickly to a smile of welcome for the guest.

'Oh, Miss Silver, do pray come in! How good of you to call!'

It would perhaps be unkind to compare Mabel's feelings with those of the wolf who, having laid elaborate plans to attack the sheepfold, is gratified by the voluntary approach of one of its choicer lambs, but it is certain that next to Althea herself there was no one in Grove Hill whom she would rather have ushered into her drawing-room. As they entered Miss Silver was saying,

'I was so much concerned at your kind visit to Miss Graham being so unavoidably cut short by her faintness that I felt I should call and let you know that she was able to get some sleep and is now feeling a good deal better. Of course the whole thing has been a most terrible shock.'

'Naturally.' Mabel was about to add other and well chosen words, when Lily broke in.

'I can't think what I should have done if I had found Mamma murdered at the bottom of the garden . . .'

There was a simultaneous 'Lily!' from both her sisters, but it had practically no effect, and she persisted.

'Of course we haven't a gazebo, and Mamma was bedridden for some years before she died. But if she hadn't been, and I had found her — perhaps in the shrubbery — it certainly would have been a most terrible shock.'

'*Lily* . . .' Mabel's tone had become an awful one.

Lily's understanding, though not bright, was capable of receiving the impression that she would do better to hold her tongue. She sat therefore in silence for some time whilst the conversation between Miss Silver and her sisters proceeded, merely turning her head from side to side so as to be able to watch the person who was speaking.

Mabel was full of inquiries about Althea.

'And you feel that she is well enough to be left?'

Miss Silver coughed in a deprecating manner.

'Oh, I should not have liked to leave her by herself. Mr Carey is with her.'

Nettie and Mabel echoed the name.

'Nicholas Carey!'

'Oh, yes. They are great friends, are they not? In fact . . .' She hesitated and broke off. 'But perhaps if it is not given out? And of course at a time of mourning like the present . . .'

It was a pity that Frank Abbott should not have been privileged to observe his Miss Silver in the role of the well-meaning friend who alternately says too much and too little about the affairs in which she has become involved. In a very

144

few minutes Mabel and Nettie were vying with each other to convince her how intimate they had been with Mrs Graham, and how complete had been the confidence she reposed in them. Between them it became established that Nicholas Carey might be a very charming young man, but definitely unreliable. Look at the way he had suddenly thrown Althea over five years ago and gone off into the wilds!

'We felt very sorry for her.'

'Really it quite changed her.'

'A most untrustworthy young man.'

Miss Silver looked from one to the other.

'Oh, do you really think so?'

Mabel Pimm's long nose quivered.

'Look what has happened as soon as he comes back!'

Lily emerged from her silence.

'Mrs Graham would not let them get married,' she said. 'Mrs Stokes who is their daily told Doris Wills, and Doris told me. She said it was ever so romantic, and now that he had come back she wouldn't be surprised if it was all on again only Mrs Graham would do all she could to put a spoke in his wheel. That's what Mrs Stokes said.'

If Mabel had been capable of producing a blush she would have blushed for Lily. It was all very well to be accurate, but there was no need to repeat Mrs Stokes' uneducated way of speaking. She gave her a look and said in a lofty voice that she never listened to gossip.

When Nicholas Carey's generally unsatisfactory character had been further dealt with, Miss Silver observed in a diffident manner that she felt herself in a very delicate situation, and that any information which could be given her by such old friends as the Miss Pimms would be most helpful. For instance when friends called to inquire after Miss Graham, since all were strangers to herself it would be of the greatest assistance to know which were really on terms of intimacy with the family.

Mabel Pimm was not one to neglect such an opportunity. Miss Silver heard all about Dr Barrington's partiality for Mrs Graham.

'People did say – but you can't believe all you hear, can you, and a doctor must see too many sick people to be attracted by them. But of course she was always sending for him . . .'

After which there was a piece about Mrs Justice.

'There is something rather vulgar about having so much money, don't you think? The girl Sophy married a distant cousin of ours. They are out in the West Indies. By the way, weren't you at the cocktail-party Mrs Justice gave the other day?'

Miss Silver smiled a little nervously.

'Oh, yes, she was kind enough to ask me. There was a time when I knew her quite well. Of course I did not expect to know many people there. Perhaps you can tell me about some of them. There was a woman who seemed to be on very friendly terms with Mrs Graham – rather a striking looking person in royal blue, with that very bright golden hair.'

Miss Mabel's thin eyebrows rose.

'If you call it gold,' she said.

Nettie came darting in.

'Of course it's tinted . . . I believe she doesn't make any secret of that. People don't nowadays, do they? They don't call it a dye any more, they just say they've had a brightening rinse. I've sometimes wondered lately whether Althea . . .'

Mabel interrupted her.

'That was Mrs Harrison. The Harrisons are newcomers to Grove Hill, but Mr Harrison is a cousin of the Lesters who used to own Grove Hill House. He bought it from Miss Lester a couple of years ago, and Emmy Lester asked everyone to call, so we did.'

Nettie took the lead again.

'She doesn't fit in very well, but Mrs Graham took her up. Of course the Harrisons have plenty of money. She has a lot of jewellery. Of course we don't know where it came from.'

'Perhaps Mr Harrison gave it to her,' said Lily.

Mabel Pimm sniffed through pinched nostrils.

'I believe she was once on the *stage*!'

Nettie continued to prattle.

'Actresses do get given valuable presents of course. She has a diamond sunburst – quite a big one. She was wearing it at Mrs Justice's cocktail-party – it made her look rather over-dressed, we thought. Perhaps you noticed it.'

146

'Oh, yes, I did. A very handsome ornament.'

Nettie went on.

'And did you notice her rings? There is a ruby and diamond, and a diamond and sapphire, and one which she always wears – five diamonds in a row – great big stones.'

'She has lost one of the diamonds,' said Lily Pimm.

Both sisters turned to look at her, and both exclaimed.

Nettie said, 'A diamond out of that ring!' and Mabel, 'How do you know?'

Lily beamed.

'Because I saw it. She was on the bus on Wednesday morning, and when she pulled off her glove to find some change to pay the fare, there was the ring. And one of the stones was gone! I said, "Oh, Mrs Harrison, you've lost a stone out of your ring!" And she said, "Oh, *no!*" And I said, "Didn't you know you had lost it?" And she said, "Oh, no, I didn't," and she turned the glove inside out to see if it had run down into one of the fingers, but it wasn't there. And I said, "Didn't you notice when you put it on?" And she said, "I don't have to put it on, because I practically never take it off. It's a little loose, and it is apt to slip round a bit, so I mightn't notice the stone being gone." And I said, "Well, it was all right last night when you were playing bridge at the Reckitts, because I always look to see what rings you are wearing, and you had this one and a pearl and diamond one on the right hand, and the ruby ring and the sapphire ring on the left, and the diamonds were all there then." I don't know why that should have made her angry, but it did, because she said, "How could you possibly tell?" So I told her.'

Miss Silver showed the most gratifying interest.

'And how could you tell?'

'I counted them,' said Lily simply. 'There are three in the diamond and sapphire ring, and three in the ruby and diamond ring, and three more in the ring with two pearls in it, and five in the one that is just diamonds and nothing else. And all the five diamonds were there! So I said, "Perhaps you lost it later on?" And she was quite cross and said, oh, no she hadn't, because all the stones were there when she dressed to come out that morning. I can't think why she should say that, when she started off by telling me about the ring slipping round on her finger so maybe she hadn't noticed that the stone was gone.'

'How strange,' said Miss Silver. 'And all this happened on the bus on Wednesday morning? You saw the stone was gone, and first she told you that the ring was in the habit of slipping round on her finger so that she might not have noticed the loss of one of the stones, and then she said that she had noticed that the stone was there when she was dressing to come out?'

Lily gave a pleased smile.

'Yes, that was what she said. She thinks a lot of that ring, you know. Some uncle or great-uncle in the family brought the stones from India. They cost a lot of money. Mr Harrison had them re-set for her as a wedding-present. She was ever so upset at losing one.'

Miss Silver then narrated an instance of a ring being lost on a beach in Devonshire and turning up some years later in a handbag belonging, not to the person who had lost the ring, but to a relative who had not been anywhere near the beach when it was missed. It was quite a long story, with a good many excursions into such irrelevancies as the exact relationship between the loser and the finder of the ring and both their previous and their subsequent histories. By the time the story was finished Mrs Harrison had receded into the background, emerging later on, no longer in connexion with the ring but introduced by Mabel for the purpose of importing Mr Worple into the conversation.

'A really dreadful young man – quite like one of those spivs you hear about in the papers. I saw them with my own eyes going into Sefton's. I had to go in myself for some buns, and there they were in one of those little alcoves at the end of the shop. I came home and told my sisters that I could *not* believe they had only just met.'

'Oh, yes, she *did*! said Nettie.

'And it turns out I was perfectly right. And who do you think he really is? You may have noticed the house-agents in the High Street, Martin and Steadman – well, old Mr Martin, the present Mr Martin's father, married a Mrs Worple as his second wife, and this is her son, Fred Worple. He went into the business when he first grew up, but he wasn't at *all* satisfactory, and after a little he disappeared and the Martins stopped talking about him. Getting on for ten years ago that must be, and now here he is back again and quite well off. Our daily maid Doris had it from Mrs Lane who works for the Martins – all these dailies will talk, you know. And I don't know where Fred Worple knew Mrs Harrison, but it seems they are quite old friends, and they have been seeing each other every day.'

Nettie came darting in.

'I wonder Mr Harrison likes it!'

'Perhaps he doesn't,' said Lily Pimm.

26

Miss Silver walked back to The Lodge in a thoughtful frame of mind. The Miss Pimms certainly had an unusual talent for gathering information. The amount with which they had furnished her provided much food for thought. Mrs Harrison had been the subject of Mabel's most serious strictures – her dress, her bridge manners, her addiction to members of the opposite sex, her treatment of her husband. She had lost her temper with him during a bridge party at Mrs Justice's only about a fortnight ago. Of course he was not a good player, and she made him worse by continually criticizing his play, but when she called him a fool with an adjective in front of it which Mabel felt she could not repeat, and finished up by throwing her cards in his face, it really did pass all bounds. A supplement by Nettie deprecated the fact that similar exhibitions were said to be not uncommon at Grove Hill House. Mrs Harrison couldn't bear to be crossed. If Mr Harrison said a word, she would flare right up. On one occasion she had thrown a decanter at his head. If it had hit him he might have been killed, but he ducked and it went smashing into a big mirror on the dining-room wall. Nettie had also quite a lot to say about the dead set that had been made at young Dr Hamilton, and at the curate at St Jude's – 'Such a nice young man, and we found that we had met an aunt of his at Brighton before the war.' There was indeed plenty for Miss Silver to turn over in her mind.

Althea had given her a key to the front door. As she came into the hall the murmur of voices in the drawing-room informed her that Nicholas Carey was still there. She hoped to see him before he took his leave, but she did not think he would be in any great hurry to go. She had reached the foot of the stairs, had indeed already laid her hand on the baluster, when she checked and remained for some moments without moving. When she did move it was to go up to her bedroom, but with a changed purpose. Leaving the door ajar, she removed her gloves and put them neatly away in the left-hand top drawer of the chest of drawers. Then, opening the right-hand top drawer, she took out a powerful electric torch, a useful gift from Frank Abbott, and putting it in the pocket of her coat made her way downstairs again. The immediate purpose of the torch did not appear. It would not be dark until eight o'clock, and it was now no more than a quarter past six.

Miss Silver went through the house into the garden and up the flagged path to the gazebo. The windows of Althea's bedroom and of the bathroom looked out this way, as did those of the kitchen, scullery and larder, but failing a spectator at any of these the place was private, a ten-foot hedge screening it from the road on the one side and massed trees and shrubs intervening to shield it from the house next door.

Miss Silver was a person whose actions were prescribed by principle, reason, and common sense. She would have claimed no other impulsion, and would have ascribed her success in the field of detection to no other cause. Yet at this moment she was obeying what Frank Abbott might have called a hunch. She would herself have repudiated the term, but there were times in her experience when thoughts and impressions too vague to attract attention would suddenly combine to form an arresting picture. Looking back upon it afterwards, she could find no better explanation for her presence in the gazebo. It would have been carefully and competently searched by the police. She had visited it herself immediately after her arrival. Every trace of the tragedy had been removed. Yet she stood at the entrance and subjected the whole interior to as careful a scrutiny as if it had never been examined before. The structure was of brick and stucco, the door, the floor, the window-frames, and some panelling, of oak. All the workmanship was very good indeed, and the woodwork had lasted well. There were four windows with glass in them, two on either side of the door so as to afford the widest possible view. In the days when the only buildings to be seen from this point would be a rustic cottage or some distant farmstead the prospect must indeed have been delightful.

In the centre of the floor there was a table. Against the farther wall was a solid bench with some quite modern deck-chairs stacked on one side of it. The floor had been swept after the removal of Mrs Graham's body, and screened as it was by trees and a tall hedge, no fresh dust had drifted in.

After some time Miss Silver stepped inside and turned on her torch. Although still quite light in the garden, the interior of the gazebo held shadowed patches, notably under the windows and where the heavy bench cast its own shade. The powerful electric beam slid to and fro across the floor under the table and the bench. She laid the torch down while she shifted the deck-chairs. The police had been thorough. There was no dust where they had stood, nothing but the swept floor and the panelling that came smoothly down to meet it. The ray moved steadily until every inch of the floor had been explored.

When the whole circuit of the place had been made and she had come back to the entrance she stood there, her hand with the torch in it hanging down, the beam switched on. Her eye, following it, had its first impression that there had been dust in the gazebo, and that it had been swept out this way. The weathering of the floor-board next the door had left a crack between itself and the sill. The beam dazzled on the crack and showed it filled with dust. She went down upon her knees and laying the torch on its side extracted a hairpin from her neat plaits and began to clear the crack.

There was grit and dust in plenty, there were a couple of small dead spiders, there was a pin, there was a strand of cobweb, there was the upper half of a press-button, there was more grit, there was fine powdered dust, there was something that the sideways-stabbing ray of the torch pricked into light. She took it up between finger and thumb and laid it in her palm. She had had no reasonable expectation that she would find it – there was no reason to suppose that it would be there to be found. She could form no certain idea as to how it had come into the crack. It might have rolled there as it fell and been covered by the dust that was later swept across the threshold. It might have been lying on the floor unnoticed when Althea found her mother's body. It might have been her desperate flying feet that flicked it into the crack, it might have been the feet of any of those she summoned. However it came there, it had remained unnoticed until now. Miss Silver looked at it with grave composure. Whatever else might be in doubt, she had no doubt at all that the small bright object in her palm was the missing stone from Ella Harrison's ring.

27

Miss Silver rang up Detective Inspector Frank Abbott. Since he had gone to town to lay the case against Nicholas Carey before his immediate superiors, she began by trying Scotland Yard, only to find that he had been there and had left again. She therefore dialled his private number, and was relieved to hear his voice in an unhurried 'Hallo . . .'

'Miss Silver speaking. I wondered whether you would be returning here tonight.'

'My dear ma'am! Even the hard-worked constabulary get an occasional half hour off! Tonight I dine out with one of my more ornamental cousins. Her husband has so much money that if they went on spending the capital for the next fifty years they wouldn't be able to get through it. Oil. The meal will be super. I shall be back on the job first thing in the morning. What did you want me for?'

Miss Silver coughed.

'It would not, I think, be advisable to discuss it on the telephone.'

A faint whistle came back to her along the line.

'An ace up the sleeve? A rabbit out of a hat? Or a cat in the bag?'

'I will let you know tomorrow.'

As he rang off he wondered what she had got hold of. He knew her too well to suppose that she had rung him up for nothing. At intervals during a most agreeable evening the thought recurred. He had known her to pull rabbits out of hats before now.

Miss Silver left Nicholas and Althea to themselves, only appearing in the hall when he made a move to go. When the door had closed behind him she went back into the drawing-room with Althea.

'Oh, Miss Silver . . .'

Miss Silver looked at her. She was flushed and trembling.

'My dear, you had better come and sit down.'

Althea pushed back her hair with one of those shaking hands.

'He has left the Harrisons and gone down to the George. He says he thinks they are bound to arrest him and it wouldn't be fair to Jack Harrison to let it happen in his house.'

'You don't think they will, do you?'

'Suppose they do – then I shan't be able to see him again . . . Oh, I oughtn't to have let him go! He could have stayed for supper – there was no need for him to go to the hotel. Oh, I don't know why I let him go – only he said he had an article to write for the *Janitor* and he wanted to get it done before – before . . .'

'My dear, pray calm yourself.'

Althea sank down upon the sofa.

'How can I? You know – he didn't do it – he didn't! Why should he? We were going to be married next day. I wasn't going to let anything stop me this time – he knew that. Your Emily Chapell was going to come – and it was all fixed. Besides he wouldn't do an awful thing like that – he *couldn't!* You must believe me! I don't only love him, I *know* him! He couldn't do it!'

All that quiet self-control was gone. This was a new Althea, ablaze with conviction, passionate in defence.

Miss Silver sat quietly down beside her.

'My dear . . .'

Althea turned a vehement look upon her.

'You don't believe me, but you've got to! If I can't convince you, how am I, how is Nicky, going to convince anyone – all these policemen, lawyers, a jury – people who don't know him – people who will believe that he did it! And he won't say the thing that would save him!'

Miss Silver raised her hand in a hortatory manner.

'I have not said I believe that Mr Carey murdered your mother. You say there is something that would save him, but that he is reluctant to avail himself of it. Pray tell me what it is.'

In her normal frame of mind Althea would hardly have spoken. But the floodgates were open, thoughts and words rushed through them without check.

'He could have an alibi, but he won't let her do it. It's because of Jack – I'm sure of it – but he won't say so. She would say he was in by eleven, and that they were together, but he won't let her do it.'

'Miss Graham, to whom are you alluding?'

Althea stared, her eyes unnaturally wide and bright.

'Ella Harrison – Mrs Harrison. He is staying with them, you know – at least he was. He has gone to the George now, but he was at the Harrisons when it happened. Jack and he are cousins, and Ella said she would say that Nicky was in by eleven, and that they were together for quite a long time after that. If she did, it would save him, wouldn't it? That woman – that Mrs. Traill who says she heard Mother call out to Nicky between twenty and half past eleven – it's what she says that is going to make them arrest him. But if Ella Harrison says Nicky was with her at Grove Hill House, then he couldn't have been in the gazebo, could he – and they wouldn't arrest him.'

'It would rather depend upon whether they thought Mrs Harrison was telling the truth.'

Althea said in a piteous voice,

'He couldn't have been at Grove Hill House and in the gazebo at the same time – he couldn't!'

Miss Silver looked at her compassionately.

'Does Mr Carey say that he was at Grove Hill House?'

Althea had a failing look.

154

'He doesn't – know – when he got in. Ella Harrison says she knows. He could not let her say he was in.'

'And he will not?'

'He – he . . .' Her voice failed altogether.

'I see that he will not. Is it because he is aware that it would not be true?'

'He doesn't know what time he got in. He says so. And if he doesn't know, then how can he tell whether it's true or not?'

Miss Silver said gravely,

'I believe Mr Carey has stated that, without being able to set any time for his return, he believes it was late before he got back to Grove Hill House.'

'He doesn't *know*. Ella Harrison says he was in by eleven. Why can't he let her say it?'

'Has he not told you why?'

Althea looked away.

'He doesn't say. I think it's because of Jack. I think – I think if she says he was in, she will say they stayed together – a long time. Oh, don't you see what I mean? Don't you see what people might think – what Jack might think?'

Miss Silver saw very clearly indeed. She saw a number of things. But before she could speak Althea broke in again.

'But it wouldn't be true, so what would it matter? Jack Harrison wouldn't believe it. Nicky is his cousin. He didn't stay with Ella after he came in – he went straight up to bed. They could tell him she was only saying it to help Nicky. Jack wouldn't believe there was anything wrong.'

Miss Silver did not speak for a moment. Then she said,

'Mr Carey would be very foolish indeed if he were to rely on perjured evidence. Perjury is both a moral and a legal crime. A person who volunteers to commit this crime must either be of an entirely unreliable character or be actuated by some extremely strong motive. In Mrs Harrison's case, have you asked yourself whether she has such a motive, and what that motive might be?'

Althea said only just above her breath,

'To help Nicky . . .'

28

Miss Silver opened the door to Detective Inspector Frank Abbott next morning and took him into the dining-room, where she settled herself in one of the two armchairs belonging to the set round the table and took her knitting out of its flowered chintz bag. The second vest intended for little Tina was now approaching completion. Frank looked at it, raised a colourless eyebrow, and said,

'How many million stitches do you suppose you knit in a year?'

She smiled.

'I must confess that I have never given the matter any attention.'

'You should do so. It may run into billions. What a lot of dressing-up the human young require!'

She allowed her eye to travel over his immaculate suit, the harmony of tie, handkerchief and socks, the elegant cut of the shoes, before replying.

'Not, I think, only the very young, my dear Frank.'

He laughed.

'One endeavours to keep the end up. I am rewarded by being constantly told that I don't look like a policeman. Which is sometimes extremely useful. Well, what have you got for me?'

She was knitting busily.

'Nicholas Carey has left Grove Hill House.'

Frank leaned back as far as it is possible to lean in a dining-room chair. He had turned it sideways so as to be able to stretch out his long legs. He had rather a languid air which might be accounted for by the fact that the attractive cousin's party had been kept up until very late. He said in a voice that matched his attitude,

'He notified us to that effect.'

Miss Silver continued.

'He was here for some time after tea yesterday, which gave me an opportunity of calling upon the Miss Pimms.'

'My dear ma'am!'

'I found it both interesting and instructive. They were extremely pleased to see me, and they imparted a great deal of information.'

'Which I suppose you are going to impart to me.'

Miss Silver proceeded to impart as much of the Miss Pimms' conversation as she considered relevant. Before she had really finished she found him looking at her with a touch of malice.

'And what am I supposed to make of the fact that Mrs Harrison is a little too highly coloured for Grove Hill society, and that the Miss Pimms accuse her of having, shall I say, a come-hither in her eye when abroad and an inflammable temper at home? Dr Hamilton and the curate at St Jude's don't seem to me to have very much to do with the murder of Mrs Graham.'

Her glance reproved him. He was reminded of her scholastic experience. He had spoken out of turn.

Without further comment she proceeded with her narration and repeated Lily Pimm's artless tale about the lost stone in Mrs Harrison's diamond ring. That it did not impress him she was instantly aware. He looked at her quizzically.

'And what am I supposed to make of that?'

Still knitting, she said without emphasis,

'I have found the stone.'

He sat up with a jerk.

'You have what!'

She loosened some strands from the pink ball in her knitting-bag.

'I have found what I believe to be the lost stone from Mrs Harrison's ring.'

'And I am supposed to ask you where you found it?'

She said soberly,

'I found it within a yard of where Mrs Graham's body was found.'

'What!'

She had no reason to complain of a lack of interest now. His cold blue eyes were intent. She said,

157

'I cannot undertake to explain what prompted me to make a particular search of the gazebo. I knew that the local police would have been most thorough in their investigation.'

'They don't seem to have been quite thorough enough.'

'I do not believe that you must blame them. Their search was of a general character. It had no particular objective.'

'And yours had?'

She said simply, 'I could not get that missing stone out of my mind.'

'Where did you find it?'

'There is a crack between the door-sill and the wooden floor of the gazebo. The stone had rolled into this crack. When the floor was swept fresh dust was deposited and the diamond covered.'

'And how did you uncover it?'

'I poked in the crack with a hairpin.'

He was gazing at her in a fascinated manner.

'You poked in the crack. With a hairpin. That makes everything perfectly clear!'

She stopped knitting for a moment, dipped into the chintz bag, and produced a small cardboard box. Putting it down on the table, she pushed it over to him.

'The diamond is inside, done up in tissue paper. I believe that it may be found to fit Mrs Harrison's ring. If so, one cannot escape the conclusion that she was in the gazebo at some time after leaving the house of some people called Reckits, where she was playing bridge on the Tuesday evening. Lily Pimm who is, I believe, an entirely accurate witness was also at the party. She takes a particular interest in Mrs Harrison's jewellery, and she says that she counted the diamonds – three in a diamond and sapphire ring, three in a ruby and diamond ring, three in a ring with two pearls in it, and five in a ring that was all diamonds. On Wednesday morning in the bus, when Mrs Harrison took off her glove in order to find some change, Lily Pimm noticed at once that there was one stone missing from the five-stone diamond ring.'

'It could have dropped anywhere. Look here, if it had been missing when she put the ring on in the morning . . .'

'Lily Pimm made the same remark, to which Mrs Harrison replied that she hadn't put it on because she never took it off,

158

adding that it was rather loose for her and apt to slip round on her finger, so that she might not notice that a stone had gone.'

He was frowning a little.

'I still say that the stone might have dropped anywhere.'

'If this stone fits Mrs Harrison's ring – if it matches the other stones . . .'

He said a thought impatiently,

'Is there anything special about it?'

'I am not an expert. It is a fine large stone and of a good colour.'

He opened the cardboard box, took out the twist of tissue paper, and unfolded it carefully. The diamond slid down upon the polished table and shone there like a dewdrop.

Frank whistled softly.

'It's certainly a sizable stone, and very bright. Five like this in a row would be a bit overpowering, I should think.'

'Lily Pimm said the ring was a valuable one. Someone in Mr Harrison's family had brought the stones from India. Mr Harrison had them re-set as a wedding-present for his wife.'

He said in a meditative voice,

'If the stone fits and matches the others, then Mrs Harrison will have to explain what she was doing in the gazebo between whenever it was she left her bridge party on Tuesday evening and . . . When did Lily go down in the bus with her on Wednesday morning?'

'They caught the ten o'clock bus from this corner.'

He was sitting up straight enough now. He said as if he was thinking aloud,

'If she dropped the stone in the gazebo – what took her there? I suppose . . .' He broke off. 'Do you happen to know whether she was here at all that evening? She was friendly with Mrs Graham – she might have dropped in to see her after the bridge party.'

'No, Frank, she did not do that. It was some days since she had been to the house, and even if she had looked in as you suggest, I am unable to think of any possible reason why she should have gone up the garden to the gazebo.'

His shoulder lifted for a moment.

'If this stone fell out of her ring in the gazebo, then what-

159

ever her motive was, she did go there. Is Miss Graham quite
sure that Mrs Harrison did not look in on the Tuesday evening?'

'She is perfectly sure.'

He picked up the diamond, wrapped it, and put it in the
cardboard box. When the box had gone into his waistcoat
pocket, he pushed back his chair and got up.

'This is where I go and see Mrs Harrison and ask her what
she was doing in the gazebo between Tuesday's bridge party
and Wednesday's meeting with Lily Pimm on the ten o'clock
bus.'

Miss Silver laid her knitting down upon her knee, but she
did not rise.

'Just a moment, Frank. There is something else which I
think you ought to know.'

'Another rabbit?'

She took no notice of this levity, but said,

'It may, or may not, have a serious connexion with what
I have been telling you.'

He sat down again.

'What is it?'

'It comes to me through Althea Graham. If she had not
been in so distressed a state as completely to break down
her self-control, she would not have repeated it.'

'Oh, she was repeating something?'

She inclined her head.

'I told you that Nicholas Carey had been here. They were
together for some time, and after hearing from her about Mrs
Traill's evidence he seems to have arrived at the conclusion
that his arrest was likely to follow. She was naturally very
much overcome. Up to now she has maintained a wonderful
degree of composure, but when Mr Carey had gone she broke
down. In these circumstances she repeated something which
I feel may be of the first importance. Mr Carey seems to have
told her that Mrs Harrison had offered to give him an alibi,
but that he had refused to let her do so. It appears she was
prepared to state that he was back in Grove Hill House by
eleven o'clock, and that they remained together for some considerable time after that. Miss Graham became more and
more distressed while she was telling me this. I formed the
opinion that whereas Mr Carey had told her very little about

160

the details of his interview with Mrs Harrison, she had guessed a good deal more than she had been told, and was convinced that the proffered alibi would compromise Mr Carey in other ways. She said repeatedly that he would not do anything that would hurt his cousin – Mr Harrison is a cousin.'

Frank Abbott cocked an eyebrow.

'The stock compromising situation – "He couldn't have done it, because he was with me"! But you know, she has already said that she has no idea when Carey got in.'

Miss Silver picked up her knitting again. The busy needles clicked.

'She is apparently prepared to unsay it. Mr Carey is refusing her offer, and Althea Graham is torn between the feeling that his alibi may save him from arrest and her natural disinclination to allow him to appear in the character of Mrs Harrison's illicit lover.'

Frank nodded.

'Quite a pretty kettle of fish, as you were no doubt about to remark.'

Miss Silver said,

'It occurs to me, as it no doubt does to you, that Mrs Harrison's motives should be subjected to the closest examination. It is, of course, possible that she is so much attached to Mr Carey as to be prepared to risk disgrace and a divorce in order to protect him.'

Frank looked at her quizzically.

'From the tone of your voice I do not gather that this explanation appeals to you.'

She was knitting rapidly.

'No, Frank, it does not. From what I have heard of her there are other considerations which should be taken into account. She is dissatisfied with her marriage – especially since Mr Harrison has had losses. She finds life in Grove Hill dull, and has shown considerable readiness to embark upon flirtations with other men. Mr Carey is attractive and has recently inherited a considerable fortune. If she gave evidence which would clear him in a murder case but which left her compromised on his account, she would no doubt expect him to marry her should her husband sue for a divorce. This would put Mr Carey in an extremely difficult position.'

'How much of this did he really tell Althea Graham?'

'I do not know. I suspect very little more than the fact that she was willing to give him an alibi.'

'You mean she is dotting the i's and crossing the t's herself?'

'I think so. She does not like Mrs Harrison, and she is in love with Nicholas Carey.'

He nodded.

'Very sharpening to the intelligence.'

'There is one more point, Frank, and I believe a most important one. An alibi for Mr Carey would also be an alibi for Mrs Harrison.'

29

Grove Hill House was well staffed, though none of the staff slept in. The parlourmaid who opened the door to Detective Inspector Abbott and Detective Inspector Sharp had been in very good service before her marriage. Now that she was a widow she had gone back to the work for which she had been trained. Her two children were in their teens and her mother lived with her, so that the arrangement worked smoothly enough. She got good wages and all her meals. She could say that for Mrs Harrison, there was always plenty in the house and you could help yourself. Of course it wasn't like working for a real lady, but the money was good, and Mr Harrison was a nice quiet gentleman if ever there was one. She showed the two policemen into the drawing-room and went to tell Mrs Harrison.

Ella Harrison took her time. When she came into the drawing-room Frank Abbott was immediately aware that there had been a fresh application of powder and lipstick. He has been credited with more cousins than anyone in England, and as the usual proportion of these were female and young, there was very little he did not know about the gentle art of making up. His standards were of necessity a good deal more indulgent than those of the Miss Pimms, but he certainly thought that Mrs Harrison should exercise greater restraint. Her hair, even if the colour were naturel, would be on the noticeable side, and natural it certainly was not. Combined with mascara, eyeshadow and a particularly vivid lipstick, it was altogether too much of a good thing. She might have carried it off in black, or brown, or navy, but not, definitely not, in a plaid skirt and a twin set in a lively shade of emerald. It was his first meeting with her, Sharp having made the original inquiries to check up on Nicholas Carey's movements. On that occasion both she and Jack Harrison had replied that they had gone to bed early, and that they had no idea of the time of Carey's return. Since none of the staff slept in the house, that appeared to be that.

They were now here on a totally different errand. The lady was said to have an inflammable temper. Rumours as to some of its more violent manifestations had not been wanting. The story of the broken mirror had reached Detective Inspector Sharp. He hoped that there wasn't going to be any unpleasantness.

Ella Harrison did not offer to shake hands. She did not even ask them to sit down. Frank Abbott thought they might have been travelling salesmen whom she had no wish to encourage. Yet she had taken the trouble to touch up her face. Sharp looked at him, and he took the lead.

'Mrs Harrison, we have called in connexion with the loss of a stone from a diamond ring. You have recently lost such a stone, have you not?'

She looked from one to the other.

'Why, yes – how did you know? I haven't reported it.'

He said easily,

'These things get about. The fact is a stone has been found. If it is the one you have missed from your ring you might be able to identify it.'

'If it is mine I should be very glad to get it back.'

'Perhaps you will let us see the ring. You are not wearing it?'

There was the ruby and diamond ring which had been mentioned on her left hand, with a less valuable pearl and diamond ring above it. On her right hand there was one ring only, sapphires and diamonds.

She said, 'No – I thought the other stones might be loose,' and went out of the room.

There was some strain, some tension – she wasn't easy. She came back with the ring.

There was a small table standing in the window. It was an old piece with a walnut top and a wreath of flowers inlaid about the edge. They were very beautifully worked in different coloured woods. The centre of the table was plain. When she came back into the room with the ring in her hand the lost diamond lay on the table, right in the middle where the dark wood showed it up. Frank Abbott put out his hand for the ring, and she let him have it. He picked up the stone and fitted it back into the place from which it had come. There could be no doubt that it was the place from which it had come. The stones were very fine. They were of an equal size, an equal lustre. They could hardly have been better matched. Frank Abbott said,

'I am afraid I shall have to ask you to let us take charge of the ring. I will give you a receipt for it.' He was putting it away as he spoke in the cardboard box which had held the stone.

Mrs Harrison's colour had risen. She said,

'Here, what do you want with that ring? It's mine, isn't it?'

'Oh, we're not disputing that. The ring and the stone are both undoubtedly yours. By the way, have you any idea where you dropped that diamond?'

'Not the slightest. Where was it found?'

Detective Inspector Sharp stood by, and was glad that he had not had to come alone. Abbott was answering her in that la-di-da way he had.

'We were rather hoping that you might have something to tell us about that.'

'Well, I haven't.'

He let her have it then, short and sharp.

'It was found in the gazebo at The Lodge.'

It was a blow – you could see that. She blinked the way a man does when he has been hit. It was a blow and it rocked her, but she got herself in hand again. She said in a sharp, steady voice,

'In the gazebo at the Grahams'? I don't see . . .'

'No? Well, that is where it was found. Perhaps you can tell us when you were last there.'

She was recovering.

'Oh, I don't know ... I'm often at The Lodge ... I play bridge there.'

Frank's eyebrows rose.

'In the gazebo?'

'Of course not! But we don't play till after tea – I might have gone up to look at the view.'

'Can you remember that you did so?'

'Not specially. We were in the garden one day last week – it might have been then.'

'Mrs Harrison, Miss Lily Pimm states that there was no stone missing from your ring on Tuesday evening when you were playing bridge at the house of some people named Reckitts.'

She gave an exasperated laugh.

'Oh, Lily Pimm – if you're going to take what she says!'

'Is there any reason why we shouldn't?'

Her foot tapped the carpet.

'Only that she's barmy – that's all.'

'She appears to be an exact and accurate observer. She told us that she admires your rings very much and always notices them. She is positive that on Tuesday all the stones were present in the five-stone diamond ring. When she met you next day on the ten o'clock bus and you took off your glove to find some change for the fare she noticed at once that one of the stones was missing. She says she pointed this out to you, and you were very much upset and said you didn't know that the stone was gone.'

The colour which Ella Harrison had applied was reinforced by an angry flush.

'Of course I knew it was gone! It had been missing for days!'

'And you continued to wear the ring?'

'I always wear it!'

'It didn't occur to you that the other stones might be loose?'

'No, it didn't!'

'But you told us just now that it was for this reason that you were not wearing the ring.'

165

Her eyes were bright with anger.

'I didn't think of it at first, and then I did! Any objection to that?'

'When did you first notice that the stone was gone?'

'I have no idea.'

'Think carefully, Mrs Harrison. This seems to be a valuable ring. Since you wear it always, it must be valuable to you. When you discovered that one of the stones was missing you would naturally be upset.'

'Anyone would be!'

'I quite agree with you. It is an unpleasant thing to happen. You would naturally speak about it to your maid – ask her to look for it very carefully in case it had dropped in the house.'

'Well, I didn't!'

Her foot was tapping again. If he would only stop these questions and give her time to think. He didn't give her a moment. He went on,

'It would seem to have been the natural thing to do.'

'Well then, it wasn't! I knew I hadn't dropped it in the house.'

'May I ask how you knew that?'

She had to make up her mind quickly. When you hadn't time to think you had to do what you could and chance your luck. She said,

'Because I knew the ring was all right when I went out.'

'Oh, you have remembered which day you missed the stone?'

She said smoothly,

'It must have been the last time I went to the Grahams', if that was where it was found.'

Frank said, 'Yes,' and gave it a moment to sink in before he went on, 'The last time you went to the Grahams' – that would be on Tuesday after the bridge party at the Reckitts'?'

'What are you trying to make me say? I wasn't anywhere near them on Tuesday evening! It was the week before – Wednesday or Thursday, I don't remember which. I was there to tea, and Mrs Graham took me into the garden afterwards to show me some plant or other.'

'Who else was there?'

'No one. It was just Mrs Graham and me.'

'I thought you said you played bridge after tea.'

'I couldn't have. There wasn't anyone to play with – even Thea was out. We were in the garden.'

'Did you say you went up into the gazebo?'

'Yes, I did. Mrs Graham wanted me to see the view.'

'She didn't go with you?'

'No.'

'And when you came home and discovered that a stone out of your ring was missing you would naturally make inquiries as to whether you had dropped it at the Grahams'?'

She met his searching look with a hardy one.

'Yes, I did.'

'Curious that Mrs. Graham should not have mentioned the fact to her daughter.'

'I suppose she forgot. She wasn't really interested in anything that didn't happen to herself.'

'You didn't mention the loss of the stone to your maid, and Mrs Graham didn't mention it to her daughter. Quite a coincidence, isn't it? I suppose you mentioned the loss to your husband?'

If Jack had been out – if she could have been certain of the opportunity of telling him what to say – but he was in the study – she couldn't be certain of anything. She took the next best chance and said,

'I didn't want him to know. It's a ring from his side of the family. He gave it to me when we were married.'

Frank thought, 'She's lying all along the line.' Out loud he said,

'You are quite sure about these dates, Mrs Harrison?'

'I'm not sure whether it was Wednesday or Thursday when I went to the Grahams' – Wednesday or Thursday last week.'

'But you are sure that it was last week?'

'Quite sure.'

'And that that was when you lost the stone out of your ring?'

'Yes.'

'Mrs Harrison, Miss Pimm is extremely definite in stating that she saw that ring on your right hand at the Reckitts

167

bridge party, and that all the stones were there. She says she counted them.'

Ella Harrison's blazing anger broke. Her furious voice leapt at them.

'Then she's a damned liar as well as a damned fool! Anyone – anyone with a grain of sense could see what she and her sisters are – spiteful old maids with nothing to do but gather up gossip and peddle it round to a lot of credulous nitwits who don't know any better than to lap it up! Just try putting your Lily Pimm in the box and see what kind of shape she'd be in by the time a lawyer had finished with her! You just try it!'

There were a number of unprintable words in this speech. Some shocked Inspector Sharp a good deal, coming from a lady in Mrs Harrison's position. In court he might have characterized them as obscene. In his own mind he set them down as low. He really wondered where she had picked them up.

Frank Abbott, waiting until she was done, saw the door open behind her and Mr Harrison come into the room – a small quiet man with greying hair and a patient look about the eyes. He said, 'What is the matter?' and Ella Harrison whirled round upon him.

'I'm being insulted, that's what! A pretty state of things when the police come tramping into your drawing-room without a with your leave or by your leave and insult you!' She swung back again. 'Perhaps you'll be a bit more careful what you say now my husband's here – bursting in and calling me a liar in my own house!'

Jack Harrison stood where he was. He had a certain half bewildered dignity as he said,

'Perhaps someone will tell me what is going on.'

Frank Abbott told him quietly and succinctly. The air of bewilderment deepened.

'A stone from my wife's ring – in the gazebo at The Lodge? Are you sure there is no mistake? But she was wearing the ring on Tuesday evening – I saw it myself. There was no stone missing then.'

The fool – the immeasurable fool! Just for a moment she couldn't think – speak – move.

Frank Abbott said,

'Are you sure about that?'

Jack Harrison said, 'Oh, yes.' He was neither quick nor clever. He found the situation confusing. His wife's anger daunted him. He steadied himself on the plain question of fact. Ella couldn't have dropped a stone out of her ring last week, because she was wearing it at the Reckitts' on Tuesday. He said so, repeating himself as he was rather inclined to do.

'Oh, yes, it was all right when we were at the Reckitts'. We were playing at the same table for part of the time. It's a beautiful ring, and I noticed it particularly. The stones came from Golconda. A great-uncle of mine brought them home and had them cut. They are well matched. They were certainly all there on Tuesday.'

Ella Harrison had been going back step by step. It was a purely instinctive movement. In a moment she would think of something to say, to do. The moment wasn't yet. She would have to wait for it. She went back until the fireplace brought her up short. There was a Sèvres jar in the middle of the mantelpiece with a delicate china figure on either side of it. Eighteenth-century figures – a lady in a hooped skirt with powdered hair, a gentleman in a brocaded coat with red heels to his shoes. She picked up the lady by her slender neck and slung her at Jack Harrison.

30

Mr Harrison ducked. The china lady in her applegreen gown and flowered petticoat smashed against the door which he had closed behind him and fell in splinters on the parquet floor. The head rolled under a small gold gimcrack chair. Ella Harrison stood against the mantelpiece, heavily flushed and breathing deep. Nobody spoke until Frank Abbott said, his voice very cool and detached.

'Perhaps it would be better to defer the rest of this interview until Mrs Harrison is calmer.'

Jack Harrison spoke.

'I think it would be better. If you want me, I shall be in the study.' He turned and went out of the room.

Ella Harrison left the hearth and came forward.

'And now we can get on with it!' Her voice was loud and dominant.

She was furiously angry, but she had got past smashing china. There were other things that could be broken, and she was out to break them. She came up to one of the easy chairs and stood there, resting her hands on the back.

'You . . .' she said, addressing Frank Abbott, 'you've been free enough with your questions. Now you're going to listen to me! I've got something to say!'

'You wish to make a statement?'

'If that's what you like to call it! I've got something to say, and if you want to write it down you can!'

Inspector Sharp found himself a chair. He got out a notebook and propped it on the edge of the table where the diamond had lain.

Frank said, 'Perhaps you would like to sit down, Mrs Harrison.'

She stared angrily.

'I'd just as soon stand! It won't take long! Quite a nice change it'll be me talking and you listening, instead of your popping off questions at me for all the world as if you were a cross-talk comedian and I was your stooge! Now, you get this, Mr La-di-da policeman – I'm nobody's stooge! And if you think you can pin anything on me, you can just set to work and think again, because I've got an alibi! And you, Mr What's-his-name Sharp, you can write that down and be damned to you!'

The veneer was clean stripped off. This was the woman who had grown up in a drunken home and learned her language from hearing her father and mother swear at one another in their not infrequent rows, who had played as a child in the gutter, who had fought and clawed her way into a children's act in pantomime, and from there with the help of good legs and a resonant voice into a variety turn. She hadn't taken anything from anyone then, and she wasn't taking anything from these policemen now. She said so at the top of her voice.

'I don't know what you think you're getting at with your

170

was I down at the Grahams' on Tuesday night! Well then, I wasn't, so you can put that in your pipe and smoke it! And why wasn't I? You see, I'm asking the questions this time, and here's the answer to that one! I wasn't down at the Grahams' because I'd got other fish to fry! And if you want to know who I was frying them with, it was Nicholas Carey! He came to this house as the clock struck eleven, and he didn't go out of it again – I can answer for that. Here he was, and here he stayed, and neither of us wanted it any different. Jack was off to bed at ten o'clock, and the servants sleep out, so there wasn't anyone to interfere with us, and that's how we wanted it to be. So now you know!'

Frank Abbott's cool detached gaze rested upon her. He was wondering how much of this was to Jack Harrison's address. Just another and more effective way of hitting him where it hurt? Some of it no doubt, and the rest the alibi foreshadowed by Miss Silver. He said,

'When you were questioned before, you stated that you were in bed by eleven, and that you had no idea when Mr Carey came in. Now you say he was in by eleven, and that you remained together.'

She had gone back to tapping with her foot.

'Yes, you don't put everything in the shop-window right away, do you?'

'Meaning that you don't always tell the truth unless it suits you?'

'Don't you go trying to make out I've said what I haven't!'

'By your own account you have said first one thing and then another with regard to your movements on Tuesday night.'

'I didn't see it was anyone's business – not then. But if you're trying to pin something on me, then it's my business to see you don't get any wrong ideas! Nicky was here with me from eleven o'clock and for the best part of the night. It didn't suit either of us for it to come out – not then. But that's how it was, and you can't get from it!'

Her flush was one of triumph now. She had flung her stone and killed two birds with it. If she had an alibi, they couldn't make out she'd been down at the Grahams' on Tuesday night, and if the alibi was going to hit Jack where it hurt, well, he'd asked for it – chipping in to say he'd seen the ring on Tuesday evening and none of the stones missing! Anyone else would have had the sense to hold his tongue, with the police in the house and a murder charge flying round. But not Jack Harrison, not her poor boob of a husband – oh dear, no! He must come chipping in with having seen the ring and noticed that all the stones were there! Well, if he liked to divorce her he could, and a good riddance to him!

The local Inspector wrote down what she had said and read it over to her. When she had signed it they both went out of the room. She heard them go across the hall to the front door. She heard it open and shut again behind them.

The warm satisfied anger in her began to die down.

31

Nicholas Carey sat at the dressing-table of his room at the George, but he was not engaged with the affairs of the toilet. The old-fashioned dressing-mirror with its five drawers, two on each side and one in the middle to take rings, trinkets, and what have you, had been pushed on one side to make way for the typewriter upon which he was rapidly tapping out his latest article. The room was furnished in a heavy mid-Victorian style, the only change which it had suffered since the days when the George was a posting inn being the substitution of up-to-date spring beds for the gloomy four-poster of a hundred years ago. If the carpet had been renewed, Mr Pickwick himself would not have been able to swear to it, and the general air of gloomy respectability remained intact.

When the telephone bell rang Nicholas stopped tapping, crossed to the space between the beds, and took up the receiver. A voice informed him that there was a gentleman to see him, 'Name of Abbott – Mr Abbott.' He said, 'Send him up,' and went back to the dressing-table, where he stood gathering up a couple of sheets already typed. He was frowning at the one still in the typewriter, wondering whether he would be allowed to finish it if they arrested him, and whether the *Janitor* would want it if they did.

There was a knock at the door before he could make up his mind. Frank Abbott came in and shut it behind him. He was alone, and the official manner was in abeyance.

Nicholas raised his eyebrows, laid down his sheets of type-script, and said,

'Mr Abbott? Is that tact or . . .'

'Well, perhaps unnecessary to give the hall porter anything fresh to talk about.'

'But I take it you haven't just dropped in to pass the time of day?'

'Not exactly.'

'Well, we might as well sit down.'

He gave Frank Abbott the armchair, sat on the side of the nearer bed, and waited. If police officers chose to come butting in they could break the ice for themselves.

Frank leaned back, crossed his long legs, and said easily,

'I thought it might be useful to have your views on Mrs Traill's evidence. Miss Graham has told you about it?'

'She has.'

'Would you care to comment on it at all? You need not of course – I expect you know that. If you do, I suppose I ought to caution you.'

'That anything I say may be taken down and used in evidence? All right, we'll take it as said. About this Mrs Traill's statement – I certainly wasn't in the gazebo at twenty past eleven on Tuesday night. I left as soon as Althea had taken her mother into the house.'

'You are sticking to that?'

'It happens to be true.'

'Mrs Traill heard Mrs Graham use your name. She is prepared to swear to hearing her say, "How dare you, Nicholas Carey!" '

Nicholas nodded.

'Yes, that's what she said before when she came out and found us in the gazebo. But you know, she couldn't have seen who it was this second time. All she could possibly have done was to see or hear that there was someone in the gazebo, and to jump to the conclusion that it was me.'

Frank thought, 'That's reasonable enough – it might even be true . . .' He said,

'There was a torch in the pocket of her coat.'

Nicholas gave a short laugh.

'No, really that won't do! If she had had the torch out and been using it, it would have dropped and rolled. It wouldn't have been found in her pocket.'

'Unless the murderer put it there.'

'Good lord, Abbott, what sort of nerve are you giving him credit for? The gazebo is right on the road, anyone may have been passing – Mrs Traill *was* passing – and Mrs Graham had called out. There may have been other sounds. Can you suppose that the man who has just strangled her is going to waste any time in getting away? Do you see him hunting round for that torch and putting it in her pocket? Because I don't. And by the way, if that's what he did, there would be his fingerprints on the torch, or if he had wiped them off, then there wouldn't be any prints on it at all. Whereas if Mrs Graham had put it in her pocket, why then, Abbott, her own prints would be there, and I suppose the police would have found them.'

Frank nodded.

'Point to you. They did. Now let us get back to what you did after the Grahams had gone in on Tuesday night. Which way did you walk – up the hill or down?'

'Up. My first idea was to go back to Grove Hill House. It's only a step, you know – up Hill Rise and just round the corner. I got as far as the corner, and realized that I didn't want to go in. It wouldn't be any good going in, because I shouldn't sleep. I went back down Hill Rise and across Belview Road. There's a lane there cutting between the houses – it's called the Dip. It has never been built over, because it's the quickest way down off the hill to what used to be farm land and water meadows. I went right down as far as it goes and turned to the left. After that I can't say for certain. Even in the last five years that part has been a good deal built up. I got into a new building estate and out of it again. I wasn't really thinking of where I was going. When I had walked as long as I wanted to I made my way back up the hill. I can't tell you where I was half the time – I just followed the rise of the ground. In the

174

end I struck St Jude's church, and then I knew where I was – ten minutes walk from Grove Hill House. I can't tell you what time it was when I got in. It was after midnight, because the street-lamps were out. I let myself in with a latchkey, and I didn't look at a clock or hear one strike. I was dog-tired. I didn't even wind my watch. I just chucked off my clothes and tumbled into bed. Take it or leave it, that's the truth.'

Well, it might be. Frank Abbott inclined to believe that it was. Nicholas Carey's voice, his manner, had been informed with a kind of nervous energy. It was as if what he had in his mind must come out, and with the least possible delay. There was not the slightest hint of aggressiveness. He had something to say and he was impatient to get it said. He had throughout the air of a man who is doing his best to remember.

Frank Abbott said,

'Well, that's your statement. I take it you would be willing to put it into writing and sign it?'

'Right away. I'll type it out now if you like.'

He went over to the dressing-table, sat down there, pulled the typewriter towards him, put in a fresh sheet of paper, and began to type. It was a rapid and expert performance. He went from one end of it to the other without so much as pausing for a word. When he had finished he extracted the sheet, took a fountain pen out of his pocket, and put a scrawled signature under the last line of the type. Then he came back to his seat on the bed, handing the statement to Frank as he went past.

'There you are – that's the best of my recollection.'

Abbott ran his eye over it. Good even typing, no mistakes, and hardly a variation from the spoken word. That word had left the impression that Carey was setting himself to remember what he had done after leaving the gazebo, and that the effort to do so had fixed it in his mind. That being so, he would not lose it again.

Nicholas said,

'Anything else you want?'

'Well, yes. You've made this statement about your movements on Tuesday night. I think I must tell you it doesn't agree with another statement that has been made.'

Nicholas gave a short laugh.

175

'I don't feel called upon to account for what anyone else may have said.'

'Mrs Harrison states that you were back at Grove Hill House by eleven.'

'Mrs Harrison is mistaken.'

'I am afraid that what she says doesn't allow for a mistake. She states categorically that you returned to Grove Hill House by eleven o'clock and that you and she remained together for the rest of the night.'

Nicholas Carey's thin dark eyebrows rose.

'How very silly of her. I suppose she thinks she is giving me an alibi.'

'You say it's not true?'

'Of course it isn't true. I'm engaged to Althea Graham. We should have been married on Wednesday if all this hadn't happened. It's a preposterous story!'

Frank was inclined to agree with him. Nicholas went on with an edge to his voice,

'It's a preposterous story, and she's a preposterous woman! I think I had better tell you she had put it up to me already and I had turned it down. The whole thing's rubbish! It must have been at least after twelve when I got back. I had a key, and I went straight to my room. I didn't see a soul. Poor old Jack, he didn't have any luck when he picked her, did he? If she goes round telling this sort of yarn it's going to hit him where it hurts. He's a nice chap, you know, but he can't cope. Honestly, Abbott, that story of hers is twaddle.'

'And you stick to your statement?'

'I stick to my statement.'

32

Miss Silver was up in the attic at The Lodge. Mrs Justice had rung up just before lunch and asked whether Althea would feel equal to seeing her if she came round at two o'clock. It was impossible to refuse so old and kind a friend.

Miss Silver left them together and climbed the attic stairs.

Since yesterday it had been on her mind that she would be glad of an opportunity to look through the books of which Althea had spoken and see whether there was indeed one which dealt with the history of Grove Hill, but until this moment the opportunity had not presented itself. But Louisa Justice was a motherly person and could be safely left with Althea. After a warm expression of sympathy she would not continue to dwell upon the tragedy. She had already informed Miss Silver that she had received some excellent snapshots of Sophy's twins and thought it might interest Althea to see them. Miss Silver could therefore devote herself to a search among Mr Graham's books.

The attic was airy and well lit, and the books were not packed away. A couple of large bookcases which had previously darkened the dining-room had been moved up here after Mr Graham's death. It would have annoyed him very much, but his widow had felt that she could now do as she pleased. The cases accommodated most of the books, and the rest stood in piles upon the floor. History appeared to have been the main interest. There were eighteenth-century memoirs, both French and English – Boswell's *Life of Johnson* in an old edition, books with fine engravings of cathedrals, an odd volume of *Ancient Abbeys and Castles,* Le Notre's *Romances of the French Revolution,* Lady Charlotte Bury lapping over into the nineteenth century, and the memoirs of the Comtesse de Boigne. These books were all together in the lower shelves of one of the bookcases. Miss Silver was encouraged to hope that what she was seeking might be amongst them, but this did not seem to be the case, and since she had no idea either of the title or the author's name, the task upon which she had embarked was not an easy one. All that she had to go on was Althea's remark that her father's books were up in the attic, and that she believed there was one amongst them which dealt with the history of Grove Hill.

She found what she was looking for in the second book-case. It was a shabby old volume by the Reverend Thomas Jenkinson, a former Rector of St Jude's. He appeared also to be the author of works on *Old Inn Signs* and *Some Interesting Epitaphs*. The book which Miss Silver took from the shelf was entitled *Residences of the Nobility and Gentry in the Neigh-*

177

bourhood of Grove Hill, with Some Remarks on the Families Residing there during the Eighteenth Century, and the date upon the title page was 1810. Miss Silver moved to an aged but quite comfortable chair and sat down to read.

The Reverend Thomas Jenkinson was one of those authors who incline to be diffuse. He had what he himself might have described as a Partiality for Capitals, and it was obvious that he revelled in the titles of the Nobility. Persons of the highest rank came and went upon his pages. There were Anecdotes sometimes verging on the scandalous. Miss Silver was obliged to consider many of them as quite unsuited to a clerical pen.

She had been turning the pages for about twenty minutes, when she came upon the name of Warren — Mr Henry Warren, a wealthy and charitable Brewer. Her attention fixed, she read on and learned that the Grove Hill Estate with a number of Profitable Farms had been purchased by this gentleman in 1749. He then proceeded to build himself a fine Mansion on the crown of the hill, to which he gave the name of Grove Hill House. There was a good deal more about Mr Warren, his two marriages, his nine children of whom not one survived him, his increasing wealth. Here Mr Jenkinson permitted himself to moralize, and Miss Silver was able to skim lightly over several pages. The Gordon Riots were dealt with at some length, Mr Jenkinson greatly deploring the Excesses of the Mob and the horrifying destruction of Property, Mr Warren's fine Mansion having been completely wrecked and destroyed, and Mr Warren himself fatally injured by some of the falling masonry.

There followed a passage which had been faintly underlined in pencil. Miss Silver perused it with attention. 'It is said that the unfortunate Gentleman had made strenuous efforts to save the more valuable of his Pictures. It was, in fact, during this endeavour that he met with his tragic End. Paintings to the value of many thousand pounds were entirely consumed in the Fires which had broken out. A better Fortune may have attended the rescue of some valuable Plate and the Jewels belonging to his late wife, all of which were in the house at the time of its Destruction. Since no trace of the Plate could be discovered among the Ruins, it is thought possible that he was able to remove it to a place of safety before being overtaken by the Fatality which terminated his Existence. His only surviving descendant being an Infant, no great search was made. It is, of course, possible that the Rioters removed the gold Plate which was of great value, but the late Mr D – L – with whom I had the Opportunity of conversing when I first came to this Parish assured me that he did not believe this to have been the case. Though he was then close upon eighty years of age he was of a perfectly sound mind and clearly remembered the excesses committed by the Rioters. He had a brother who was a Physician and who was called in to attend the unfortunate Mr Warren. He informed Mr D – L – that he found Mr Warren *in articulo mortis,* but not quite gone. He said the dying man constantly muttered to himself some such phrase as "The gold is safe," or, "I have saved the gold." The Physician inquiring of him, "What have you done with it?" and "Where is the gold?", Mr Warren gazed about him as if having no knowledge of his surroundings and muttered words which were only partly intelligible. Not long afterwards he passed into a state of Insensibility from which he did not rally. Mr D – L – maintained that the Truth of the foregoing could readily be established, since there were several persons present, including a young woman afterwards married in Yorkshire. This person, Mrs M – n, after an absence of many years is now returned and is a parishioner of my own. On referring to her for corroboration of Mr D – L – 's story, he being now deceased, she confirmed it in every particular, even to repeating some of the words let fall by Mr Warren when he lay a-dying. These I do not feel should be set down in print lest they should give rise to false hopes or to the Cupidity of unprincipled persons.'

Here the account ended, the Reverend Thomas branching off into speculations concerning a spring in the Long Meadow, said to be one of the superstitiously named Trouble Waters which were supposed to indicate by their flooding the approach of some National Calamity. Interesting as this subject might prove, Miss Silver did not pursue it. Instead, she got up and went to stand immediately under the unscreened electric bulb which lighted the attic. Even at some distance she had thought she could discern faint pencil marks between the initial M and the final N of the name by which the Reverend Thomas

179

Jenkinson had designated the lady who had married in Yorkshire and afterwards returned to his parish. Held immediately under the light, there was no doubt that this was the case. The name had been filled in, but by whom? If by Mr Jenkinson, the addition must have been made a good deal more than a hundred years ago, if by Mr Graham possibly no more than twenty. The letters were not easily legible. They faded into a page already discoloured by age and damp. But they made a certain impression upon the eye.

Miss Silver looked away and then back again several times. The impression became stronger. The pencilled letters between M and N certainly suggested a name, and that name was Martin.

33

On the following morning, Althea being provided with the company of Nicholas Carey, Miss Silver took a bus into the town. She got out half way down the High Street and made her way to the offices of Martin and Steadman, House-Agents. Asking for Mr Martin by name, she was presently ushered into his pleasant room at the back of the house. The day being very mild, a glass door stood wide upon a garden which fairly blazed with autumn flowers. If Miss Silver's exclamation of admiration and pleasure was not quite uncalculated, it was entirely genuine. She had, it is true, been informed by Althea Graham that praise of his garden was the one sure way to Mr Martin's heart, but her appreciation was perfectly sincere. The display of dahlias, chrysanthemums, late roses, carnations, and michaelmas daisies, was quite a dazzling one. There was warmth in her voice as she said,

'What a lovely garden!'

Mr Martin accepted the tribute. It was a not unaccustomed one, but repetition had no power to render it less pleasing. In the course of a short interchange on the subject of suburban gardening she informed him with regret that she herself could not speak from experience, since she lived in a flat.

'But the gardens here are delightful. The soil must be good.

I am staying with Miss Althea Graham at The Lodge, Belview Road.'

Mr Martin's look changed to one of concern.

'Then perhaps you can tell me how she is bearing up. I was very much shocked by Mrs Graham's death. We attended the same church, and I usually pass the house on my way to business. I have known Miss Graham since she was a child. I am glad too, that she has someone staying with her. There are no near relatives, I believe.'

'I believe not. I am very glad to be here. My name is Silver – Miss Maud Silver. Miss Graham has told me how kind you have always been.'

He moved a paper on his desk and said with a trace of embarrassment,

'I have tried to do my best for her. I expect she will have told you that I have a client who has been very anxious to purchase the house. It is perhaps too soon to expect Miss Graham to come to any decision in the matter, but from the business point of view it might be better if she did not delay too long. Mr Blount's last offer was a very handsome one, but I cannot be at all sure that it will stand. A tragedy like this – a *murder* – well, there is nothing which can so depreciate the value of a property. In Mr Blount's case his reason for being willing to make such a good offer for the house was the fact that Mrs Blount, who is more or less of an invalid, has taken the greatest possible fancy to it. She seems to be very difficult to suit. He doesn't want to be too far out of London, and he tells me they have looked at above a hundred houses, first in one suburb and then in another, and that Mrs Blount has turned them all down. He said he could hardly believe it when she took such a fancy to The Lodge. "I give you my word, Mr Martin," he said, "if I can get her into a house that she likes and she'll settle down there, it will make the whole difference to my life. Peace and quiet, that's what I want, and I'll pay anything in reason to get them." And of course when you come to think of it, what is the good of anything if you can't have a bit of peace in your home?'

Miss Silver agreed, after which she inquired whether he had had any communication from his client since Mrs Graham's death.

Mr Martin took up a pencil, poised it as if he were about to write, and put it down again.

'Well, no. No, I haven't. And that is what makes me a little uneasy. You see, Mrs Blount being the kind of nervous invalid he says she is, she may have gone right off the house. These nervous ladies are like that, I am afraid – all over a thing one minute, and right off it the next. Miss Graham will probably not wish to stay on in the house, especially if it is true that she expects to be married very soon. If I may say so, I think that everyone who knows her would be very glad to hear that this is the case. I remember Mr Carey very well. We put through the sale of Grove Hill House for his aunt, Miss Lester. It was a family arrangement, but we saw to the business side of it. Mr Harrison who bought the place is a cousin, but it is always wise to leave professional details in professional hands. Mr Carey used to be about a good deal before Miss Lester moved – spent his holidays here, and always great friends with Miss Graham.'

Miss Silver gave a gentle cough.

'They are on very friendly terms now, but it is perhaps not quite the moment to make any announcement.'

'No, no, of course not – I quite understand. But in the circumstances, I feel that if Mr Blount repeats his offer, or comes anywhere near to repeating it, there should be no unnecessary delay. His offer is, or rather was, an outstanding one. Miss Graham could not expect as much from any other quarter. Even if he were to make a much lower offer, I think she would do well to consider it.'

Miss Silver surprised him. She gave a bright sideways look which reminded him of a bird, and said,

'You expect the price to come down, not so much on account of Mrs Graham's tragic death and its possible effect on Mr Blount as because Mr Worple is no longer competing.'

Mr Martin repeated the second of the two names.

'Mr Worple?'

Miss Silver inclined her head.

'Yes. I happened to meet him when he called to inquire after Miss Graham.'

Mr Martin frowned. Every time Fred Worple's name was mentioned it gave him the idea that there was something shady going on. Where had Fred got the money to go bidding a house up to something quite above its market value? A lucky win on an outsider – that was Fred's answer. But why sink the money in buying a house in Grove Hill where he would be nothing but a fish out of water? He wished with all his heart that Fred would clear out. Mr Martin's suspicions about him had a nasty way of spreading to his own client Mr Blount. The more he thought about any of it, the less he liked it. And here was this Miss Silver saying,

'Mr Worple is a relation of yours, is he not?'

Practice had perfected Mr Martin in a formula which set Fred Worple at as great a distance as possible. He produced it now.

'He is my step-mother's son by a former marriage. I really know very little about him.'

'I see. I understand from Miss Graham that your family has a long connexion with Grove Hill.'

Mr Martin smiled for the first time.

'My grandfather started the business, but we had connexions here before that.'

Miss Silver beamed.

'Then you are probably an authority on the local associations. I have come across an interesting book on the subject whilst staying at The Lodge – a history of the neighbourhood by the Reverend Thomas Jenkinson.'

'Oh, yes. I remember my father had a copy, but I don't know what has become of it. Curious how things disappear, isn't it? Of course my stepmother may have it knocking about somewhere. I shouldn't be at all surprised if she had. Curious your mentioning it now – I haven't thought about that book for years. Rather a prosy old gentleman Mr Jenkinson, but there was a piece about the Gordon Riots . . . Now let me see, my father thought there might be something in that – some story his grandmother used to tell. She was from these parts, and came back again as a widow. She remembered the old Grove Hill House being burned down by the rioters. She had some kind of post there, I don't know what, and my father could remember her telling him about the mob breaking in and Mr Warren losing his life – a very nasty business, and a lot of property destroyed. A good job we don't have that sort of thing now!'

There was a little more talk during which Mr Martin kept

the conversation firmly away from Mr Worple. In the course
of doing so he dwelt on the recent growth of the suburb and
said that his father remembered the High Street as very little
more than a row of village shops.

'Those houses in Belview Road, they were the first to be
built somewhere in the nineties – ninety-six, ninety-seven or
thereabouts. That was when the Lesters began to sell off parts
of the old Grove Hill Estate. The house had been rebuilt, you
understand, after the Riots – but I think not for some time
after, and they kept that and the garden, but most of the park
land was sold and built over. Land was getting expensive to
keep up, and of course once we were into this century and
Lloyd George came along with his land duties and his death
duties all these estates started to break up. Wonderful to think
of income tax ninepence in the pound on earned income and
one-and-three on unearned! Well, we shall never see that
again, shall we?'

Still discoursing in this safe strain, he escorted Miss Silver
to the street door, produced a final message for Althea Graham, and was just about to step back into the outer office,
when he changed his mind and hurried after her.

'Miss Silver – if you'll excuse me – you might perhaps
be interested. That is Mrs Blount just getting off the bus.'

34

Miss Silver was very much interested. The woman whom Mr
Martin had pointed out as Mrs Blount did not at all correspond
with his description of her as the spoiled delicate woman so
much indulged by her husband that he was willing to pay an
extravagant price for her fancies. Mrs Blount really did not
look like that at all. She had unmistakably the air of a woman
who has lost interest in everything. Her hair and skin quite
obviously received no attention. Her clothes, originally of a
fair quality, had a neglected look. There were wisps of hair
on the collar of the coat, and the hem of the skirt sagged

lamentably. Her stockings were twisted, and her shoes had not been cleaned for at least a week. But above and beyond all these things it was her face which fixed Miss Silver's attention. Under the limp felt hat, it had a lost and hopeless expression. Someone past emotion, beyond any expectation of relief, might look like that. In the course of her experience, Miss Silver had seen a great deal of trouble, suffering, fear, and guilt, but even against this background there was something about Mrs Blount which gave her a feeling of dismay.

Moving slowly towards her, she saw that she remained standing at the bus stop. The other passengers were dispersing, but Mrs Blount just stood as if the effort that had brought her there had petered out. Miss Silver was reminded of a child's clockwork toy that has run down. She came up close and said in her pleasant voice,

'You are a stranger here. Can I help you at all?'

Mrs Blount looked at her vaguely. She picked out one word from what Miss Silver had said and echoed it.

'Help . . .'

Miss Silver put a hand on her arm.

'I think you are not very well. Can I help you?'

The vague look persisted. The dry lips said,

'No one – can – help me.'

Miss Silver regarded her with compassion.

'There is a very nice café at the corner. If you can walk as far as that, we could have some tea or coffee together. A hot cup of tea is very refreshing.' She kept her hand on Mrs Blount's arm and took a step in the direction of the café.

Mrs Blount moved too. She did not seem to be either faint or giddy. In Miss Silver's opinion she was suffering from shock. She was certainly in no fit state to find her way alone in a strange town. It would do her good to sit down quietly in one of the shaded alcoves at the Sefton Café and have a nice cup of tea. She guided her kindly and firmly in that direction and met with no resistance.

The time being now a little after twelve, the midmorning rush was over and it was as yet too early for anybody to be thinking of lunch. Miss Silver ordered a pot of tea and conducted Mrs Blount to the end alcove at the back of the room. Since there were four empty spaces screened off from one another by curtains in a vivid shade of emerald green between this alcove and the one in which an aggressive lady appeared to be laying down the law to a meek friend over coffee-cups whose dregs had long since congealed, Miss Silver could feel assured of privacy. She had not at that time any idea of how valuable this might be.

The waitress brought the tea on a green tray and departed. Mrs Blount leaned back in one of the ornamental wicker chairs, her eyes fixed as if upon some image of despair. Miss Silver poured her out a cup of tea and inquired whether she took milk and sugar.

The stiff lips moved, but they did not relax. They said first 'No,' and then 'Yes', and then 'It doesn't matter.'

Miss Silver added milk and sugar and set the cup before her. Mrs Blount put out a hand to take it, lifted it as an automaton might have done, and drank from it in a series of spasmodic gulps. When the cup was empty she put it down. Miss Silver filled it again. The lifting and the gulping were repeated.

When the cup had been put down for a second time Mrs Blount leaned back again and closed her eyes. She had not slept since midnight. She had not been able to swallow any breakfast. Mr Blount had gone out early, upon what business she did not know. By half past eleven she could no longer bear the solitude of her room, nor could she face the lounge. She had dressed and gone out. The bus happening to stop at the corner just as she came to it, she had got in and allowed it to take her down into the town. Once there, she had no idea what to do next. At the first sip of the hot tea she had realized how parched her mouth was. She drank eagerly, and was a little more aware of her surroundings. Her eyes opened and she looked at Miss Silver and said,

'You are – very kind.'

'I do not think you are well enough to be out alone.'

'I am – quite well.'

'You have had a shock.'

'Yes – a great shock. I don't know what to do.'

'Is there any way in which I could help you?'

Mrs Blount's head moved in a slow negative gesture.

'I don't think so. You see – he is my husband . . .'

Miss Silver said nothing. The slow, heavy voice went on,

'Perhaps he will kill me – I don't know. If he thinks I heard what he was saying, I think he will. I don't think I mind – not really. It's just not knowing when it will happen or how he will do it. It's dreadful not to know, but I haven't got – anything to live for.'

Miss Silver said firmly,

'There is always something to live for.'

Mrs Blount made that slow movement of the head again. 'Not for me . . .'

Miss Silver took one of the hands which lay ungloved in the shabby lap. It felt cold and slack.

'Have you no family of your own – no relations?'

'They didn't want me to marry him. I would do it. They said I would be sorry.'

'Mrs Blount, why are you so much afraid of your husband?'

She pulled her hand away and stared with eyes that were definitely frightened now.

'I don't know you! How do you know my name?'

'I am staying at The Lodge with Miss Althea Graham. Your husband is trying to buy the house. You were pointed out to me.'

The frightened eyes shifted, looked away.

'I shouldn't have said – anything. He doesn't like me to talk about his business.'

'Why are you afraid of him?'

Mrs Blount stiffened.

'There isn't anything – to be afraid of. He is – very good to me. He is buying the house because I like it so much.'

Miss Silver felt a deep compassion. The poor thing was repeating what she had learned by rote. It was a lesson in which she had been drilled. She said,

'That is what you have been told to say, is it not?'

Mrs Blount looked at her, and suddenly she broke down. That large flat face of hers began to crumple and quiver. Her hands went up to cover it and she said in a shaking whisper,

'Oh, I can't go and live there – I can't – I can't – I can't! I'd rather he killed me – I would – I *would*!'

Miss Silver looked anxiously about her. The dogmatic lady

and her acquiescent friend had gone. There really was no one within hearing, and fortunately Mrs Blount had her back to the shop. She leaned forward and said,

'Are you not perhaps being a little fanciful? Is there any reason why your husband should want to harm you?'

Mrs Blount's hands dropped back into her lap. Her tears were running down without restraint. She said in that whispering voice,

'Oh, there's reason enough — reason enough and to spare. He always said to keep out of his business, and reason enough for that. I've known for a long time there was reason enough and I've kept out. I've always known I'd do better to keep out, and I've done it. Only last night ... last night ...' She choked on a sob and began to grope for a handkerchief.

Miss Silver said,

'What happened last night?'

Through the folds of a large crumpled handkerchief Mrs Blount's voice came in a succession of gasps.

'It's not — my fault — if he talked — in his sleep — but he'll kill me for it. I wish I was dead — before he does it! Oh, God, I wish I was dead! And he'll kill me — as sure as death he'll kill me — if he ever comes to know what he said!'

Miss Silver said in a calm, even voice,

'Why should he know, Mrs Blount?'

Mrs Blount stared at her.

'He's got ways,' she said.

35

Looking back upon the interview, Miss Silver could not feel any satisfaction. It provided much food for thought, aroused both suspicion as to the past and anxiety as to the future, yet supplied none of the answers which these speculations and doubts demanded. After Mrs Blount's burst of crying she had pulled herself together and would say no more. Like so many people who are threatened, the mere fact that she had spoken of her fears had to some extent dissipated them. As Miss

Silver had said, how was Sid to know that he had called out in his sleep and said ... Her thought shuddered away from what he had said.

The hot tea had done her good. Things are always worse on an empty stomach. She ought to have eaten some breakfast, but her throat had closed up against it. She caught the bus back and got out at Miss Madison's guest house, which was about half way up the hill. Lunch was just going in – a really good stew with dumplings in it like her mother used to make, and an apple pie. The people down here called them tarts, but that was nonsense. A tart was an open pastry case filled in with fruit or jam, and with maybe a criss-cross of pastry on the top, but a thing that had the fruit in the middle and was all covered in was a pie, whether it had apples in it, or plums, or anything else you liked. Her mother came from the north, and people in the north gave things their proper names.

She ate some of the apple pie and then went up and lay on her bed and slept for a while. It wasn't a very quiet sleep, because it was full of rushing dreams. In one of them Sid was angry with her because she had baked an apple pie and the pastry had gone sad. He took the helping she had given him and threw it at her plate and all, and the edge of the plate cut her like a knife, so that the blood soaked through her dress and she knew that she was going to die. And then it was all different and she was in a dark cave that wound and turned and she couldn't see where she was going, but there was a footstep that followed her all the way. She began to run, but she couldn't get away from it. It was Sid's footstep, and Sid's voice calling after her to stop, only she knew that if she did he would kill her, and she knew how. Those two strong hands of his would come round her neck and wring the life out of her. In her dream they touched her and she screamed. And' woke up screaming.

Mr Blount shut the door behind him and clapped his hand over her mouth.

'Crazy – that's what you are!' he said in a low furious voice. 'You don't want everyone to think I'm doing you in, do you?'

She pushed at his hand, and he took it away from her mouth.

'Oh . . .' she said on a long-drawn sob. And then, 'I was dreaming.'

'Overate yourself at lunch I shouldn't wonder! What were you dreaming about?'

She said faintly,

'Someone – running after me . . .'

He stood over her with a frowning look. No one would have thought him jovial now. After a moment he turned away.

'Well, get up! I want to talk to you!'

She hadn't undressed, only loosened her stays and pulled the eiderdown over her. She got up now, laying everything straight on the bed and putting back the pink coverlet. When she had finished he came back from the window where he had stood tapping on the glass and dropped a hand on her shoulder.

'What's all this about last night?' he said.

He could have asked no more terrifying question. Her face went blank with fear.

'Last night . . .'

He swore under his breath.

'You heard. When I came in just now, there was Miss Madison wanting to see me – very nicely spoken and all that, but the first and the last of it was there had been a disturbance in the night and it had waked those two women down the passage – Mrs Doyle and Miss What's-her-name.'

'Miss Moxon.'

'I'm not bothering with her name – I want to know what they heard! All I could tell Miss Madison was that I slept all night, and that if there was any disturbance it must have been you! Anyone say anything to you about it?'

'No, Sid.'

'Sure about that?'

'I didn't get up.'

'Breakfast in bed – they'll charge extra for that!'

'I didn't have – breakfast. I had some coffee in the town.'

'No one spoke to you at lunch?'

He kept staring at her, and she couldn't look away. She was beginning to feel confused. She tried not to speak, but she heard herself say,

'Only Miss Moxon.'

'Did she say she had been disturbed?'

'Something like that.'

He said, 'I'll have what she said, or I'll cut it out of you!'

The knife – that was her terror. His hand moved towards the pocket where he kept it. 'Oh, God – any way but that!' Words were jerked out of her.

'She only – said – someone called out – and waked her.'

'What did you say?'

She had never found it easy to tell lies. They just don't come to you if you haven't been brought up that way. She stared helplessly.

'*What did you say?*'

'I said – you – called out.'

He took her by the other shoulder too, held her face right up to his, and cursed her under his breath. Even if someone had been just outside the door they wouldn't have heard what he said, but she had to hear it. She had to hear it. What it led up to was,

'You told her *I* called out?'

She was sick with fear. It was no use trying to hold anything back. She got out two words on a gasping breath.

'She knew . . .'

He let go of her suddenly and stood back. Perhaps he was afraid of what his strong hands might do. He couldn't kill her here in Miss Madison's Pink Room. He walked away, getting as far from her as he could before he turned and said,

'You said I called out. Was that true?'

'Yes, Sid. You were dreaming.'

'Did I just call out, or did I say something?'

'You – called – out.'

He made a step towards her.

'If you lie to me, I'll slit your throat!'

'No, no, I won't – I'll tell you.'

'What did I say?'

He wouldn't stop asking her until she told him. There was no strength in her to hold anything back. She told him what he had said. As soon as the words were out of her mouth she knew what she had done. She tried to undo it.

'She didn't – hear what you said. She only heard you call out. Nobody heard what you said – except me.'

He repeated the words quite smoothly and quietly,

'Nobody heard except you? But you heard me – or you say you did. How many people have you gone blabbing to?'

'No one – no one.'

He said,

'And you'd better not! D'you hear? And now you'd better get busy and pack! We're off just as soon as we can be ready!'

'Where – where are we going?'

He said, 'You'll know when you get there!' and began to take his things out of the chest of drawers and throw them into a suit-case.

36

Miss Silver laid her hands down for a moment upon her knitting.

'I believe I have told you everything that passed between us. I should like to know what you think about it.'

Frank Abbott did not reply immediately. He looked at her, neat and earnest, with the half-finished vest in her lap. He knew from experience that the description of her interview with Mrs Blount would have been a most carefully accurate one. Just what it all amounted to was another matter. He said so, adding,

'There might be quite a simple explanation, you know.'

'Yes, Frank?'

'Mrs Blount may be off her head.'

She picked up her knitting again.

'That was not my impression.'

'It would cover your account of her behaviour.'

She coughed gently.

'No account of anyone's behaviour can convey more than a bare outline. Mrs Blount was very much afraid.'

'She might be afraid and yet have no cause for it.'

'In my opinion she was suffering from shock.'

'Well, you saw her, and I didn't. But, you know, it sounds a good deal like persecution mania. That "Perhaps he will kill me – I don't know. If he thinks I heard what he was saying. I think he will" – it sounds rather that way, you know.'

Miss Silver shook her head.

'It sounded to me as if the poor woman had overheard something which had terrified her into a breakdown. Her husband had talked in his sleep. She did not tell me what he said, and I could not press her, but it had thrown her into a condition of shock in which all the natural restraints had ceased to operate and she talked out what was on her mind. I feel sure that only a great shock would have put her into the state she was in when I met her. The Blounts are staying at a guest house half way up the hill. Whatever it was that had shocked her probably happened at some time during the night, since she spoke of her husband having talked in his sleep. I think that she herself had not slept again, and that she had eaten nothing. I think she had come out because she could no longer stay in the house. When I spoke to her she was standing aimlessly at the next bus stop with, I believe, no idea of what she would do next. I am particularly glad that you have called, because I felt that I should see you without delay. I believe that Mrs Blount may be in serious danger.'

Twenty-four hours ago he might have laughed at her. Now he was conscious of no desire to take the case of Mrs Blount too lightly. He said,

'You know, you asked if we could dig up something about Blount and Worple . . .'

She raised her eyes to his and said, 'Yes?'

'Well, there isn't very much for you, but there is something. If Worple isn't the rose, he's been near it. In other words, if he isn't a proved criminal, he's been mixed up with people who are. He is full of money at the moment, his own account being that he had a lucky win on an outsider – no details given as to when, where, or how. He fancies himself as a ladies' man. He calls himself a commission agent, and he's got a tongue as long as your arm.'

Miss Silver's glance reproved this metaphor.

'And Mr Blount?'

'Oh, Blount has rather a respectable background. His father had a second-hand shop in the Edgware Road. Blount himself is supposed to have been a bit of a rolling stone. Then he came in for the business and settled down. Mrs Blount had some money of her own. Her people didn't want her to marry him. There was a family quarrel, and they don't speak. The parents are dead, and the brothers and sisters didn't like the money going out of the family. She was middle-aged, and they thought they could count on it staying put. There's been some talk about Blount. He's away a good bit, and when he's back she goes about looking frightened. Worple and Blount have been pretty thick for a year or two. That is the lay-out. Nothing much to go on, nothing you can take hold of. I should say offhand that both Worple and Blount are fairly shady characters. For some reason or other there is an impression that Blount is a bad man to cross. He was married before, and his wife fell under a train. It might have been an accident, it might have been suicide. He was supposed to have been miles away when it happened.'

'Supposed, Frank?'

He said,

'I gather that the present Mrs Blount's family have made slanderous insinuations, but the general opinion is that whatever happened or didn't happen, nobody was going to catch Blount out.'

'Rather a strange attitude if there was nothing against his character before the accident occurred. Did he come into money from his wife?'

Frank cocked an eyebrow.

'That, my dear ma'am, is one of the things which started people talking.'

'One of the things, Frank?'

His light, cool gaze rested upon her.

'There seems to have been an idea that the Blount family was rather too prone to accidents.'

'There were others?'

'Blount's father broke his neck falling down an appropriately antique flight of stairs in his second-hand shop one dark night. He was alone in the house, and when they found him in the morning he was dead. His son had gone down into Sussex on a job.'

'Then why was there any talk about it?'

194

'Oh, just their nasty minds, I expect. He really did go down into Sussex, and he really did have a job there, but as some of the nasty-minded pointed out, he had a motorbike and he could have come back, done what he had planned to do, and returned to finish his job in Sussex. It's just one of those things. If he had wanted to do it, I suppose it could have been done. He came into a paying business and the old man's savings.'

Miss Silver said gravely,

'Two accidents, and both of them profitable to Mr Blount. Do you really think that the present Mrs Blount may not have good reason to be afraid? She too has money of her own. Last night he talked in his sleep. It was what she heard him say that had induced the state of shock in which I found her. It must have been something of a very serious nature. Nothing less would account for her condition. In my own mind I feel very little doubt that it was something which would connect him with the murder of Mrs Graham.'

"My dear ma'am!"

She looked at him steadily.

'I do not need you to tell me that there is no evidence of such a connexion. Mrs Blount would not be available as a witness, and in any case I do not imagine that words uttered by a sleeping man would be admissible in a court of law. But consider for a moment Mr Blount's character and behaviour. His father and his first wife both meet with accidents from which he profits. He marries a second woman with money of her own, brings her here, and begins to bid for Mrs Graham's house. Then Mr Worple turns up. They bid one against the other until they have reached the extravagant price of seven thousand pounds, at which point Mr Worple withdraws his pretensions to the house but continues to pay marked and unwelcome attentions to Miss Graham. I do not know how you would interpret the situation up to this point, but in the light of what you have just told me about a previous intimacy between Mr Blount and Mr Worple it seems to me probable that, whatever their object in acquiring The Lodge, they had come to the conclusion that partnership might prove more profitable than rivalry.'

He was looking at her with great attention.

'Whatever their object might be in acquiring The Lodge – what exactly do you mean by that?'

'I am unable to believe in the motive put forward by either of them. Mr Blount is not the man to spend a large sum of money in order to gratify a whim of his wife's. Nor does Mr Worple seem to me to have shown so much attachment to his family and his early surroundings as to make it at all credible that he should wish to sacrifice a large sum of money in order to acquire a totally unsuitable house.'

'And you think that he has now agreed to share The Lodge with Mr and Mrs Blount?'

She looked down thoughtfully at the small pink vest and measured it against her hand.

'No – that is not what I think. I do not believe that either Mr Blount or Mr Worple has any intention of residing at The Lodge.'

'They were prepared to spend seven thousand pounds on a house without any intention of living in it!'

'If Mr Blount was prepared to pay seven thousand pounds for The Lodge, it was because he expected to make a handsome profit. If he and Mr Worple have come to some agreement, the purchase price would be shared between them, but the profit would also have to be shared. Since their rivalry has been eliminated, they will naturally not expect the price to be so high. Only this morning Mr Martin the house-agent intimated that the circumstances of Mrs Graham's death must seriously affect the value of the property.'

'Well, it would, wouldn't it? But let us come back to the point. How do you suppose Mr Blount expects to turn a handsome profit upon an ordinary suburban house for which he was willing to pay seven thousand pounds? And he does seem to have been willing to pay that when he and Worple were still bidding each other up. The profit couldn't possibly come from a re-sale, you know. What do you suppose he was after?'

Miss Silver gave a meditative cough.

'I believe he may have wished to dig in the garden,' she said.

37

It took quite a lot to startle Frank Abbott, but at this he pulled himself up in his chair and said,

'*What!*'

Miss Silver reproved him with a glance and repeated her remark.

'I believe he may have wished to dig in the garden.'

'My dear ma'am!'

'Or in the gazebo. Yes, I think it would probably be in the gazebo.'

She laid down the almost completed vest and took out of her knitting-bag that copy of the Rev. Thomas Jenkinson's book which had engaged her interest. There was a neat white marker between the pages, so that it opened readily at the chapter on Grove Hill. She handed the volume to Frank, directing his attention to the paragraph which dealt with the Gordon Riots. Reading on, he would come naturally to the passage which had been marked by a faint underlining. Whilst his attention was engaged with the narrative she returned to her knitting and remained in silence. She could have guessed the moment when he reached the description of the unfortunate Mr Warren's last moments. At the report of the Physician who was Mr D – L – 's brother his colourless eyebrows rose, but he read on to the end without speaking. Then, and not till then, he said across the open page, and quoting from it,

' "The dying man constantly muttered to himself some such phrase as, 'The gold is safe,' or, 'I have saved the gold.' " This, I suppose, is the nub of the whole thing, the gold being presumably the gold Plate which is mentioned as being of great value. All very interesting, my dear ma'am, but highly speculative. Where did you come across this book?'

'Althea Graham told me that her father had been much

interested in the early history of Grove Hill. She spoke of some connexion with the Gordon Riots and told me her father's books were in the attic, and that an account of the Riots was to be found in one of them. When I had a little time on my hands I looked for the volume and found it.'

'That accounts for your being informed about the last moments of the unfortunate Mr Warren. But how do you suggest that Blount and Worple got to know about them?'

'My dear Frank, Mr Worple was the stepson of the late Mr Martin whose own son, the present Mr Martin, is the leading house-agent in Grove Hill. In a conversation I had with him this morning he told me that his grandfather had founded the firm, and that his father had been much interested in local history and had possessed a copy of Mr Jenkinson's book. Since this was the case, Mr Worple would have had access to it. This passage might well catch his imagination. Just what brought it to the forefront of his mind we have no means of knowing, nor just why he should have passed on his thoughts and speculations on the subject to Mr Blount, but . . .'

Frank Abbott threw the book down open on to the dining-table.

'You know, I'm not at all sure you haven't got something there. At least you may have one bit and I've got another. You didn't ask me what Blount's job was, apart from associating with crooks and keeping a second-hand shop, but it may have a considerable bearing.'

'He had a job?'

'A more or less hereditary one.'

'My dear Frank!'

'Well, his mother came from a Sussex village, a little place called Cleat. Apperantly Blount used to spend a lot of time down there with his grandfather, who was the last of a highly respected line of – what do you think? I give you three guesses.'

She smiled.

'I think you had better tell me.'

He said,

'Dowsers. And I won't insult you by asking whether that means anything to you or not.'

She said sedately,

'Water diviners, are they not?'

He nodded.

'Grandfather Pardue was highly skilled at the job. He operated all over Sussex. If your well went dry you asked him to come and find you another. Or if you wanted to build, he could tell you if there was likely to be a water supply on the spot. Quite a famous old boy in his way, and he taught his grandson. We got all this from the Sussex locals. They say Blount lapped it up and is almost as good as the old man was. He charges quite a tidy fee, and he still gets called in.'

Miss Silver said in a thoughtful tone,

'It used to be considered a mere country superstition. I believe a forked stick is employed, preferably hazel. It is supposed to dip when it is held over ground which covers water.'

'It is not only supposed to – it does. My cousin Charles Montague had an ancestral mansion which he turned over to the National Trust. He kept a few acres to build a cottage on, and water being essential, a dowser was called in. He asked me if I'd like to come down and watch the performance, and I did. The chap walked round for about twenty minutes, and there was nothing doing. Then we went to another place, and the rod started to twitch. The chap went on walking and holding it out in front of him, and presently it began to dip and twist until it was all he could do to hold it. He told them where to dig, and they found a first-class spring about a hundred feet down.'

Miss Silver's 'Yes' had a questioning note in it. She added, 'Pray proceed.'

'Water isn't the only thing a good diviner can find.'

'I believe not.'

'There is an idea that metals can also be located. Blount's grandfather was called in by the local police after the Mickleham robbery in 1922. A good deal of valuable plate was taken, and there was an idea that the thieves had buried it. The old boy found it and got a handsome reward. But whether he did it with his divining rod, or because he knew something that the police didn't, don't ask me to say. Villagers often know a lot more than they ever spill.'

Miss Silver folded her hands upon Tina's pink vest.

'I do not suppose Mr Blount to have been looking for water

in Mrs Graham's back garden, but he might have wished to confirm a theory that Mr Warren's gold plate had been concealed under, or in the neighbourhood of, the gazebo. I do not know whether you noticed the reference in Mr Jenkinson's account to a young woman who was present during Mr Warren's last moments, and who must therefore have heard his references to having saved the gold. I would like you to return to the passage.'

Frank ran his eye down the page until he reached 'a young woman afterwards married in Yorkshire'. Continuing from there, he read aloud. 'This person, Mrs M – n, after an absence of many years has now returned and is a parishioner of my own. On referring to her for corroboration of Mr D – L – 's story, he being now deceased, she confirmed it in every particular, even to repeating some of the words let fall by Mr Warren when he lay a-dying. These I do not feel should be set down in print, lest they should give rise to false hopes or to the cupidity of unprincipled persons.'

Having reached the end of the passage, he looked up and said,

'Mrs M – n?'

'If you will turn the book to the light you will see that the intervening letters have been pencilled in.'

He did so, and exclaimed,

'What do you make of it? Looks like Martin to me.'

Miss Silver said,

'During my conversation with Mr Martin this morning he mentioned that his father's grandmother had been employed in some capacity at Grove Hill House at the time of its being burned down by the rioters. He said his father could remember her telling him about the mob breaking in and Mr Warren losing his life. Do you not think she may have told him rather more than that, and that the story may have caught his step-son's fancy? Something of the kind, I think, must have occurred in order to bring Mr Worple and Mr Blount upon the scene. Mr Worple has this story of buried treasure. Mr Blount is believed to be able to locate the presence of metal underground. It would be a reason for their association, would it not? But Mr Blount endeavours to steal a march upon his partner. He gets here first and makes an offer for the house.

But Mr Worple follows him. There was probably an angry scene, and for a time they bid against each other, but in the end they decide to join forces again. Mr Worple withdraws from the bidding, and at this juncture Mrs Graham is murdered.'

Frank laughed.

'It's an ingenious and fascinating tale, but of course it would be impossible to prove any of it. And even your ingenuity would be strained to find a reason for the murder of Mrs Graham!'

She shook her head.

'It was not, of course, premeditated. Of the three, or perhaps we may say four, suspects, there are only two against whom there is any evidence. In the case of Mr Carey there is Mrs Traill's statement that she heard Mrs Graham call out "How dare you, Nicholas Carey!" at a time which must have been very close to that of the murder, and when according to his own account he would have been at some considerable distance. This is evidence that Mrs Graham returned to the garden after her daughter had taken her in, and that she became aware of an intruder whom she took to be Nicholas Carey. It is no proof at all that it *was* Nicholas Carey. The second suspect is Mrs Harrison. As late as seven o'clock on Tuesday evening her diamond ring was undamaged. At ten o'clock on Wednesday morning one of the stones was missing. In the interval Mrs Graham had been murdered. Later the missing stone is found in a crack at the entrance to the gazebo and Mrs Harrison goes to extravagant lengths to provide herself with an alibi for Tuesday night. Mr Worple must come in for some suspicion, but there is nothing that really connects him with the crime, and in both his case and Mrs Harrison's it is difficult to imagine what would take them to the gazebo at such an hour, unless of course they had an assignation there.'

He laughed.

'A little far-fetched, don't you think?'

'Perhaps. And the motive for murder would be a weak one. But in Mr Blount's case he could have had a quite compelling reason for silencing Mrs Graham. It is obvious that he had no opportuniy of carrying out a really thorough test in the neighbourhood of the gazebo. When he came to view the house he doubtless went into the garden, but Miss Graham would certainly have accompanied him. I do not know to what extent a divining rod could be employed without its being plainly in evidence, but anyone who contemplated sinking a large sum of money in a project of this kind would certainly wish to make the strictest possible tests before committing himself.'

'So Blount went to the gazebo to wave his divining rod and make sure of the gold?'

'I will not go farther than to say that he might have gone there for such a purpose.'

'And then?'

'He knows that the household at The Lodge keeps early hours. What he could not know was that Mr Carey and Miss Graham would be meeting in the gazebo at half past ten, and that their meeting would be interrupted by Mrs Graham. Owing to this, she was awake at an hour when she should have been safely asleep. I think he must have used a torch – no doubt with great caution – and I think she must have seen it from the bathroom window. Certainly something took her up the garden again in a great hurry. She reaches the gazebo and calls out. You have to imagine the effect on the person whom she has surprised. He takes her by the throat, perhaps to stop her screaming. The rest follows.'

Frank nodded.

'A good tale, and even a likely one! And not one single solitary shred of evidence to put before a jury! But in Carey's case – well, I think it would be touch and go for him, depending on who was briefed for the defence and upon just what impression he made in the witness box.'

'And if you were on such a jury, which way would your vote go?'

He laughed.

'That would be telling!'

She said demurely,

'I should very much like to be told.'

'Very well, strictly between you and me I don't think Carey did it. From what I have heard I should imagine she would have been an appalling mother-in-law, but I shouldn't think he would go to the length of murdering her to avoid the relationship – too much awkwardness all round, and not enough incentive. He was marrying the girl anyhow, and as Mrs Graham had already found him in the gazebo once, it really didn't matter whether she walked into him again.'

He received a look of intelligent commendation.

'That is precisely the argument I should have put forward myself. But to return to the Blounts. I feel extremely anxious on her account. If he becomes seriously alarmed as to what she may have overheard, I fear for her safety. She is in just that vague shocked condition which would make it comparatively easy to stage an accident. She is, in fact, in a frame of mind conducive either to accident or suicide. And there would be no proof that it was not just a case of another neurotic woman laying down the burden which she feels no longer able to carry. Of course as long as she is here and in a guest house . . .'

He interrupted her.

'They have left the guest house. I called in there on my way up, and they had gone. All very sudden and unpremeditated. Miss Madison was put out enough to want to blow off steam, and she told me all about it. It seems two of the guests were alarmed by Mr Blount calling out in his sleep last night. She said she just mentioned it to him when he came in in the early afternoon and he didn't say anything then, but a little later he came down and said he had been called away in a hurry, upon which he telephoned for a taxi, paid the bill, and departed to catch the four-thirty. She seemed to think that he had taken offence.'

Miss Silver was looking exceedingly grave.

'Did she say anything about Mrs Blount?'

He nodded.

'She said she didn't look as if she was fit to travel.'

38

The Blounts travelled by a slow train. It stopped at a great many stations, and every time it stopped people got in or got out. Sometimes the compartment was so crowded that Mrs

Blount felt as if she couldn't breathe. The morning had been cold, but the sun had come out and the afternoon was muggy. Most of the people who were travelling were far too warmly dressed, but nobody seemed to want to have a window open. The air became heavy with the smell of moth-ball and warm people and tobacco smoke. Mrs Blount shut her eyes, because when she tried to keep them open everything kept slipping out of focus. She couldn't see how ill she looked – those pale eyelids closed and the dark marks like bruises underlining them. With her head tipped back and her colourless lips fallen apart, it really did seem as if those drooping lids might never rise again. Mr Blount in the opposite seat was stirred to anger. What did she want to go and make a show of herself like that for? Why couldn't she behave like any of the other women in the compartment? There was one of them reading just the kind of rubbishy paper Millie was so fond of. Another was sucking peppermints, and a thin wiry woman in spectacles had got up quite a brisk argument with the person next to her. He leaned forward and touched Millie on the knee.

'Here, you'd better not go to sleep, had you? You always say it gives you a headache if you sleep in the train.'

She started, looked at him nervously, and spoke in an undertone.

'I just felt giddy.'

He began to wish he had left her alone. But perhaps it was all for the best. If anyone was going to remember seeing them, it would be recalled that her behaviour had been odd, and that he had been solicitous for her comfort. He said in his most agreeable voice,

'Oh, well, you must do just what makes you most comfortable, my dear.'

She knew why he spoke to her like that. He was never sharp or angry with her in front of people. He had been the same with his first wife, the one who fell under a train. There had been some talk about that. He wasn't there when it happened – or he wasn't supposed to be there. And no one could say they had ever heard them quarrel. She shut her eyes again and tried not to think about Lucy Blount who had fallen under a train nearly four years ago.

Sid hadn't told her where they were going yet, but she thought that it would be Cleat. His grandfather was dead, and his Aunt Lizzie lived on in the old thatched cottage which visitors always thought so picturesque. Sid often did quite well out of taking pieces out of stock and putting them into the cottage – a chair, or a table, or some china figures. Visitors used to see them, the table and a chair outside in a casual sort of way, and the figures up in the window close to the glass. They would pay good money and go off as pleased as Punch, thinking they had got a bargain. Lizzie Pardue was very good at selling things like that. She was daily help at the Vicarage, a little bit simple but a good worker. She didn't know anything about the things Sid brought down for her to sell only what he told her, so that the people who bought them just thought she had no idea of the value which she hadn't, and that she was a simple soul who had never been out of a village in her life which was perfectly true.

They had to change twice before they got to Cleat. It was only the third time that Millie Blount had been there. A faint reassurance came to her as Lizzie Pardue opened the door of the thatched cottage and made them welcome. Sid must have rung up the Vicarage and said they were coming, because their rooms were all ready, and a nice meal too. He must have done it at the station when he left her in the ladies' room and they were waiting for their train. The reassurance came from the homely surroundings and from Lizzie Pardue herself. Sid took after his mother's people. Lizzie had the same florid colouring, the thickset build, the strong arms and hands, but there the resemblance ended. Her features were soft and blurred and her eyes were very kind. Kindness – that was the thing you noticed about her at once, and went on noticing. She had a shy half hesitating look for Sid's wife who was still a stranger, and a soft almost whispering manner of speech. Mrs Blount didn't say to herself in so many words that Sid wouldn't try anything on in front of his Aunt Lizzie, but there was that kind of feeling in her mind. She ate a good supper, and thought that she would sleep.

There were three bedrooms in the cottage. Lizzie had the one which looked to the front. The big double bed was the one in which her parents had slept all through their married life. When old Mr Pardue died she had moved in quite simply

205

and as a matter of course. The cottage belonged to her now and all the furniture, so it was only right she should have the best room. The other two bedrooms were small, with narrow truckle beds.

Millie Blount would rather have slept on the floor than have shared a room with Sid. She didn't feel as if she could ever share a room with Sid again. Suppose he was to call out in his sleep like he had in Miss Madison's Pink Room. Suppose he was to say what he had said before. Or words. Everything in her shook at the thought of it. But here she could lie down on a narrow bed and pull the bedclothes right up over her ears and she wouldn't hear anything at all. The cottage was strongly built, with thick walls, and the thatch all over it to deaden sound. Even if Sid called out she wouldn't hear what he said.

Just before she went to sleep it came to her that he might want her to have a room of her own just as much as she wanted it herself. He might want to be alone at night just as much as she wanted it, because then if he talked or called out there would be no one to hear him. This comforting thought went with her into a deep and dreamless sleep.

It wasn't till next day when Lizzie Pardue had left them alone and gone off to the Vicarage that it occurred to Millie Blount to wonder why they had come down to Cleat, but she knew better than to ask any questions. If she could have heard Lizzie talking to the Vicar's wife it might have started her worrying again. Lizzie had worked for Mrs Field for a great many years and felt quite at home with her. They were making beds together, and she had a lot to say about her nephew Sid and his wife.

'Very worried about her he is, Mrs Field. That's why they're down here. "Country air," he says, "and your cooking, Auntie Liz," he says, "and if that don't make her well, nothing will. Right down melancholy, that's what she is." And what with his first wife throwing herself under a train, poor thing, it's only natural he should take it to heart.'

Mrs Field said,

'Did she throw herself under a train? How dreadful! No, the sheet isn't straight, Miss Pardue – it wants pulling up on your side.'

Lizzie pulled it up.

'She threw herself right under the Brighton express. Sid he took it to heart something dreadful. She left him a nice bit of money, but it don't make up for losing your wife. And he said to me last night, "I'd never get over it if anything like that was to happen again, Aunt Liz," he says.'

'Miss Pardue, that's the Vicar's pillow you've got, not mine. You don't mean to say there's any reason to suppose . . .'

Miss Pardue shook her head in a mournful way.

'There's no getting from it she's melancholy. And I'm sure there isn't a kinder husband than Sid anywhere. But he's worried, I can see that, and he says she talks funny.'

'The eiderdown is behind you, Miss Pardue. How do you mean, "She talks funny"?'

Lizzie Pardue picked up the eiderdown and spread it across the bed.

'It's the things she says, and the way she says them if you know what I mean. Sid don't like talking about it, but when it comes to saying she don't think she can go on and he'd be better off without her, well, it gives you a bit of a turn, what with poor Lucy throwing herself under a train and all.'

'She ought to see a doctor,' said Mrs Field in her most decided voice.

In the cottage with the thatched roof Mrs Blount was sitting at the kitchen table peeling potatoes. There were some sprouts to see to too. Sid had picked them and brought them in, and she was very pleased to get everything forward so that there would be as little as possible for Aunt Liz to do when she came home at half past twelve. At the other end of the table Sid had a bottle of ink and a writing-pad. He got out his pen and dipped it.

He hadn't written more than a line or two before he stopped and began to rub his thumb and the side of his hand. She kept her eyes on the potatoes so that she needn't watch him. He didn't like being watched, and she didn't like looking at his hands. They were strong and coarse, and there was hair on them. They frightened her. He began to write again, and went on to the foot of the page. Then he said, 'Ow!' and wrung his hand with the pen in it. A blob of ink splashed down on to the white scrubbed table. Lizzie Pardue wasn't going to like that. Mrs Blount got up to get a cloth, but he shouted to her not to fuss and she didn't dare. She went and sat down again, and there he was, nursing his hand and saying he had put the thumb joint out, and how was he to finish his letter.

'And it's got to catch the post whether or no. There's a chap I half said I'd go into a deal with, but I've thought better of it. Heard something about him as a matter of fact, and he's not the sort I want to get mixed up with.'

Mrs Blount was very much suprised. They had been married three years, and she never remembered his telling her anything about his business before. She didn't say anything, because she didn't know what to say. He went on grumbling about his hand.

'It's no good thinking I can hold a pen, because I can't. And that letter's got to catch the post. You'll just have to make the best job of it you can. I'll tell you what to say. You'd better come round here and take this chair. And wash your hands! I don't want my business correspondence all messed up with dirt off those potatoes!'

There wasn't any dirt on the potatoes, because of course they had been scrubbed before she sat down to peel them, but she didn't say anything.

She went and washed, and he swore at her for being so long. By the time she was set down and had the pen in her hand she was shaking. He put the block in front of her with a clean page on it. He had finished the first sheet and laid it aside. She said, doing her best to keep her voice steady,

'Do I put a 2 at the top?'

He swore at her.

'You don't put anything down but what I tell you! And don't start too near the top. There'll be only a sentence or two to come, and it'll look better that way.'

She sat waiting for him to tell her what to write. He stood over her, watching everything she did, and began to dictate. It made her so nervous that her hand shook worse than ever. She wrote in stumbling letters:

'I can't go on with it. It's no use. I don't feel I can.'

He was looking over her. When he saw what she had written he pulled the block away and swore again.

'How do you think I can send a scrawl like that! I'll just have to try and get him on the phone!'

He tore the sheet off the block and looked at it. The writing was barely legible, and pulling the block away had made the pen run off at an angle.

He stood behind his wife's chair and smiled approvingly. He thought that what she had written would do very well.

39

Jack Harrison was in a most dazed and uncomfortable frame of mind. He was not a man of marked ability in any direction. He had entered a family business, Harrison and Leman, General Importers, at the age of eighteen, detached himself from them to serve through the first World War, and returned when it was over with a wounded shoulder which still occasionally gave him trouble, and an immense thankfulness at finding himself back in the office. He was not clever, but he was painstaking, courteous, and trustworthy. In due course he became a partner and inherited a considerable fortune from two bachelor uncles. He was universally liked, but after a slightly patronizing manner. At least one woman had cared for him deeply, but he had most unfortunately married Ella Crane. He would have been happy with Emmy Lester and he was not at all happy with Ella, but it never occurred to him that there was anything he could do about it. He did what he could to avoid rows and the occasions for them, but it was uphill work and he wasn't very good at it.

That there should have been a row, and a major one, in front of two police officers, one of them a member of the local force, was a terribly shaming thing. The figure destroyed by Ella's uncontrolled rage was Meissen ware and had belonged to a several times great-grandmother. He might have received a cut over the eye which could have affected his sight, and worst of all, the scene, its sound, its fury, its violence had blown upon the smouldering resentments of the last two or three years and fanned them into flame. It wasn't right to hate your wife, to wish vainly that you hadn't married her, and that there was any way in which you could be rid of the burden of her presence. And if this was wrong, what was to be said about the promptings of which he was now and then aware. It shocked him very much that there were moments in which he was conscious of a desire to strike Ella, to see her shrink away from him and be afraid.

Into this unhappy frame of mind there came like a catalyst a note from Nicholas Carey. It had been dropped in at the letter-box by Nicholas himself, after which he rang the bell and walked away without looking back or waiting for Mrs Ambler the daily parlourmaid to open the door. She brought the note to Jack Harrison in his study and told him she had just seen the back of the gentleman going down the drive — 'He didn't wait any time at all, just dropped it in and walked away.'

He opened the note and read what Nicholas had written.

Dear Jack,

I think I'm practically certain to be arrested today. It's a stupid business, and I shouldn't think it would come to anything, but there you are — an arrest is indicated, and I imagine that most people would vote for me as the likeliest suspect. I don't know where they'll put me, but you can come and see me if you like. You had better collect some dope as to who would be a good solicitor for this sort of thing. I don't imagine that the old boy who settled up Uncle Oswald's estate would make much hand of it. Sorry for the general upset and scandal.

Yours,
Nick.

The confusion in Jack Harrison's mind cleared. As long as there were several courses open you could turn first to one and then to another and consider following it. You could, and probably did, reject them all and just stand still and do nothing. But as he read Nick's letter the uncertainties which had surrounded him like a fog thinned away and he could see quite clearly what he had to do. He couldn't let Nick be arrested. Nobody in their family had ever been arrested as far as he knew. Nick was engaged to Althea Graham. They had been on the point of marrying. Althea was a nice girl and a good daughter, and she hadn't had a fair deal. And then there was Emmy. If Nick was arrested it would hurt Emmy very much indeed. She was kind and good. She didn't deserve to be hurt. He couldn't allow Nick to be arrested. He put the note in his pocket, went into the hall, and considered whether he should put on a coat. No, the afternoon was a warm one, and there was no sign of rain.

He put on his hat, opened the front door, and went down the drive. If Nick expected to be arrested he would go and see Althea Graham first. It was quite probable that he would be there now. He didn't want to butt in, but he couldn't, no he really couldn't let Nick be arrested.

40

The front door of The Lodge having been opened to him by Miss Silver, Mr Harrison found himself rather at a loss as to what his next step should be. He went into the dining-room because Miss Silver seemed to expect him to go into the dining-room. In a vague kind of way he remembered hearing that Althea Graham had someone staying with her, and he supposed the lady who admitted him to be this someone, though he did not know her name. She relieved him of this part of his embarrassment by pronouncing it clearly and firmly, to which he responded by giving her his own and explaining his presence.

'I have no wish to intrude, I do assure you of that, but Nicholas Carey is my cousin and I am very anxious to see him – very anxious indeed. I thought perhaps he might be here.'

Miss Silver inclined her head.

'He is in the drawing-room with Miss Graham. I do not feel that they should be disturbed.'

Jack Harrison took hold of one of the dining-room chairs. He did not know how hard he was gripping it until afterwards, when he discovered with surprise that there was a red weal across his palm. At the time he did not feel it at all. He only felt a painful increase of the confusion and distress in his mind. He heard his own voice.

'He is saying good-bye to her. I had a note from him. He expects to be arrested.'

'Did he tell you that?'

'Yes — he wrote me a note. He said he thought he was certain to be arrested. I can't let that happen, can I?'

Miss Silver observed him with care. He was in a state of considerable distress, and he had something on his mind. She was too experienced to mistake the signs, and in fact Jack Harrison was past making any effort to conceal them. He said, straining at the words,

'I didn't want to have to say anything. You see, my wife comes into it — but I can't let Nicholas be arrested. He hasn't anything to do with it, so I can't let them arrest him, can I?'

She said, 'No, Mr Harrison,' and looking past him, saw through the window the gate on Belview Road swing in. Frank Abbott and Detective Inspector Sharp came through it and began to walk up the flagged path towards the house. She said, 'Just a moment, Mr Harrison,' and went to let them in.

After one glance over his shoulder he stood where he was, bearing down upon the chair and watching the door. Miss Silver closed it behind her. He heard a murmur of voices and thought, 'She is telling them what I said.' These were the police officers who had come to his house yesterday. They had come to question Ella. He would have to tell them his story. Here. Now. It was too late to go back. Miss Silver was telling them what he had said. There was no going back. In a way it was a relief. He would tell them just what had happened and be done with it.

They were coming into the room now, the Scotland Yard man, and Inspector Sharp, and Miss Silver. Chairs were pulled out and they sat down. He sat down too. His hand and arm were numb. The Scotland Yard Inspector said,

'Miss Silver tells us that you want to make a statement with regard to the murder of Mrs Graham. Is that correct?'

His own voice astonished him. It was louder than usual and at a higher pitch as he said,

'You are going to arrest Nicholas Carey, aren't you? He wrote and told me. I didn't want to have to say anything, but I can't let him be arrested. It wouldn't be fair, because he really hadn't anything to do with it at all.'

Frank Abbott said,

212

'Just a moment, Mr Harrison. If this statement involves yourself, I had better warn you . . .'

Jack Harrison shook his head.

'No – no – I hadn't anything to do with it either. It's just that my wife is involved – to a certain extent – and of course not in the murder. But . . .' He broke off. 'Perhaps I had better tell you what happened.'

Inspector Abbott said he thought it would be a very good plan, and Inspector Sharp got out a notebook. Jack Harrison waited until they were ready for him. Miss Silver, sitting at the end of the table, watched him. They all watched him. When he began to speak his voice had lost the high strained pitch, it was lower and more natural. He sat back in his chair, his right arm hanging stiffly. An earnest, conscientious person who had been much perplexed in mind and was now doing his best.

'It was that Tuesday evening. We had been to a bridge party at the Reckitts'. We got back at about half past seven. When we had had our meal I went into my study – I generally do in the evening. I left the door ajar. I wanted to know if anyone came to the house, or if my wife went out. After the daily maids have gone there is no one in the house but ourselves.'

Frank Abbott said,

'Mrs Harrison was expecting someone?'

'She was meeting a friend. I didn't know where they were meeting.'

'What friend?'

'A man called Worple – Fred Worple. My wife had been on the stage – she knew him then. He turned up here a week or two ago. He has relations in the town. He met my wife again, and they have been seeing a good deal of each other. I didn't care for the friendship. Worple is a shady, flashy type, and I told my wife that it wouldn't do her any good to be seen about with him. She was angry, and she said she would do what she liked.'

'Yes, Mr Harrison?'

There was rather a long pause before Jack Harrison went on. He was looking at Mrs Graham's polished dining-table, but what he saw was his own study table with the ink-stained blotter, and the telephone fixture on the right. He saw himself putting out a hand and lifting the receiver. He said,

'I had a call to make. When I took up the receiver my wife was talking on the extension in her room. She said, "All right, Fred – half past ten or a quarter to eleven," and then she rang off. So you see, I knew that she was meeting Worple, but I didn't know where. At a quarter to ten I went into the drawing-room and told her I was going to bed.'

'You have separate rooms?'

'Oh, yes.'

'Next to each other?'

He shook his head.

'It's a big house. It's been in the family a long time. I have the room I used to have when I came to stay as a boy. My wife's room is at the other end of the house.'

'Well, you went to bed?'

He shook his head.

'No, I went to my room and waited. One of my windows overlooks the side door. I thought if my wife was going out, or if she was letting anyone in, that she would use this door. The front door bolts make quite a noise when they are drawn back. So I put out my light and sat by the window and waited. I went on waiting and nothing happened. I thought I wouldn't do anything until a quarter past eleven, and that then I would go along to my wife's room and see whether she was there, because there were two other doors which she might have gone out by. My watch has luminous hands. At twenty past eleven my wife came out of the side door and went on round the house and out of sight. I was all ready to follow her in a dark raincoat and tennis shoes. It takes just five minutes to walk from Grove Hill House to The Lodge. I want to make it clear that I could see my wife in front of me all the way. When I turned the corner into Hill Rise she was standing still – in fact I very nearly ran into her. On the other side of the road a woman was running down to the corner, and the bus was coming down Belview Road. When it came to the corner by The Lodge it stopped and the woman got in. I was only about three yards away from my wife. As soon as the bus had gone she ran the rest of the way and went in by the tradesmen's entrance of The Lodge. It is right on the corner and runs along by the hedge to the little yard outside the back door. As soon as she turned in like that I guessed that she had been meeting this man Worple in that kind of a summerhouse at the top of the Grahams' garden. They call it a gazebo. Of course you will have seen it, because that is where Mrs Graham's body was found. I don't know why she went there. She always goes to bed very early. I let my wife get round the house, and then I followed her. When I came out on to the path that goes up the garden I could see her ahead of me. I want you to be quite clear that except while I was following her round the house she was never out of my sight. Is that quite clear?'

Inspector Sharp nodded and said, 'Oh, yes, Mr Harrison.'

Jack Harrison went on in the same precise and methodical manner which he had used throughout.

'I could see her, partly because I was looking for her, and partly because I have very good night vision. Neither she nor any other person could or did see me, because by the time they were heading my way I was standing still against a dark background.'

Frank Abbott said sharply,

'The other person? What other person?'

Jack Harrison looked faintly surprised.

'There was a man in the gazebo. As you know, there are steps going up to it. When my wife had reached the top step, a man rushed past her, knocking her down.'

'Do you mean that he hit her?'

'Oh, no, I don't think so. He was just in a hurry to get away.'

'Mrs Harrison must know whether he hit her.'

The surprise became more apparent.

'I haven't spoken about it to my wife. She has no idea that I was there.'

'All right, go on.'

He did so in a meditative tone.

'If she lost a stone out of her ring as you say she did, then I think it must have happened when she fell. Her hand could have struck the jamb.'

'Very likely. But go on about the man.'

'He came running down the path very fast. I stepped into

a garden bed to avoid him. There is a little step down to the yard outside the back door. He must have forgotten it, because he tripped and came down sprawling. He was up again in a moment and ran round the house and away.'

'Did you recognize him?'

Jack Harrison shook his head.

'Not in the way of seeing his face. But it wasn't Mr Worple.'

'How do you know it wasn't?'

'He wasn't tall enough. Mr Worple must be not far off six foot. As this man went past me he was not much taller than myself, but there was a good deal more of him. Not a tall man, but broad. A heavy man by the way he fell.'

Miss Silver had said nothing all this time. She listened, and she watched with keen attention. She did not herself feel any difficulty in identifying the man who was broad but not tall, and who fell heavily, with Mr Blount.

Frank Abbott said,

'What happened after that?'

Jack Harrison replied in the simplest manner.

'He got up again.'

'You did not try to stop him?'

'I had no reason to do so. It was not until next day that I had any reason to suspect that he had probably murdered Mrs Graham.'

Frank Abbott said,

'Well go on. He got up . . .'

'And rushed away. My wife was getting to her feet at the entrance to the gazebo. If she was expecting to meet Mr Worple, and I think there is no doubt that she was, it must have been a great shock to be knocked down by a violent stranger. She came limping down the path towards me, breathing in a distressed manner. I stood perfectly still behind a clump of hollyhocks and let her go by.'

Frank Abbott leaned forward across the polished table.

'Did she go into the gazebo?'

Jack Harrison shook his head.

'Oh, no – she hadn't a chance – she was knocked down on the threshold.'

'But afterwards – when she got up again?'

'Oh, no. She was groaning and getting up – I could hear

her all the time. I think her one idea was to get away. She came down the steps and down the path and went round the house and out into the road. And then she went home.'

'You're sure about that?'

'I followed her. When she got inside the drive she stood for a bit. There is a path that goes off to the left through a shrubbery. I went that way because I wanted to get in first. I had some thoughts of locking her out, but I considered that she had been very badly frightened, and that it would be a cruel thing to do, so I just went up to my room and left the door unlocked.'

'You are sure she came in?'

'Oh, yes. I waited by the window until I saw her come round the house and go in. I had set my door ajar, and I heard her come up the stairs and go away to her own room.'

'You didn't speak to her about what had happened, either then or next day?'

'No.'

'Why didn't you?'

'I didn't wish to have a scene with my wife.'

Having been privileged to witness one of these conjugal scenes, the two Inspectors believed him. Frank Abbot said,

'You said nothing to her at all even when you had heard about Mrs Graham's murder?'

'No, I didn't say anything.'

'Mr Harrison, you must have realized the importance of your encounter with this man on the scene of the murder. He was at any rate an intruder upon private property, and his behaviour is, to say the least of it, highly suspicious. He hasn't any business in the gazebo. He knocks a woman down and makes a bolt for it when he is discovered there. You must surely have realized that it was your duty to go to the police?'

'Oh, yes. But you see my wife was involved.'

Frank Abbott's light, cool gaze rested upon him.

'We have a witness who heard Mrs Graham speaking to someone in the gazebo at just after twenty past eleven. This witness was frightened and ran down to the corner to catch the bus. If, as you say, the bus was at the corner and a woman was running down towards it when you turned into Hill Rise, this witness's statement is confirmed, and it becomes clear that Mrs Graham was murdered between the time when she was heard to call out and the moment when you saw this man whom you have described rush out of the gazebo.'

'I suppose so.'

'You did very wrong not to report the matter at once.'

Jack Harrison said,

'I suppose I did. But I wouldn't have let an innocent person be arrested – I had quite made up my mind about that. That is why I have come to you now. My cousin said he was going to be arrested, and I couldn't let that happen.'

'Well, I think we shall have to have another interview with Mrs Harrison. You're sure she doesn't know you followed her?'

'Yes, I'm sure. What I wanted was to avoid having a scene.'

He hesitated, and then came out with,

'There's just one thing more . . .'

'What is it?'

'When this man fell there was a sound as if he had dropped something. He might have had it in his hand, or perhaps it fell out of his pocket – I don't know. The yard is paved and it made a sort of metallic sound against the stone. I had a torch in my pocket, and when my wife had gone away round the house I switched it on. I found the thing quite easily, and by hurrying after her I was able to come up as near to my wife as I wanted to.'

Frank Abbott said,

'And what did you pick up?'

Jack Harrison dived into the pocket of his raincoat and produced an object wrapped in tissue paper. He unwrapped it, holding it gingerly, and laid it down upon the table. It was a forked rod made of metal. Frank Abbott looked at it, Inspector Sharp looked at it, Miss Silver looked at it. Jack Harrison said,

'I don't know what it is, but I took care how I picked it up. I really only touched the ends of the fork – if you want to try it for fingerprints.'

Frank Abbott said in his most expressionless voice,

'The really up-to-date dowser affects a metal rod.'

41

Nicholas and Althea had been together for an hour. They had
not spoken very much. He had come to say good-bye. Memory
brought back to both of them that other time five years ago
when they had said good-bye in the gazebo. Then it had been
for five long, cold, sterile years which had taken youth, joy,
everything. But he had come back. The dead years were restored
again. Life flowed in and the wilderness blossomed. If he
went now, not to the risks and dangers of far places but to the
cold unsparing judgement of the law, perhaps this was the very
last time that they would see each other except with bars
between them – the very last time that they would touch, or
kiss, or say a word that others did not hear. And yet on the
edge of such a separation they had no words to say. And if
they were to touch, how could they bear to part? To each
of them there was present the thought that it would be better
to make an end, to wrench away and have done with this long
unconscionable dying of all that had been just within their
grasp.

When presently Miss Silver came into the room there was
half the width of it between them – Althea in the sofa corner,
her face quite drained of colour, her hands clasped rigidly
upon the black stuff of her skirt; Nicholas at the window with
his back to her, staring out at the path and the road beyond
the gate. Three men had come through the front door and
shut it behind them. They went out by the gate and turned the
corner into Hill Rise. They were Detective Inspector Sharp,
Detective Inspector Abbott, and Jack Harrison. Nicholas
wondered why they had not arrested him. Behind his back
Miss Silver gave the slight cough with which she was wont to
call an audience to attention and said,

'Mr Harrison has made a very important statement.'

The two Inspectors and Jack Harrison walked up Hill Rise

and turned into Grove Hill Road. Frank Abbott noted that it did take just five minutes to reach the front door of Grove Hill House. In the porch Jack Harrison said apprehensively,

'You won't want me, will you?'

The reply being in the negative, he exhibited considerable relief, remarked that they had better ring the bell, and slipped away round the house to the side door.

When the maid had gone to summon Mrs Harrison and the other two were alone in the drawing-room, Sharp said,

'I wonder what she'll smash this time. The poor chap's afraid of her, you know. What do you think about that statement of his?'

'I should say it was true.'

And with that the door opened and Ella Harrison came in. She wore the same plaid skirt as before, but the jumper and cardigan were scarlet instead of emerald, and the effect was even more startling. She had on a good deal of make-up, and she looked as if her temper might get away with her at any moment. Without even the slightest of greetings she said,

'Well, what is it now? I suppose you think I've got nothing to do but answer a lot of stupid questions! And I don't have to answer anything I don't want to – I know enough about the law to know that!'

She had a challenging look which Inspector Sharp avoided. Frank Abbott met it coolly.

'I think it would be better it we were to sit down. I think you can help us, and I think you would be well advised to do so. The fact is, a very detailed statement has been made with regard to your movements on Tuesday night.'

'What do you mean about my movements? I hadn't any movements! We came home from the Reckitts' at seven o'clock and we didn't go out again.'

'Mrs Harrison, if you persist in that statement you may find yourself in a very serious position. You did go out on Tuesday night at about twenty minutes past eleven. Perhaps you do not know that you were followed, and that the person who followed you has made a detailed statement as to where you went and what you did.'

The shock was overwhelming. It was abundantly plain that Jack Harrison had spoken no more than the truth when he stated his wife had no idea that he had followed her. She took a hesitating step with her hand out before her as if she could not see. When Sharp brought up a chair she dropped on to it and sat there panting, her colour mottled and patchy under the rouge and powder. Frank Abbott said,

'We have this statement, and I believe it to be a true one. If you will tell us just what happened from your own point of view, and the two accounts correspond, I think you will find that you have nothing to be afraid of. What you must understand is that nothing but the truth is going to clear you.'

She said in an altered voice,

'Who followed me?'

'Your husband. He says you were only out of his sight three times, and that for the briefest possible space, from the moment of your leaving the Grove Hill drive until your return to it. If you will give us your account of what happened during the same period, we shall be able to compare it with what your husband says. If the two accounts agree – well, you can see for yourself that their credibility will be considerably strengthened.'

He was talking partly to give her time. She had received a sudden and unexpected blow. She said in a difficult voice,

'He followed me?'

Frank Abbott said briskly,

'And has given a most circumstantial account of everything that took place. Now, Mrs Harrison, only a very stupid woman could fail to see that from your point of view it is absolutely necessary that your statement and your husband's should correspond. If you and he are describing the same incidents and you are both telling the truth, they will, but the slightest deviation from what really happened, the least shade of falsehood, and you will be aggravating the dangers of your position. As you say, you needn't speak if you do not want to, but you will be very foolish indeed if you refuse.'

He could see that she was pulling herself together. Her colour was returning to normal. She took one or two long breaths, straightened herself in her chair, and said,

'My husband really did make a statement?'

'Oh, yes.'

'How do I know you're not having me on?'

221

'You can ask him yourself.' Then, turning to his colleague, 'Do you mind, Sharp – I expect he will be in his study.'

While the Inspector was out of the room Ella Harrison sat eyeing Frank Abbott. The beautiful grey suit, the tie and the handkerchief in discreet shades of bluish grey, the immaculately polished shoes, the mirror-smooth hair, the long elegant hands and feet, the cool assured manner, produced an odd mingling of antagonism and respect. She had an impulse to disturb that polished calm, to scream, to throw anything that came handy, but it was an urge that died frustrated. There wouldn't be any china broken at this interview. Something shrewd and commonplace got the upper hand, something which knew which side its bread was buttered, something that had always made it its business to take care of number one.

When Jack Harrison and Inspector Sharp came into the room she swung round on them. Jack looked nervous, and well he might. He only came just across the threshold and stood there against the door when he had closed it. She said sharply,

'So you followed me on Tuesday . . .'

'Yes, I followed you.'

She gave an angry laugh.

'Taking a bit of a risk, weren't you? If I had really met Fred he'd have knocked your head off!'

Frank Abbott intervened.

'Mr Harrison is here to satisfy you that he did follow you on Tuesday night, that you were only out of his sight whilst turning the corner between Grove Hill Road and Hill Rise, and for the brief time that it took you to skirt the Grahams' house on your way to the back garden, and on your return from it. Is that correct, Mr Harrison?'

He said, 'Oh, quite.'

'Then we needn't trouble you any further. I take it, Mrs Harrison, you are now satisfied that your husband did follow you, and that he has made a statement as to what he saw and heard. What about it?'

She watched Jack Harrison go out of the room and shut the door before she answered. If she could have had five minutes alone with Jack to find out what he had told them . . . She might as well think about having the moon. There was

222

nothing for it, she would just have to stick to the truth. She turned round, gave Frank Abbott a hardy look, and said,

'All right, I'll play.'

She made her statement, and Sharp took it down. There was some gloss at the beginning. Fred Worple appeared as the old friend whom she couldn't ask to the house because Jack couldn't bear her to speak to another man.

'You've really no idea how dull it's been. Not what I should say was the best way to keep your wife fond of you, but if a man's jealous he's jealous, and that's all there is about it. So when Fred turned up – and mind you, we'd been real good friends – what was the harm in slipping out to a cinema or meeting him somewhere?'

'And you met him in the gazebo at The Lodge?'

She hesitated, bit her lip.

'Well, I did once or twice. The Grahams used to be in bed by ten o'clock unless Winifred was playing bridge, and she didn't often play at night. She was by way of being an invalid, you know, but if you ask me it was mostly put on. She liked being fussed over and she didn't want Thea to marry . . . Where was I?'

'Meeting Mr Worple in the gazebo.'

She gave him an angry look.

'It was just once or twice when the weather was fine. I wasn't going there on Tuesday. He was coming here, but he didn't come.'

There was rather a prolonged pause.

'Yes, Mrs Harrison?'

'Oh well, you might as well have it. He was making up to Thea, I'm sure I don't know why, and I got it into my head that he might be there with her.'

'That wouldn't seem very likely.'

She tossed her head.

'You don't think about what's likely when you've been expecting someone and they don't turn up! I thought he might have done it on purpose – I thought he might be with Thea – I thought perhaps he might be expecting me to come to the gazebo. So I went.'

She went on from there to turning into Hill Rise. She had seen a woman run down to catch the bus at the corner of

Belview Road. She had slipped in through the tradesmen's entrance at The Lodge, and she had gone round the house and up the garden to the gazebo.

'I went up the steps, and just as I got to the top one I had the most awful fright. Someone came barging out and knocked me over. I was thrown against the door and came down smack. I suppose that was when the stone came out of my ring. I know I hit my hand, because it hurt all night afterwards.'

'It was a man who knocked you down?'

She said quickly, 'It wasn't Fred Worple – not tall enough. Besides Fred wouldn't.'

'Do you know who it was?'

'I could make a guess.'

'Well?'

'That man Blount that was offering for the house. What did he want it for? I thought it was him at the time, snooping round after everyone was in bed and asleep.'

'You thought it was Mr Blount. Did you recognize him?'

'No, I can't say I did.'

'Well, go on, Mrs Harrison.'

She stared at him defensively.

'There isn't any more. You don't suppose I was going to stay there after being knocked down like that? I got up and I went back home as quick as I could.'

'Did you go inside the gazebo?'

Her temper flared.

'How do you mean, did I go into the gazebo? What do you take me for? I suppose poor Winifred Graham was lying there dead, wasn't she? If I'd gone into the gazebo I'd have fallen over her! Do you really suppose I'd have come away and left her lying like that? Because I wouldn't! I don't know what you think people are made of! Why, she mightn't even have been dead!'

The Inspector wrote that down, as he had written all the rest. Frank said,

'Oh, I don't think there is any doubt that she was dead.'

42

The inquest on Mrs Graham was held next morning. Althea described how she had found her mother's body, medical evidence was taken from Dr Barrington and from the police surgeon who had carried out the autopsy, after which the police asked for an adjournment. The funeral took place early the same afternoon. Miss Silver was thankful when both these events were over.

Althea gave her evidence simply and clearly and took part in the funeral service with quiet self-control. Nicholas sat beside her in the church and slipped a hand inside her arm at the graveside, but it was necessarily a day of severe and continued strain.

Nicholas came back to the house, and Miss Silver left him and Althea together. As far as their personal problem was concerned the outlook had brightened. Nicholas had not been arrested, and in the light of the Harrisons' statements it was now in the highest degree unlikely that any charge would be brought against him.

Frank Abbott went up to town to confer with his superiors, and presently found himself making for Cleat in a police car driven by Sergeant Hubbard, who was wearing a suit the twin of his own in everything but cut, and a handkerchief, a tie, and a hat which were reverential copies. Imitation may be the sincerest form of flattery, but it must be admitted that when owing to a calamitous difference in personal appearance the imitation approximates to parody, the result may be a severe strain upon the temper of the person imitated. There were times when Detective Inspector Frank Abbott was amused, and there were times when he was exasperated. This was one of the times when he was exasperated.

But the afternoon was a fine one, Sergeant Hubbard a very good driver, and once clear of London and its suburbs the scenery extremely pleasing. There was also the satisfaction of feeling that the case was practically in the bag, and that Jack Harrison had been prompted to unburden himself in time for the mistake of arresting Nicholas Carey to be avoided. The Press is not backward in looking after its own. The *Janitor* had a reputation. He thanked his stars that it had not been afforded a chance of living up to it.

Down at Cleat it was a very pleasant day. Mr Blount suggested an expedition to the cinema in a neighbouring town. Rillington was only five miles away, an agreeable bus ride. He invited Lizzie Pardue to accompany them and offered to stand treat, first tea at the Arcadia and then the cinema conveniently placed on the other side of the Square. Lizzie was thrilled. She hadn't been brought up to have treats, her father having had very strong views as to woman's place being in the home. What did they come into the world for if it wasn't to do the cooking and the scrubbing and the bearing and rearing of the children, and where did all these things take place if it wasn't in the home? Outings, junketings, gallivantings and such like – you'd only got to look around and you could see what come of them! Lightmindedness! Tittle-tattling! Gossiping! Idleness! And downright evil doing! 'Look at those there suffragettes! What like of shameful carrying on do you call that? See'd it with my own eyes I did, forty years back and more! Votes for Women, they said! And what come of it? Two great wars and bombs adropping all over the place!'

Under this régime and with her nose very firmly held to the grindstone, Lizzie grew up with very little to distract her from the stricter ways of industry, and old Mr Pardue had his house kept like a newpin and an obedient daughter always at hand. Tea at the Arcadia and a cinema to follow were the height of dissipation. She put on her church-going clothes, a black coat and a skirt handed on by the Vicar's wife after the Vicar had gazed disapprovingly at it and remarked, 'Really, my dear, I don't think you can wear that any more even at a funeral,' and a rather crushed black hat with a piece of red ribbon tied round it and a bunch of daisies to cover the knot.

Mrs Blount wore the shapeless clothes in which Miss Silver had seen her. She had travelled down in them, and she put them on just as she put on her hat without so much as looking in the glass. If it crossed her mind to wonder why Sid who never took her anywhere should be taking them to the cinema, it was in the vaguest possible manner. In fact everything in her mind was vague. It was a relief to be at Cleat, it was a relief to be with Lizzie Pardue, it was a relief to have a room of her own. She had slept heavily on the narrow truckle bed. She didn't feel very far off sleep as they sat in the Rillington bus. In fact she did nod and sit up again with a start when Lizzie nudged her. After that she kept her eyes wide open and fixed them on the road. It made her feel a bit giddy, but anything was better than to have Sid notice that she had nearly dropped off.

She need not have worried. Mr Blount was perfectly aware of her confused state of mind and very well satisfied with it. It wouldn't do for her to go to sleep in the bus, but all to the good if she were to appear vague and drowsy. They had had a pot of tea after their midday meal, and the tablet which he had dropped into her cup should just do the trick nicely. It wouldn't send her off, but it would make things easier all round.

The Arcadia Café was very full and very noisy. Lizzie Pardue enjoyed it to the full – the clatter of plates, the buzz of voices, and the continual rush and roar of the traffic outside. She had two cups of tea, scone and butter, three fancy cakes, and two chocolate biscuits. Milly Blount drank two cups of tea. They were scalding hot and they made her feel better. Aunt Lizzie kept pressing her to eat, but she didn't feel as if she could. Every time that Lizzie Pardue pressed her Mr Blount felt a difficulty in restraining himself. He couldn't even frown because of wanting everyone to notice that his wife wasn't herself and how kind and considerate he was being. But if he had to pay for two teas like the one Aunt Lizzie was having, it was no good saying he wasn't going to be put out about it, because he was. Fancy cakes and chocolate biscuits for a woman who was going to be dead and out of his way before the day was an hour older – well, there wasn't any sense in it, was there? Fortunately Milly was having enough sense to say no. He said loud enough to be heard by the people at the next table,

'You're not eating anything, my dear. Are you not feeling well?'

She was glad when they came out into the air, but when they had crossed the pavement and came to the kerb she hung back. The cinema stood at one corner of a four-cross-way, and they were on another. There was a lot of traffic, and the noisy rush of it made her feel giddy again. When the lights changed Sid put his hand on her arm and guided her to the island in the middle of the road, and there they had to wait until they could cross to the other side. A lot of people were waiting too, the island was crowded.

Rillington is an old place with narrow streets and picturesque houses which motorists would like to see pulled down and antiquarians are prepared to battle for to the death. The struggle continues in the Press and in the local Council Chamber, but so far the antiquarians have held the position. The four wide roads which converge upon the town become four bottle-necks as they discharge their contents into what is known as the Square. It follows that cars and buses must of necessity pass very close to the islands. They stop when the lights are against them, but as soon as the green light goes on they go forward as fast as the local speed limit will allow, and sometimes a good deal faster. A bus-driver with the way clear before him and no policeman in sight is apt to chance his luck.

The police car which contained Detective Inspector Abbott and Sergeant Hubbard turned into Rillington High Street and approached the Square. Held up by the red light before they reached it, Frank Abbott noted the Arcadia on the right and thought briefly that a cup of tea would be agreeable but they had probably better not stop and anyhow there wouldn't be anywhere to park. As his gaze travelled back across the street it rested upon the crowded island just ahead of them. It looked as if a lot of people had crossed from the side where the café stood and been caught up there. The red light ahead had changed to amber, and as his eye reached it the green came on. The whole line of traffic began to move and their own car with it.

It was at this moment that Frank saw and recognized the Blounts. Mrs Blount was on the very edge of the island. There was a woman next to her in a black coat and skirt and a black hat with a red ribbon round it. Mr Blount was not next to his wife nor immediately behind her. Frank opened the near-side door and got himself and his long legs out on to the pavement. He called out to the astonished Sergeant Hubbard, 'Get her parked and come back!' and proceeded across the traffic in the direction of the island in a highly dangerous and exasperating manner. So far his actions had been largely automatic. Looking back upon them, he was aware that they had been prompted by the simultaneous and vivid appearance in his mind of a number of pictures. There was Miss Silver saying earnestly, 'I am deeply concerned about Mrs Blount.' There was Mrs Blount herself on the edge of a stream of traffic which would presently be going very fast. There was the crowd on the island behind Mrs Blount. And there was Mr Blount, not so near his wife as to come under suspicion but near enough to exert pressure at a critical moment. And away in the mental background but still discernible, Mr Blount's father who had broken his neck falling down the stairs in his own house, and the first Mrs Blount who had gone down under a train. Money in it for Mr Blount on both these occasions, and money to come to him if anything were to happen to the present Mrs Blount. Dead men tell no tales. If Mrs Blount had a tale that she might tell, she wouldn't be able to tell it. Not if she was dead.

All these things were suddenly and menacingly present as he came up out of the traffic and stood in the lee of the island. There was no standing-room on the island itself. He didn't want to attract Mr Blount's attention, but he had got to be within reach of Mrs Blount. He began to edge along in front of the island. Two women looked at him angrily, and a man said, 'Where are you shoving to!' The cars that had been waiting for the lights to change had all got away now, and the oncoming traffic behind them had put on speed to get across the Square before they changed again. Everyone was watching them go by. Time was getting short – the lights would go again at any moment. A scarlet bus was speeding up to get across in time. It was going to pass so near the island that the people in the front row made an involuntary movement to step back. Only there wasn't any room to step back. The people behind began shoving in order to keep their places. Somebody shoved Mrs Blount so hard that she lost her footing on the stone kerb and plunged forward just as the bus came roaring past. Lizzie Pardue screamed and made an ineffectual snatch at her coat sleeve. Mrs Blount herself didn't scream. She felt a paralysing terror, a paralysing certainty that this was death. And then, quick and hard, the grasp of a hand upon her outflung arm. It was a man's hand and it was strong. It held her back from where she would have fallen under the front wheels of the bus. It jerked her sideways past Lizzie Pardue and the bus went by. The scarlet paint on the side of it brushed her shoulder and left it sore and hot right through the stuff of her coat.

When her mind began working again the lights had changed and the traffic had stopped. Room had been made for her on the island. The man who had saved her had his arm about her shoulders, holding her up. Lizzie Pardue was sobbing and crying, and Sid was standing looking at her and saying,

'What happened, Milly – what happened?'

Milly Blount said, 'You pushed me.'

43

Frank Abbott came to The Lodge in the evening and told Miss Silver all about it.

'If you hadn't managed to put the wind up me about Mrs Blount she'd have been dead by now. There we were just driving along peaceably through Rillington, when I saw her on the island and had a come-over. There she was, and there Blount was, and there was the traffic, and it up and hit me in the eye that if I was a crook and wanted to get rid of a woman who had a packet in the bank and who knew too much about me, I couldn't possibly ask for a better opportunity. The next thing I knew I was out of the car and half way across the road. I should have felt all sorts of a fool if nothing had happened, but as you know something did. Blount and I were twin souls with but a single thought. The possibility of a jam on an island and a shove at the right moment had not escaped him. As a matter of fact the whole thing must have been very carefully planned. He had never taken his wife and the aunt to anything in Rillington before, and when they searched him at the police station he had one of those folding-up rulers in his pocket. Just the sort of thing to slip through the row between him and Mrs Blount. Opened to a foot length it would be quite long enough and strong enough to do the trick. She said he pushed her, you know, and she said her back hurt her, so the police surgeon had a look at it, and there was the mark where the ruler had bruised her. I told you Hubbard turned up just after it happened. Blount tried to carry the whole thing off with his wife being suicidal. Well, he'd planned for that too. Tucked away in his wallet there was a scrawled sheet in Mrs Blount's writing which said, "I can't go on with it. It's no use. I don't feel I can." She says he was writing a letter in the kitchen. He pretended it was about a deal he had thought of going into, but he'd made up his mind not to go on with it on account of having heard something he didn't like about the fellow. All of a sudden he said his thumb joint had slipped and he would have to get her to finish the let-ter for him. He dictated that "I can't go on" stuff, and then snatched it away from her and said he couldn't send anything so badly written and he'd have to ring the man up. She says he had made her so nervous beforehand that she could hardly hold the pen. And you know, if that wretched scrawl had been produced at an inquest any jury in the world would have brought in a verdict of suicide. As it is, he has been charged with the attempted murder of his wife, but as soon as the Harrisons' statements have been gone into he will probably be brought here and charged with the murder of Mrs Graham. They've got some fingerprints off the metal rod he dropped when he tripped in the yard. If they are identical with his own, he'll be for it all right.'

Miss Silver coughed gently.

'Mrs Blount has indeed had a providential escape.'

'I think she's been afraid of him for a long time. I don't think there's much doubt that he contrived the deaths of his father and his first wife. That gave him the idea that he could get away with anything. I should think Worple may be en-couraged to come across and give some useful information. By the way, we're all set to investigate the gazebo on Monday morning. Whether Mr Warren's gold plate will be found there or not, I imagine that both Worple and Blount were convinced it was there for the finding, and that they meant to be the finders. For that they would have to be in lawful possession of the premises. I don't know what an eighteenth-century service of gold plate would be worth in the market. It couldn't very well be sold here for what it was, and it would be difficult to get the gold out of the country if it was melted down. Of course there are ways! Crooks are always thinking up new ones. But that seven thousand Blount was offering for the house – you know, that sticks in my throat. I can't bring myself to believe that the money would ever have been paid over. Of course they would expect to get some of it back on a re-sale, but I shouldn't have said that the market price of the house would be more than four thousand. And they couldn't count on getting that.'

Miss Silver had begun a new piece of knitting. It was to be a cardigan for her niece Ethel Burkett for Christmas. She had started upon the back. Three inches of ribbing and two inches of the pattern appeared upon the needles. The wool was very soft and the colour a deep smoky violet. Ethel had put on a little lately and the shade would be becoming both to face and figure. She had lately bought herself a grey skirt with a purple line in it. Miss Silver had obtained a pattern of the stuff and intended to knit a twin set to go with it. She said now in a thoughtful voice,

'The Reverend Thomas Jenkinson mentions jewellery as well as the gold plate – jewellery which had belonged to Mr Warren's late wife. The term might cover a good deal, or very little. There would almost certainly be some valuable rings. There might even be a diamond necklace.'

Frank laughed.

'And there might be no more than a twopenny-halfpenny brooch or two!'

She was knitting placidly.

'I think it improbable that a couple of brooches would be dignified by the name of jewellery. I also think it probable that Mr Worple, and through him Mr Blount, possessed rather more information than we do. Mr Worple's step-father, the elder Mr Martin, remembered his grandmother talking about the

Riots. You will recall that she was the young woman who married into Yorkshire but returned to Grove Hill as a widow. She is quoted as having been present when Mr Warren died, and as being able to corroborate what took place during his last moments. She told Mr Jenkinson things which he did not consider it prudent to set down in print lest they should "excite the cupidity of unprincipled persons". What she said to her Vicar she may very well have repeated to her grandson. We may not know exactly what it was, but I think we may fairly deduce that either by word of mouth or in writing it ultimately reached Mr Worple and was passed by him to Mr Blount. If anything should be found in or under the gazebo, can you tell me just what the legal position would be?'

He raised his eyebrows.

'Is there really anything you don't know? It's not in my line, but I have an idea that it would rank as treasure trove. If a man conceals something in the ground or otherwise with the intention of recovering it at a more favourable moment, I believe his heirs can claim it even after a considerable lapse of time, but if he doesn't dig it up himself and there are no heirs, it is treasure trove and in theory it belongs to the Crown. As a matter of modern practice, if the find is of any archaeological or historical value it is passed on to the appropriate museum. You may remember that is what happened to the find of Roman silver at Traprain in Scotland, which is now in the Edinburgh museum. But whereas there used to be only nominal compensation for the finder, which resulted in a great many valuable and interesting things being melted down for the bare value of the metal, it is now the practice to hand out what is considered to be the real value.'

Miss Silver inclined her head.

'That agrees with my own impression.'

He said,

'Two minds with but a single thought!' and then went on hurriedly, 'As regards Worple, from what I have heard about him I should think he will be prepared to cut his coat according to his cloth. In other words, I should say that he would come clean. From our point of view there really isn't anything against him. There is nothing criminal in wanting to buy a house, even if you think there is something valuable buried

in the garden. I don't imagine for a moment that he would
have mixed himself up in a murder. Shady financial transac-
tions are his line, not physical violence, and he has generally managed to keep on the safe side of the law. They may
want him as a witness, in which case I've no doubt he will be
willing to oblige.'

Miss Silver dismissed Mr Worple in the fewest possible
words.

'A meretricious person.'

44

On Monday morning a carpenter took up the floorboards of
the gazebo – good solid oaken boards which had endured
through successive generations since they had been laid there
somewhere about the year 1750 at the orders of the wealthy
brewer, Mr Henry Warren. He could not at that time have
foreseen a day some thirty years distant when, having been
warned by a sure hand of violence planned against the Catho-
lics, he would secretly and under cover of night be lifting the
end board against the wall where the heavy oak bench was
designed to stand, with the purpose of concealing beneath it
a service of gold plate which he did not yet possess and the
jewels and trinkets of his wife not yet deceased. Yet without
such premonition, the octagonal shape of the gazebo and the
space beneath its floor lent themselves to such a purpose. The
last board against the wall was a short one. On that night of
terror Martin Hickley had taken up that last short board
under his direction. They had carried down the plate together
and wadded it with its own baize covers. The plates and
dishes were pushed as far under the boards as they would go.
The two great salt cellars took some stowing away, but in the
end all was disposed of and a hollow made to take the jewel-
case. When the board was nailed down again and a little dust
scattered over it there was nothing to show that it had ever
been taken up.

The ephemeral violence of the Riots flared itself out and left a ruined house and two dead men behind it. Martin Hickley died when the roof of the hall fell in as he was carrying one of his master's pictures to safety, Henry Warren being struck down at the same time by a fall of masonry in the portico before the front door, and surviving for no more than an hour or two. An old story and three parts forgotten, but reaching across the nineteenth century and into the twentieth to affect the lives of half a dozen people, and to bring two of them to their deaths.

There were some such thoughts in Miss Silver's mind as she watched the workman at his task. Frank Abbott, passing near her, took a moment to stand beside her and look down with a quizzical gleam in his eye. He said in a voice pitched for her ear alone,

'I feel that this demands a quotation. Don't tell me that Tennyson is mute.'

A slight cough reproved the impertinence. She said sedately,

'I can give you a most apposite one, but you will have heard it before.'

'What is it?'

She said, 'The lust of gain in the spirit of Cain.' And with that the board came creaking up and he left her and went forward.

Nicholas and Althea were watching too. They stood together, her hand just slipped inside his arm. It was a bright morning. The carpenter's voice said,

'There's something there, and pretty heavy too.'

Inspector Sharp said, 'Better take up a couple more of those boards.'

In the end Henry Warren's gold plate came up out of the dark place where he had thrust it in 1780. Its appearance would certainly have shocked him very much. The green baize in which it was wrapped had rotted away to a murky slime. Gold being gold, it would return to its primitive lustre, but for the moment it certainly did not look as if it could be worth a man's honesty or a woman's life. Mrs Warren's jewel-case had practically ceased to exist. Wood and leather had cracked and disintegrated. Drought had reduced it to powder, and periods of rain to slush, but somewhere in the resulting mess was the jewellery which it had contained. A little man of the name of Benchley who had been brought in as an expert pronounced the plate to be gold — a full service for twenty people. He refused to commit himself as to its value.

Just how Henry Warren came to be possessed of so extravagant an appointment was later explained when it appeared that it had been deposited with him by the eccentric and notorious Mr Wavenham when he fled from his creditors in the latter part of 1779. Since Mr Wavenham was killed a year later in a duel in Italy and left no heir, the disappearance of the plate had never been explained. Mr Warren's concern to preserve the trust committed to him by his friend certainly redounds to his honour. But a good deal of patient research would be necessary before these particulars could be established. At the moment the gold plates were piled one upon the other and Mrs Warren's jewellery was laid out upon the oak table.

Mr Benchley made lists of everything. He asked for a cloth and a bowl of soap and water, and stabbed at the stones in a necklace, bracelets, rings.

'Necklace. Diamonds. Fine stone. Centre one about five carats.'

'Pendant in the form of a cross. Diamonds and rubies. Probably French.'

'Five rings . . .'

The catalogue went on, very dry and precise like Mr Benchley himself. And when it was all done and the floor boards put back again, the police went away and took the plate and the jewellery with them. There would have to be an inquest to decide whether the find was treasure trove or not. Whether it was or whether it wasn't, it would certainly be a very long time before the matter was finally settled.

Frank Abbott remarked irreverently that you couldn't hope to hurry a government department, and that when you got a museum mixed up in it at the other end it might quite likely be 1980 before anything got settled, which would make it a round two hundred years since the stuff was buried.

They were in the drawing-room, and he was taking his leave. Nicholas Carey put an arm round Althea.

'Well, I hope you're not counting on wearing the diamond necklace, Allie,' he said.

He was startled to see how pale she turned.

'Oh, I *couldn't*!' she said with a shudder.

He shook her a little, lightly.

'Darling you won't get a chance.'

Frank Abbott had a sardonic gleam in his eye.

'Well, I suppose you two will be getting married.'

'If I'm not being haled to prison. Can I take it that the arrest is definitely off?'

'I think so. You'll be wanted to give evidence when Blount comes up before the magistrates – both of you. And again at the trial. So don't take a honeymoon in Timbuctoo or the Gobi desert. I don't think we want to risk Blount being let loose on society again. The other things won't be brought up against him at his trial, but between ourselves and strictly off the record, I haven't the slightest doubt that he contrived the accidents which removed his father and his first wife. And as you know, the attempt upon his present wife came within an ace of succeeding. He used a footrule to push her with, one of those folding ones, and he probably employed the same technique in the first wife's case. She fell under a train, and he was supposed to be somewhere else at the time so he got away with it. But this time I think we've got him. Of course you never can tell with juries. But I can't see twelve ordinary people having any reasonable doubt that Mrs Graham disturbed him when he was going over the ground with his divining rod. She took him for Carey, which was natural enough, and called out using Carey's name. He tried to stop her and – succeeded. When Mrs Harrison came on the scene looking for Worple I think she had the world's narrowest escape. However by that time I expect Blount's nerve wasn't so good. He must have heard Mrs Traill run down to the corner. She was frightened when she heard Mrs Graham call out. And she ran for the bus, but he wasn't to know that. He wasn't to know how much she had heard, or whether she wouldn't start to scream and give the alarm. Then he heard the bus and waited to let it go by. And when Mrs Harrison came along all he wanted was to get away, so he blundered past her, knocking her over. Then he tripped at the step coming down into the back yard and lost his divining rod. Definitely his luck was out. And on the top of all that he talks in his sleep and his wife hears what he says. It must have been a bit of a jolt. He has probably been thinking of getting rid of her for some time. Now it's a case of needs must and the sooner the better. He takes her down to Cleat, ropes in his respectable aunt who can't say enough about his kindness to his wife, and prepares for another fatal accident. This time there would have been a perfectly good suicide motive. He must have thought the plan completely watertight. But I don't think he is going to get the chance of murdering anyone else.'

He shook hands all round and departed with Detective Inspector Sharp. Miss Silver following them out of the room, he had a word with her at the door.

'You will be giving the bride away?'

A look reproved him.

'It will naturally be an extremely quiet wedding.'

There was a sparkle in the cool blue eyes.

' "The bride wore crape and a mourning wreath"?'

Miss Silver said composedly,

'No one has worn crape for at least the last forty years.'

'My dear ma'am, you know everything! I withdraw the crape. I like Carey, but I don't suppose we shall ever come across each other again. I shouldn't have cared to have had to arrest him, but you know it very nearly happened. When do you go back to Montague Mansions?'

'Althea would like me to stay and see her married. I do not feel that she should be here alone.'

'Will you be back by Sunday? And if you are, may I come to tea?'

Miss Silver smiled indulgently.

'Hannah tells me we have had a delightful gift of honey in the comb from Mrs Rafe Jerningham. She will make you some of her special scones to eat it with.'

Althea and Nicholas stood together in the drawing-room. Both his arms were round her as he said,

'When are we going to get married, Allie?'

She answered him in a soft, trembling voice.

'I don't know. I think we ought to wait.'

He said grimly,

'Another five years? You had better think again. I want to take you away and look after you.'

She said,

'Away?'

He nodded.

'Somewhere where nobody has ever heard of Grove Hill. Spain if you don't mind trains and buses that don't arrive, and plumbing that doesn't work.'

'I'm not passionate about them. Did you think I would be?'

He laughed.

'I thought perhaps a plunge into the Middle Ages would be a complete change. But I tell you what, we can start off in the South of France and just wander. If you know the ropes it can be done very agreeably. And we needn't make any plans. When we've had enough of one place we can go to another. Now that I'm not going to be arrested, I'll get a car. A chap I know is selling an Austin which has only done four or five thousand miles. He's going to America, and I can have it any time I like. So what about getting married on Thursday?'

Althea looked up at him. There was something she was going to say, but it didn't get said. It came over her in a rush of feeling that yesterday was gone – that all the yesterdays of the last five years were gone, and that nothing and nobody could bring them back again. They had been dreary and endless in the living. They had dragged upon their way and halted on their going, and at the end they had gone out in tragedy and terror. There had been enough of them and to spare. They were done, they were over, they were gone, and she and Nicky were free. They were together and they were free. She looked up at him, and she said,

'Yes – yes – yes.'

MORE BOOKS BY THE SAME AUTHOR
AND AVAILABLE FROM CORONET

All these books are available at your local bookshop or newsagent, or can be ordered direct from the publisher. Just tick the titles you want and fill in the form below.

Prices and availability subject to change without notice.

Hodder & Stoughton Paperbacks, P.O. Box 11, Falmouth, Cornwall.

Please send cheque or postal order, and allow the following for postage and packing:

U.K. – 55p for one book, plus 22p for the second book, and 14p for each additional book ordered up to a £1.75 maximum.

B.F.P.O. and EIRE – 55p for the first book, plus 22p for the second book, and 14p per copy for the next 7 books, 8p per book thereafter.

OTHER OVERSEAS CUSTOMERS – £1.00 for the first book, plus 25p per copy for each additional book.

Name ....

Address...

....